REBWAR - HOUSE OF SUREN

OLS SCHABER

RORSCHACH PRESS

GET YOUR FREE PREQUEL NOVELLA
TO THE REBWAR SERIES

Just visit www.olsschaber.com and sign up. You'll also get news on forthcoming books and deals.

PROLOGUE

He checked his digital watch, which read 11:56, and he put his black leather glove back on. He wrapped his scarf tighter around his neck and walked on the spot to warm his cold feet, the dried leaves underneath crunching to his rhythm. Wind rattled and banged through the bare trees around him but he kept listening for someone to approach the clearing he was in. His worry was that it would be someone walking their dog or a couple on a romantic walk. He'd chosen this area for a couple of reasons but one was for its remoteness. He took out a box of cigarettes and flipped the lid. There were three left. He thought about taking one but decided to wait; he'd already had two and had kept the butts. He coughed, feeling a cold coming on – or was it this damn cold country. He heard his name spoken, turned around and saw him.

The man walked over and they greeted each other. He offered the cigarette, which he refused, and they walked towards some trees, explained how he had this amazing offer, getting this man excited and engaged. They passed the pine tree and, pointing up into the sky, he showed the man a bird of prey. It was a distraction. His colleague flung a rope around the man's neck and pulled hard. He too joined in and helped him to hoist the man. Kicking and struggling for breath, the man clung on. They held him, their arms growing tired, the rope bouncing and flicking, as the man fought for his ebbing life. Not long now. A little longer. Both hung on as the tight rope slackened.

ONE

A bitter icy breeze blew across the muddy fields surrounding the cemetery. Rebwar drew hard on his cigarette as if he was trying to draw in its fire. The grey sky sucked out all the leftover colour. He looked over to Dinah, who had buttoned her woollen black coat right up to her chin. She gave him a warming smile. Rebwar's last funeral had been a couple of years before in Chelsea. It had been for Bijan's old mistress. This one was just as tragic. Dinah's nephew, Izah Sasani, he'd been found hanging off a tree in Epping Forest. The whole family and friends had come out to send him off. Rebwar looked around him, unsure if he was at a mobster's funeral or whether the black suits just made it look that way. His police whiskers had tingled on seeing the fancy parked cars. This was a family that liked to show off their wealth. Dinah had briefly mentioned her auntie. They were apparently related to the House of Suren, part of the seven great houses that ruled Iran back in the Parthian period. Dinah had tried to give him a brief history lesson but as he'd been brought up on the streets of Tehran, he'd never been interested in old tales. Or that's what he told himself, as his ex-wife Hourieh was obsessed with her past and was convinced that she was an aristocrat, which added to his contempt of people having a birthright to privilege.

'That's Jaleh,' said Dinah trying to point her out in the crowd. 'Doesn't she look beautiful?'

Rebwar tried to find her. Dinah had sent Jaleh a black suit and cashmere coat from her boutique. He hadn't seen it, so didn't know what he was looking for. To the sound of murmurs and crying, they walked along a tarmac path towards a chapel in the middle of the grounds. It was small but unmistakable, rectangular and with three large stained glass windows on its side. They passed it and behind it was a plot awaiting the coffin.

'And that's her daughters, Nahid and Sarah.' Dinah nodded to them.

They looked beautiful. One was dressed elegantly in a black throw, which partially covered her face. The expensive jewellery sparkled. Her sister wore a tight-fitting dark grey turtleneck with a single gold chain over it. Her black leather skirt showed off slender legs. Dinah tutted. They found a place to stand, which was on the fringes of the main pack. This was Dinah's remaining family. Her parents had passed away when she was in her twenties. Six men carried the coffin out of the chapel. As it came closer, the guests comforted each other. Dinah grabbed Rebwar's hand and gripped it. Tears streamed down her cheeks. The men placed the coffin by the freshly dug grave. The priest held his hands together and began his sermon. Rebwar craved a cigarette but pulled Dinah close in. He could feel her shaking. He'd never met Izah, but heard that he'd been a nice boy, running the family business and going places. His girlfriend, Liz, looked devastated and kept staring at the coffin.

Liz was what they called 'a social influencer'. Dinah had tried to explain what she did exactly. It still made little sense to Rebwar. All he knew was that she liked to post lots of glamorous photos of herself in amazing locations.

The six men fixed some ropes around the shiny wooden coffin and carefully lowered it. They hadn't found a note, so it was unclear why Izah had committed suicide. But there was plenty of speculation. Dinah thought he had been suffering from depression. Ever since his dad had died in a car accident, he'd never been the same. The mourners filed past the hole, throwing flowers into it. Next to it was Farhad Sasani's headstone. Dinah headed towards her aunt to share her condolences and gave her a hug. Rebwar politely shook her hand, feeling an awkwardness on what the protocol was. Jaleh wiped her tears and looked at the mourners following behind him. They walked slowly back to their cars which were parked outside the grounds.

'She's everything to me,' said Dinah, 'I feel her pain.'

Rebwar took out some cigarettes and offered one to her. They both lit up. 'Couldn't imagine losing my son,' he said.

Dinah grabbed his hand and they walked off. Rebwar looked into the distance, hearing the gentle murmur of the London orbital traffic. He had a shift coming up in his Uber taxi.

TWO

The Shishawi on Edgware Road was Rebwar's sanctuary where he would regularly have a coffee before starting his shift. With its loud, Persian-themed decor, it was a piece of home that he liked to hang on to, even though the clientele was a mix of tourists and Arabs. Cigarette in hand and sitting outside under a patio heater, he read a copy of the Hamshari, one of Iran's bestselling newspapers. As it was a mouthpiece for the government, he'd skim over the headlines and head over to the sport to see how his beloved football team Persepolis were doing. It was good news. They had won 3-1 against Pars Jonoubi and kept their unbeaten record. It made him smile.

'I thought you'd been to a funeral?' said Berker, coming over to Rebwar's table. 'Did your horse come in?' Rebwar just showed him the newspaper, which to Berker was a series of dashes and squiggles. But the numbers were understandable. Berker tapped his nose in recognition. 'Brandy with your coffee?'

Rebwar nodded and checked the time. He had an hour before his ten o'clock shift would start. He'd known Berker since coming over to London, a Kurdish Turk who had fled over to London to make a new life for himself. Though they had few common points of interest, Berker had helped him in the past, getting some info on people. The area was nick-named Little Cairo and as a waiter, he would pick up all sorts of gossip. He was a useful ally.

Rebwar's phone lit up. 'Musa,' Rebwar stubbed out his cigarette and leaned back in his metal garden chair. 'Fancy watching Chelsea play?'

'Got tickets?' Rebwar's son said excitedly. 'When?'

For a moment Rebwar thought of bluffing and finding some. But he'd been caught out before. 'Thought we could go to a pub. Have a few drinks.' Since Musa had turned seventeen, Rebwar had tried to entice him with visits to pubs. He strangely missed them since Geraldine had disap-peared. Geraldine had been his partner in crime and handler for Plan B. It had been a month or so since he had heard from them. He really should have been celebrating the fact, as they had coerced him into making illegal investi-gations. He still didn't know who Plan B were, but suspected that they were a secret operation of the govern-ment and to that everyone who worked for them had some kind of debt to pay.

'I've got a party to go to.' Replied Musa, 'Mate's birth-day. Next match, hey?' replied Musa.

'How's school?'

There was an audible sigh of disappointment.

'I'm worried, want the best for you. Can't be driving an Uber like your father.'

Musa laughed then left an awkward silence. 'Dad...'

Rebwar felt bad. He wanted to help but it always wound Musa up. 'Yeah son.' He lit another cigarette.

'Can I borrow hundred quid?'

Rebwar dragged on his cigarette weighing up his answer. 'Sure, but I've only got cash,' to which he got a sigh. 'Never met a banker that I would trust...'

'OK, Dad, I'll come and meet you tomorrow. The usual, I guess. And mum's doing alright before you ask.'

Rebwar had heard that his ex-wife Hourieh had fallen and broken her wrist. He'd bought flowers but got nothing from her. 'Is she walking?'

'With a stick which she uses to hit people. And job's OK. Still haven't been fired. I'll come tomorrow?'

Rebwar took another draw on his cigarette. 'Yeah, call me before.'

Berker put down a coffee with a glass of brandy. 'How's Musa?'

'Teenager. He's still got that job your friend gave him. Or I think so... what was it?'

Berker laughed. 'Garage. He's making tea for the boys. He's a good boy.'

'Well, tell them to pay him more. He's still asking for money.'

Berker picked up an empty coffee cup. 'Should have told him to study law.' He walked off.

Rebwar's phone rang again. It was a withheld number.

'Like to talk to Rebwar Ghorbani,' said a woman's voice.

He touched his face, feeling his day's growth, 'Speaking.'

'I'm Jaleh Sasani, Dinah passed me your number. I'm looking for a detective. Have been told that you were a policeman back in Iran.'

Rebwar tried to remember her from the funeral and what Dinah had said about her. There wasn't much to go on apart from her being a widow and grieving her son. 'Yes, what you looking for?'

'A murderer. But I think it's best if we meet in person. Tomorrow for lunch? I'll send you my address.'

Rebwar's immediate thought was that Izah had committed suicide but held back on asking her questions. 'See you tomorrow and hope I can help. Inshallah.' Rebwar stared back at the phone, thinking of calling Dinah, but his shift was about to start.

THREE

Still feeling groggy from his nightshift, Rebwar finally found the road he was looking for: Forest Side, up in Epping. The house, which was not far off the M25, looked grand. Large black cars were parked on the commanding gravel drive. He hadn't chatted to Dinah about her aunt but had texted her to mention that he was going to meet her. It wasn't a simple message. He parked the car and walked up to the big glossy black door. Before he could ring the doorbell, it opened and a large, suited man greeted him. His chiselled looks and dyed black hair made him look menacing, which was probably the idea.

'Jaleh is waiting for you in the drawing room.'

Rebwar checked his watch; he was on time. The house looked expensive and the drawing room was with large flower arrangements and there was a big painting of the surrounding countryside. Jaleh sat in a black dress on a white leather chair. Her smile was warm and comforting. Expensive gold jewellery adorned her. She had dark piercing eyes that followed him.

'Mr Ghorbani, would you like a coffee?' He nodded and

followed her gestures to a waiting chair close to hers. There was a coffee table laid out with sweets and cups. 'I see you met Jake Hayden, my faithful butler. He knows everything and was my husband's butler. I inherited him.'

Hayden poured a cup of dark black coffee into a cup. Rebwar had noticed that he carried a gun which was tucked in a holster. 'Thank you for inviting me.'

'Let's get the pleasantries over,' said Jaleh. 'My son was murdered. And I need to know who did it. I understand you were a policeman in Tehran and work as a private detective.'

'Mrs Sasani—'

'Call me Jaleh. You are family, Dinah is my precious niece and I love her like a daughter.'

'Jaleh...'

She smiled.

'It is correct. I have arrested and put people away for murder. Can you tell me about Izah, if you can.'

She looked down as a veil of sadness passed over her. 'He was my son, my only precious son and...' She reached for a handkerchief.

Rebwar a felt a lump grow in his throat but he knew that if he was going to take on this job, people were going to have to deal with their grief. She held her hand as she looked away.

'Sorry... He ran the family business since my husband passed away. He was the heir... and now... I hope that my two daughters choose well. Not that Sarah has.'

'Now you know I will need access to everyone and I will need to ask them questions,' said Rebwar. 'Awkward, insensitive questions. You might not like what I find.' Rebwar sipped the coffee, which was strong and sweet, just as he liked it.

'I will pay whatever it takes, I need to know who, before I avenge the murder.'

'Have you got an idea who might have done it? Enemies, rivals?'

Jaleh picked up a small silver table bell and rang it. 'I have my suspicions. But I want you to have a fresh look and not to lead you down the wrong alley. There was enough grief and pain when my husband died.' Hayden walked into the room. 'I need a sherry. Would you like something to help you relax?'

Normally with his old friend, Bijan, he'd have one of his expensive malt whiskies, but in this case, he wasn't sharing tales from the old days. 'I'll have another cup of coffee.' He took out the notebook that he had brought along with him. 'You say you have two daughters?'

'Yes, Nahid and Sarah. Both in their twenties and living their lives of leisure. I'm still waiting to be a grandmother. They stayed out of the business. Unlike me. My son was only sixteen when his father...' She looked up. 'You're going to ask me how he was killed?'

Rebwar nodded.

'Drunk, and he drove into a tree, or that's what they said. He... was drinking at the time. But he would have taken a taxi or...' Jaleh looked away towards the window.

Rebwar saw some family pictures in silver frames dotted around the room. He got up and went over to one. 'May I?'

With teary eyes, she nodded.

Hayden walked back in with a tray and glass of sherry which he placed on the coffee table. He eyed Rebwar as he looked at the pictures. They were of the family on holidays, smiling faces and large sunny villas.

'You married?' asked Jaleh.

'I was. Have one son who's here.'

'Whatever you find, you tell me first. I don't want gossip and you might hear stories of my husband. He didn't have an easy start in life. He had to fight for his business. And we are the House of Suren. You know that.'

'Yes, Jaleh, Dinah mentioned it. I didn't have a traditional education and, like your husband, had to fight for my position, so I respect what people have to do. Family is everything.' Rebwar carried on walking around the room trying to find as much information as he could. He would have to ask around on who the Sasanis were. Even if Jaleh offered to be an open book, it wasn't so simple. There was an edge to her and she wasn't to be crossed. He knew he was dealing with gangsters. What bothered him was that Dinah had not been frank about this side of her family. Even though Jaleh had reassured her he had carte blanche to investigate, he was going to tread on people's feet. Jaleh wasn't going to be happy with a quick and simple verdict that it really was suicide. He was having second thoughts on what he had got himself into. And he said to himself '*Che daste gol be âb dâdi?*'[1]

FOUR

The portrait was of General Bijan Achmoud in full dress uniform with all his medals. Rebwar had seen them but never studied them or asked about them. In the picture, Bijan looked full of life, thick black moustache, strong cheekbones and a piercing gaze that commanded attention. Both had served in the Iran-Iraq war and each had their own views on it. Rebwar let the old general tell his stories through his rose-tinted glasses. Bijan was an old friend and had helped him in the past, so, sometimes, Rebwar had to bite his tongue and keep his emotions and opinions to himself. He had stared death in the face whilst men like Bijan had ordered it. Dinah kept telling Rebwar to get himself checked out for PTSD, but survival was enough for him.

'That was taken in my office in Qom...'

Rebwar looked over at Bijan's fading gaze. Each time Rebwar saw Biajn, he thought it was going the last time. 'Didn't know there was a base there.' Bijan just nodded back, not replying to his remark.

'How's Katerena?' Bijan just looked over and stared at

him. The last time Rebwar had asked that question was a couple of months before, when he was looking for his ex-wife, Hourieh. With his friend, Raj, he had found them in a luxury flat in the docklands. Bijan had been hiding them there.

'Stealing my money, the whore,' Bijan replied at last. And then looked away.

The door opened and Bijan's butler came in with a tray with tea and traditional Persian sweets – or that's what Rebwar hoped. Each time he paid Bijan a visit, there was another manservant. He seemed to change them on a weekly basis. He laid down the tray with tea and Bijan waved him away like an annoying fly. He winked at Rebwar, which was the sign for him to get him a whisky, which, of course, he wasn't supposed to have. Bijan had multiple health issues and it was frankly a miracle that he was still alive. Maybe it was those sneaky drinks that kept him going. Rebwar reached for the key above the antique cupboard and opened it to find the usual collection of old whiskys. From his visits, he'd slowly got to know a few. His favourite were the smoky ones. He picked up a Laphroaig and poured two generous measures into two glasses.

'Haven't you sent her back?' said Rebwar.

Bijan used his two hands to cheer and take a large gulp. His left foot tapped the floor as it went down. Rebwar sipped his, enjoying the smoky burn and cleansing feel.

'I've tried,' said Bijan, 'but she just keeps coming back like a bad smell. Bitch. Should have never set eyes on her. How's Hourieh?'

Rebwar showed his hand with its missing wedding band.

Bijan squinted and smiled. 'Her father was a good man. Sorry to hear. Musa OK?'

'Doing good. Has a job but still asking me for money. What can you tell me about the House of Suren and the Sasani family?'

Bijan tapped on his empty crystal glass which gave a sharp bell-like sound. Rebwar took it and went over to the cabinet for a refill. 'Bunch of crooks. Father was an ambitious upstart. Decided to associate himself with pseudo royalty. Even got a historian to dig up some rubbish about their family being related to them. As if an old myth about the seven great houses of Iran would give them any credibility? It makes you an enemy of the state. Idiots. No one believed it. You involved?'

Rebwar brought back his glass. 'They're asking me to investigate their son's suicide.'

Bijan gulped his drink and let a sigh out. 'SAVAK [1] will know or the British?'

Rebwar dismissed Bijan's conspiracy theories. 'Did you know Farhad Sasani?'

Bijan swept back his thinning grey hair. 'He wanted to do some business with me. I politely declined... No, I told him where to go.'

'What's their business?'

'Import-export, he told me... drugs or anything illegal in Iran.' Bijan moved around his chair trying to find a comfortable position.

Rebwar needed Bijan to focus. He still wanted to know what he had got himself into. 'What happened to Farhad?'

Bijan sized Rebwar up. 'Digging up old stories, drove himself into a tree.'

'Suicide?'

Bijan laughed. 'If only.' He tapped his nose. 'Rivals I heard.' He shrugged his shoulders. 'Or Jaleh. Now, she is an interesting woman. You watch out for her, my friend. Black widow they call her.' Rebwar caught a little smile and wondered whether something had gone on between Jaleh and Bijan.

'And Iza, the son?'

'Always he was a wet one. Which makes the suicide scenario plausible, but maybe that's what they want you to think. Enough of these old stories. Let me show you what I just bought myself.' And he slid to the front of his chair.

Rebwar went over to help him out. 'I got a call from Farrouk.' He was his former police partner back in Tehran and the reason he had to flee. But Farrouk had kept sending him cryptic postcards. But it was a way to tell him that he knew what he was up to.

Bijan looked up. 'Wasn't he executed?'

'That's what they wanted me to think. Had an agent visit me and show me a picture of him hanging off a construction crane.'

He shook his head. 'That government, they don't even have shame on how to hang people. And?'

'He called me a few weeks ago. I was at a Chelsea match with my son and said he could see me.'

'You sure it was him?'

'Sounded like him... and he asked about Musa.'

Bijan leaned on his cane and shuffled his way to the door. 'They want something from you. He's always been up to no good. I'll ask around. Come, come... I have a surprise.'

FIVE

The sun reflected off the placid boating lake and made
Geraldine shield her eyes as she walked out of The Long-
holme cafe. Carrying a tray with two coffees, she made her
way to a table occupied by a couple and served them a
cappuccino and an Americano. The elderly lady said her
thanks whilst her husband watched people row their little
Viking-like boats around the water. The pond was on a
small island that was banked by the river Great Ouse.

'Sorry, dear. De's forgotten to recharge his 'earing aid. I
think he does it on purpose. Could I trouble you for a one of
those cakes?' And she pointed over to the table next to
them.

Geraldine looked over. 'Carrot cake?'

The lady nodded politely.

'With cream I guess.'

She smiled back.

Geraldine walked back into the cafe and went over to
the cooled display cabinet to cut a piece of cake.

'Hey G,' It was Nadia, the young brown-haired waitress
with the wide smile. 'There's a man asking for you?'

She winked at Geraldine.

'Me, a man?'

'Looks foreign. Holiday fling?'

'Nadia...' Since getting this job she had kept her head down and kept herself to herself. Nadia wasn't to know that she batted for the other team. 'You sure? Who?'

'Table Three.'

She tried to look over, but whoever it was, was concealed by customers and a pillar. She had been expecting a visit from Plan B. It had been naïve to think she could simply disappear in Bedford, but she'd hoped to have a few months of peace before moving on again. She glanced over to a mirror on the far end of cafe. She hadn't bothered with a disguise or even a fake name. She looked tired with bags under her eyes and messy hair but, to be fair she hadn't been looking after herself. 'Sure he's not trying to get your number through me?'

'Well don't.' Nadia came over to her. 'He's a bit creepy.'

Who had they sent? Now she was curious. Her ex? She put a slice of carrot cake onto a plate and went out. She looked over to Table Three. The man had curly dark hair, wore an oversized brown leather jacket. He had a tanned completion and wore a short, trimmed beard. It wasn't who she had expected to see. Possible Plan B operative? She served the cake to the old lady.

'Sorry to be a pain, but you forgot the cream.'

Geraldine looked down. 'So I did. Sorry I'll run back and get it.' Her husband took the fork and dug into the cake.

'Make that another cake.'

Geraldine nodded and then went over to the other table. 'Can I help you?'

'Yes, I am looking for Geraldine.'

She hesitated in answering. He didn't feel like a Plan B

type even though she couldn't pin exactly why if she was asked. But there was usually a procedure or some kind of call. This was too casual. 'And you are?'

'We have a friend in common. Coffee?' He smiled, revealing a set of gold teeth.

There was something Middle Eastern about him – sure, Rebwar would have narrowed it down to a country. She didn't think this man was the right sort, which would have fitted in the Plan B category. He didn't have that look of protocol that they had. Or was this a test? 'I'm working here.' She checked her watch. Her shift ended in an hour. 'What's your name?'

'Mr Serid. Like I said, we have a friend in common. You will be interested.'

Geraldine's senses told her to walk away but her curiosity got the best of her. 'The Flower Pot. At six.' And she walked away.

SIX

Rebwar parked his car along Chester Row, around Sloane Square. Large bricked three-storey houses faced each other. With white rendered ground floors, it gave the street a dramatic perspective. With glossy black doors, flower boxes and expensive cars, he got the measure of what he could expect of the eldest daughter. He rang the doorbell and waited. A voice responded.

'I'm here to see Nahid Sasani. I'm Rebwar.'

The door buzzed and he pushed it hard. He entered the reception, which had a striking black and white marbled floor. Nahid's stiletto shoes echoed as she made her way to him. Her short black skirt barely covered thin, slender legs, which was a contrast to her tight polo neck white jumper that showed off her slim figure.

'Mr Ghorbani. My mother warned me...' She flicked her black wavy hair. Her dark eyes fixed on him. Her classic Persian looks captivated Rebwar and he struggled to find something to say. Even though he had seen her at the funeral, there was something mesmerising about her. She looked away, 'You embarrass me...'

'Sorry? You just remind me of someone in Iran.' He lied to buy some time. 'A film star.'

'Sorry, just painted my nails.' She turned around and walked off towards a large room down the hall, her hips swaying rhythmically along.

He followed, perusing the art and furniture that looked both expensive and modern. The back room faced onto a lush green garden, the high window giving a view of the neighbouring houses. The white and gold striped wallpaper made the room seem taller.

'Drink?' she said standing by a bar.

He shook his head.

'Oh sure? I can't tempt you with a Manhattan?' She picked up a metal shaker and poured herself a drink.

Rebwar sat down on a bright green couch. The awkward angle made it impossible to lean back. 'I'm driving.'

She laughed. 'Uber is such a lifesaver. Think I'd be in jail without it. What can I do for you?'

'You know why I'm here?' He took out a notepad where he'd jotted down some questions.

'Mother. She's got it in her head that my poor brother was murdered.' She took a large gulp of her drink. 'He was a troubled soul. It was coming. Frankly, I'm amazed it wasn't sooner.'

'What makes you say that?'

'He was a manic-depressive. And he tried twice when he was a teenager. Sad, but what could I do? What could anyone do? I loved him. He was caring and made sure...' She carried on walking around the room. Repositioning furniture and vases.

'Made sure?' She looked away as if she was hiding something. 'Did he have enemies?'

She stopped and faced him. 'Enemies?'

'Anyone who wanted him out of the way? Rivals? Lovers?'

'Mr Ghorbani, you make me laugh. Who do you think we are? Mafia? No, no and no.'

'Money troubles?'

She carried on walking around, looking at herself in the large mirrors around the room. 'He wasn't a gambler, if that's what you're asking.'

'But you got along with Izah?'

'He was my little brother. Mr Ghorbani you are wasting your time.'

Rebwar checked his notes. 'Could I get a coffee?'

Nahid looked at Rebwar as if he was asking to be waited on. 'Sure, sure... There's a machine in the kitchen...' She laughed nervously and her cheeks flushed red. 'I've never used it.'

Rebwar got up, taking the opportunity to look around. 'Sure, I can work it out.' As he walked out, he glimpsed Nahid pouring herself another drink. The kitchen was clean and looked like it had only recently been installed. The cooker's clock flashed midnight, as did the microwave. He spotted the coffee machine on the counter. It took pods like the one Dinah had at her home. He looked for a cup and the coffee. Each cupboard was immaculate, with matching sets of colourful plates. He opened the fridge to find three bottles of champagne, a couple of juice cartons, eggs and a six-pack of beers.

'Do I need to order a delivery?' Nahid had followed him into the kitchen.

'No, no, all good.' He loaded the coffee machine with a pod and waited for it to deliver an expresso shot. The rest of the kitchen looked devoid of anyone living in the house.

Even a showroom would have had a bit more character. He ran his finger on the ceramic cooker. There were traces of white powder and he put it down as cocaine. 'Do you live alone here?'

Nahid took another large gulp from her drink. 'Yes.'

'Did you get along with Elisabeth?'

'Liz? Yeah sure. We're like...' She intertwined her index and middle finger. 'Bezzies.'

'Could she be involved?'

She flicked her hair. 'What do you mean? Involved?'

'In the business?'

She sat down on the couch facing him. 'If you are trying to dig up some dirt, I'd ask my mother. It was a suicide, simple as that. Ask yourself why my mother hired you, Yes, I don't get along with mother and that's why I'm here. Since dad died, she's never been the same. She wants me to marry and have children and be a submissive wife like she had been. Times have moved on.' She stood up and walked over to a mirror. 'Sure you don't understand, Mr Ghorbani? Sure it's no different in Iran. Is it?'

For Rebwar, Iran seemed like a distant memory. Even though he read a few newspapers and gossiped with some old friends, it was all in the past. 'I'd be a foreigner if I went back there.'

'You a fan of the Shah?'

'My wife is or my ex. Did he use drugs?'

'Mr Ghorbani. Drugs? Are we just brats to you?' And she grabbed her mobile from a table. 'My mother is going to hear about this.'

Rebwar got up and went up to a glass display that was filled with photos and trophies. They were of her tennis achievements. The silverware dated back a decade and she had won a few. He recognised Wimbledon where she had played as a junior.

'What do I expect?' Nahid was complaining on her phone. 'Well, some respect for starters and he's rude and a brute.'

The pictures were of her smiling in various tennis outfits. He hadn't spotted that spark in her today. It was as if a previous life had been put away in that glass box for people to admire.

'I don't care that he's a policeman. Can't you just mourn Izah like anyone else? He took...' She looked down, wiped a tear from her face and threw the phone into the couch. 'Bitch!'

SEVEN

Rebwar arrived in St Mark's Road in Hanwell, West London. He had a pickup and was driving down the long residential road, which was lined with semi-detached houses. He tried to find a space to park whilst he announced his arrival. He took the opportunity to call Raj, his technical wizard and old friend. Raj called him 'Uncle' as he had helped his father back in Iran. Rebwar had never had to learn any computer skills, so Raj was his go-to person. He also had an incredible appetite and every meeting involved some kind of fast food.

'Uncle, I was just thinking about you.' He gave a high-pitched giggle.

'You're hungry?'

Raj giggled on.

'I need you to dig up some information on a family called Sasani.'

'What Dinah's? What has she done?'

'It's her extended family. Need to go.' Rebwar dropped the call as he saw an old Indian lady approach his car, laden with large blue and white striped bags. He got out to help her.

'Couldn't you have come earlier? You're all the same.'

Rebwar popped the boot open. 'Going on holidays?'

'Never you mind. Now, you be careful with that.'

As he put the bags into the back of the car they clanked as if full metal objects and there was a strong smell of spices.

'Ealing station?' Rebwar confirmed.

'Yes, yes, can't you see? My daughter sorted it out. Go, go, there is no time to waste. I have people waiting for me.'

Rebwar put the car into gear and followed the instructions on his phone. 'Your daughter's not coming with you?'

'You keep your eyes on the road, mister. And she is to be married to a good family. She is not for you.'

He indicated to take a left. 'Arranged?'

'I am not having her choose any old husband. Surely you understand that. Have you got a daughter?'

'A son, Musa. He's seventeen.'

'Well, I'm sure you are looking for a suitable bride. Have you chosen?'

He noticed a text flash up from Raj. He was already on the case and wanted to meet. 'I will let my son make his own choices. In Iran, we don't have that tradition anymore. But it's not unheard of.'

'Well, it's our tradition and I will pair her off like I was, as was my grandmother. Look at this country and what it's becoming, a mix of inbred dogs.'

Rebwar looked at her angry wrinkled face. She had a collection of gold earrings and piercings on her ears and nose. 'You from India?'

'Pakistan. It was once a great country. But you know now... everyone thinks we are terrorists. Like you.'

He'd ferried his fair share of unpleasant people over the

years, but he wasn't too sure where this one wanted to go with her rant. His phone flashed with Dinah's number. He hadn't spoken to her since meeting her Auntie Jaleh and he was struggling with having to investigate her family. He let it go to voicemail.

'Over there! Drop me.'

Rebwar looked over to the station. 'Madam, I'll get a ticket. Have to drop you—'

'No, not over there. Otherwise I'll give no stars.' A fine would take out most of the day's profits, so he drove past the entrance to the station. She grabbed the back of his seat and shouted into his ear. 'Stop the car! Now! Did you hear me?'

Rebwar flicked his head out of the way and made the car swerve and it mounted the curb. He compensated and strayed into another lane. With a car honking and narrowly avoiding him, he stopped the car.

'You crazy driver,' she said. 'Did you not listen to me?' Undeterred, she got out of the car, rushed to the boot and opened it.

Rebwar didn't know where to look, with angry drivers giving middle fingers and abuse. 'Hey, what do you think you're doing?' Before he could get to her, she was swiftly walking away with her large clanking bags. His instincts told him to run after her but he slammed the boot shut and got back into the car. He lit a cigarette and drove off.

———

He arrived at West Acton tube station where Raj was waiting. His imposing mass made him stick out in the crowd outside the square, bricked station. Rebwar thought it looked more like a toaster than a modernist building. He stopped by the crossing, whose lights had turned red, wound down his window, and whistled Raj over. He spotted Rebwar and held out his hands as if Rebwar was meant to come over to pick him up to which Rebwar waved him over again and swore to himself.

'In a mood?' said Raj, filling the passenger seat and waiting for Rebwar to fist pump him back.

Rebwar silently swore to himself. 'So?'

'All right, all right, keep your hair on. Hello, nice to see you too. Oh thanks, how was your day?' Rebwar drove off, letting Raj have his own little private chat. 'You can just drop me off...'

Rebwar lit a cigarette. 'KFC?'

Raj put his index finger up, 'Chicken Kitchen on 265 High St. It's got five-star reviews.'

'Is this going to cost me?'

'I'm widening my palette, seeking fresh adventures.'

Rebwar checked him out. 'You got a girlfriend?'

Raj just giggled and blushed a bit. 'On the internet...'

'What's her name?'

Raj just shrugged.

'Oh, come on...'

Raj covered his eyes with his hand. 'Sexy212.'

Rebwar tried to make sense of what he had just said. 'A phone number?'

'Uncle, it's her handle. Look...' Raj showed him a picture on his mobile. Rebwar leaned in to see a blonde semi-hidden face, her hoodie and hair obscuring most of her features. 'She's from Estonia.'

'Are you sure she exists?' Rebwar looked for a parking space close to the fast-food restaurant.

'She's not a bot, if that's what you're saying.'

In the restaurant, Rebwar sat with a coffee, waiting for Raj to come back from ordering at the counter. He listened to Dinah's message. She was asking what he wanted for dinner. He smiled, thinking how she made him happy.

'Uncle... so here is what I've found. And are you sure you want to know?'

'Why?'

'Dunno, feels kind of weird looking into your girl-friend's family. Are you getting married?'

Rebwar leaned back and waved Raj away. But it was a valid question, and Dinah had a reputation for being a gold digger. Not that Rebwar had a fortune to his name. In fact, it was the opposite, particularly with having to pay child maintenance. And that was a struggle. 'It's a job. Her auntie has doubts about her son's suicide.'

Raj brought his soft drink and took a large sip through its straw. 'Successful business, but it's a classic front for laundering money and moving contraband.' He held his hands up. 'Haven't found anything. They look clean but their rep is on the shady side. They have had a few acci-dents in their warehouses. They pay good money...' Rebwar crossed his arms. 'Hear me? When you don't have to pay well but do, then it's suspect.'

'OK. And the family?'

Raj looked down at his phone and scrolled over the screen. 'Second generation Iranian. Both grandparents came over before the First World War. Farhad Sasani passed away in a car crash.'

'I need to know more about that.'

'You might need to ask Geraldine for that info. Pre-internet and a file somewhere in an archive. Where is my favourite cop?'

Rebwar could have asked the same question. 'Missing. Phone is dead.'

'Oh, and? You worried or...?'

It was a question he had tried to avoid and had hoped the answer would come knocking. But it hadn't. 'What about the suicide?'

'They did a post-mortem and have sent you the doctor's email. He hanged himself on a tree in Epping Forest and was found by a dog walker. Like his girlfriend.'

Raj showed him her Instagram page. He was still trying to understand what Instagram was all about. 'What does she do?' He instantly regretted asking the question.

'Well, look!' Raj blew out his large cheeks and took a big bite of his fried chicken burger. 'Can I join you when you interview her?'

Rebwar shook his head. Even though Raj would stop him from asking silly questions, he also didn't need someone to make her feel uncomfortable.

'But she's an influencer. You need me there. She'll be offended when you don't look impressed at her followings or how many views she's had with the latest Gucci handbag. Or been to that latest party.'

Rebwar still struggled with the concept of someone making money out of some pictures or mentioning a brand. Who the hell cared? Maybe Raj did have a point. How did she fit in with the Sasanis? 'OK, but behave. And make sure you... you know...'

Raj giggled and fist bumped him.

EIGHT

Geraldine sat in one of the corner benches in The Flower Pot, a cute little pub in the centre of Bedford that was her new local. On the outside it looked more like a sixties council house but the landlord had made it welcoming with hanging baskets and a fresh coat of light mint green paint. Inside it was a cosier affair with big black wooden beams and traditional furniture. She had chosen a seat where she could see onto the busy street and the entrance. She sipped her pint of Doom Bar and checked her watch. It was just past 7 pm and the man she was meeting was now late. Her nerves twitched, since she had no actual idea about who it was. Her gut told her to run away, but this wasn't going to just conveniently go away, as he had found her. There had also been no news from Plan B or anyone else. She checked her phone for a message from Rebwar. She had hoped that he would have called by now. Around her were couples and families having their Sunday dinners. It was busy enough for her to feel confident that he wouldn't try anything stupid. Derreck, the landlord had looked out for her before and wouldn't shy away from a fight. Then, by the back door appeared the man. His long black beard and thick dark eyebrows gave him an intense look. A large broken hooked nose completed the thug like impression. He had come in using the secret garden. With no real acknowledgment, he walked over to her and sat on the stool. A waft of stale cigarettes hit her.

She presented her hand and, after a hesitant look, he shook it firmly. 'Can I get you a drink, Mr Serid?'

He shook his head. 'You are Geraldine and partner of Rebwar?'

She took another sip of her beer. He was making her feel nervous. 'Something like that.' She tried to stay calm and courteous. 'What can I help you with?'

'I am looking for him.'

'You found me. Surely he isn't hiding. And how did you find me?'

A smile revealed perfect white teeth. 'I cannot find him. He is an old friend. We used to work together back in Iran. We were detectives in the police; I have old contacts.'

'It's been a couple of months since I've heard from him. Sorry but I can't really help you.'

'But you are Geraldine Smith and you work for police?'

'Did.'

He clicked his fingers. 'I have found the right person. My government is looking for my old friend and I am here to help him. He needs to know that he is in danger. They are looking for him.'

Geraldine leaned back, wondering what was really going on. How had he really found her? 'Farrouk Serid isn't it? It's because of you he had to escape Iran.' He reached for his Mehr branded packet of cigarettes. Which looked like counterfeit Marlboro Golds and with the lack of government warnings, they were from the black market. 'You can't smoke here.' To which he smiled and left the box on the table. 'And you call this a free country with all your laws and cameras. And that is no replacement for God. I know you know where he is. You have been friends for a long time and helped him out.' He pointed with his index finger to the ceiling. 'I know this.' He held his heart with his other hand.

She crossed her arms and looked at him. There was something menacing about him. 'No comment. Now, I can pass on a message if you like and maybe it will reach him.'

He waved his finger at her. 'Now, you just told me you know him. Yes, you are a good friend. You will tell him he is in danger. And I can help him. How is his wife and son?'

Geraldine shrugged and drunk her beer. 'Not my business.'

'I hear that they divorced. She is an honourable woman, well respected. Sure I can find her too. Wonder what he will say?'

She leaned forward towards him. 'Is that a threat?'

'Just talking about old days. You are an intelligent woman. You have studied. Did he work for you? I thought he was just an Uber driver. That is what he told me.'

'I thought you were in jail?' She remembered Rebwar mentioning this a few years before.

'It is very political over in Iran and...' He pointed to himself. 'If you have ambitions like me...'

'And corrupt. Look, Mr Serid, I can pass on a message but I don't know where Rebwar is. And I'm sure you can order an Uber and find him.'

'I just hope they don't find him first. Jail is not nice and he doesn't have many friends.'

Geraldine thought back on Rebwar's stories about Iran. Everyone doubted everything. 'How will he know you are who you say you are?'

He laughed and wagged his finger at her. 'I see you have met him. Tell him I know who commander is. I have taken enough of your time. Inshallah and may you be blessed.' He bowed to her and left.

Geraldine sat there puzzled about why he had sought her out. Was he trying to rattle Rebwar or her? It was certainly working.

NINE

The Pizza Express in Chelsea was in an imposing building with had a small white arch as an entrance. Rebwar sat at a table in the courtyard outside where he could smoke. Large lit rectangular umbrellas covered each table. For a chain restaurant, this place had a grand air to it, with its statues and columns. From what he'd heard from a few of his fares, the building had had a colourful past being an artist studio to a bohemian disco. From where he was sitting, he could see onto King's Road. He sipped his half pint of beer. Rebwar had picked the place to finally officially introduce his relationship with Dinah to his son, Musa. They were both late. He'd offered to pick up Musa with the intention of having a chat with him. A couple of months before, Rebwar had told Musa about Dinah at a Chelsea game. He should have waited till the end of the match as he got the blame for them drawing to Manchester United. But was there a good time? Musa still wanted his family back. Rebwar and his ex, Hourieh, had struggled with him. First, he'd been taken away from Iran and then had to make new friends. Rebwar was having doubts if he was going to come.

He looked around and saw couples having romantic dinners and a couple of families. He glanced at the menu again and doubled checked if they had pepperoni pizza. It was Musa's favourite. He looked at his phone. There was a message from Raj. He took a deep breath. He was regretting taking on the Suren job. What was he going to find? And what was he going to say to Dinah?

'Another beer?' asked the young black-haired waitress. Rebwar nodded.

'Can I interest you in some garlic bread or olives?'

Her smile froze as he thought about it. 'Just the beer.' He got up, walked outside and lit a cigarette. It helped for a moment. But what was Musa expecting? A new family? He read Raj's message. It was the address for the Dr Kalvin Roe who performed the post-mortem on Izah Sasani. There was a picture attached. He stretched out his arm to get a better look at it. A portly ginger-haired man with an intense gaze.

'Making a selfie?'

Rebwar looked up to see Dinah, smiling and dressed in a white puffer jacket with faux fur on its hood. He put his phone away and gave her a kiss. She presented her cheek.

'Lipstick my love.' And she took his cigarette from his hand and took a deep breath. 'You nervous?'

He nodded and took the cigarette back. 'He's still on his way. He better make it.'

Dinah grabbed his arm and they walked back into the restaurant to sit down. 'It's all right if he—'

Rebwar stood up again and went over to the archway. Musa stood underneath with I paused my game to be here printed on his T-shirt. Rebwar wanted to give Musa a comb but refrained. He shook his hand and gave him a hug. 'Thanks, son, I know you didn't want to come over.'

With his head lowered, Musa made his way over and

flopped into the chair. Dinah got up and gave him a kiss on his cheek. Musa managed to give a forced smile back.

Rebwar pushed over the menu to him. 'They've got your favourite.' He scanned the menu, shook his head and pushed back it back. 'It's here.'

'Hawaiian.' And he took out his phone and a pack of cards.

'Sure, they'll make it for you,' said Dinah waiving down one of the servers.

Rebwar looked through the menu again. How had Musa got it wrong? Or had he? It wouldn't be the first time he had changed his mind. And this was a perfect way to show him up. As Dinah asked the waiter to see if they had the pizza for Musa, Rebwar tried to get his attention. 'Son, there's other ones.' Musa was laying out the cards to play patience. Their suits glowed in the dark. 'Cool cards.'

'Present from Raj.'

'Musa, dear,' said Dinah. 'He's going to ask. OK?'

Musa just shrugged. Rebwar couldn't even mention Chelsea as they had just lost to Leicester City.

'What game did you pause?' Musa just made a face back and Dinah, also feeling frustration, squeezed Rebwar's hand.

'Should have worn my first choice.'

'Oh, what was it?' said Dinah with a curious smile.

He showed them a picture from his phone: A T-shirt with a slogan that read I didn't want to come.

'Oh, creative. Now I heard you're a Chelsea supporter.' Musa leaned back and carried on looking at his phone. Rebwar was about to intervene, but she held his hand down. 'Heard of Olivier Giroud? Well, his wife came into the shop to buy a dress.'

'Did you ask how Celia is doing?'

Rebwar and Dinah looked at each other, wondering who that was.

'Like you two, she cheated on him.'

Rebwar clenched his teeth and took a deep breath.

'Should have seen her car,' said Dinah. 'Bentley. And she flashed the cash...'

'He's got a Ferrari 458 spider, red.'

The waiter brought over some more drinks and said they could do a special request. Rebwar finished his beer and ordered another one.

'Did one of your exes have one?' Musa asked Dinah.

'Yeah, but he was a cock. Sorry for my Arabic. Glad to have seen the back of him. Jealous and angry. Nice car. So where are you working now? Sure you don't want to go back to my boutique? Oh, I've got a better idea. What about I ask my Auntie Jaleh?'

Rebwar had to hold his immediate answer, which was no. It had become complicated enough.

'Doing what? No dishes?'

'It's a big company. Wouldn't that be a great idea?' And she looked over to Rebwar.

He forced a smile and hoped they would forget it by the next day. 'Shall we order?'

'Can I drive their limo?'

'There's better jobs, Musa,' said Rebwar.

'What about your mate, Bijan? He's got a Rolls-Royce.'

'Sure we can ask. I find it cute. Like father and son. And one day you can have a fleet of them.' Dinah got her phone to make a selfie and lifted her glass to cheer. 'Come on, guys, it's a family moment.'

Rebwar's phone lit up. It was a number he didn't recognise. He got up and stepped outside to take it.

———

Raindrops peppered the pavement around Rebwar as he answered the phone. 'Hello.'

'Hey.'

He recognised her soft voice, which had a hint of nervousness to it.

'Are you being watched?'

Since taking the job, it hadn't crossed his mind that someone could be watching him. But it wasn't a bad shout. He looked around him, scanning the cars and people passing by. 'Who should I be looking for?'

'A friend of yours. Mr Serid.'

His old partner from Tehran. He felt a cold shiver run down his back and leaned forward. 'Go on.'

'He asked me to pass on a message. That there's people from the government after you.'

He lit his cigarette. 'Tell me what he looked like.'

'Beard, thick dark eyebrows, large broken beak nose, creepy.'

Rebwar rubbed his stubble. 'Did you get a picture?'

'No, but he told me to say that he knows who the commander is. Mean anything?'

It did. It concerned an old case regarding a mysterious serial killer in Tehran. 'Yeah, is that all he wanted to say?'

'He fucking found me more than you did. What's this all about?'

He leaned back against the white wall. 'I don't know. I got shown a picture of him being hanged. And then got a phone call from him. Someone is playing me.'

'Well, keep me out of this, OK? I'm quite happy serving cakes to old people.'

'Nice to—' She hung up. He didn't even get to ask how she was doing. Rebwar returned to the table.

'Where's Musa?'

'Gone.' Dinah downed her glass of white wine. 'Back to his game, I think.'

Rebwar swore to himself, anger mounting as he ran back onto the street, hoping to see Musa. He tried phoning him but his call went to voicemail and he knew better than to leave an angry message.

TEN

Rebwar drove up Carr Road which was not far from Epping Forest and the Sasani's family home. The red bricked row of houses were simple two-floor suburban projects from the fifties. It was a haven for families with its large practical cars and a diverse collection of bicycles. He parked his car and went up to the address that Jaleh had passed on. Weeds lined the short stone path to the door. Black bin bags were lined up in the front garden. He rang the bell and waited. He was greeted by a smiling young woman.

'Hi, you must be Rebwar,' she said out of breath. 'I've only got a few minutes. Got to walk the dog.' She waved him in. The hallway looked bright and had crayon marks along the walls. 'Carry on to the end. Tea? Only got herbal.'

Rebwar shook his head and found the living room. Children's toys were scattered over the floor like an unfinished jigsaw puzzle. Plates with half-eaten food cluttered the table. The kids were outside in the garden playing, which surprised him as it was a brisk, cold December day.

'Sorry for the mess. Been looking after the neighbours'

kids. They wanted to use our trampo. Mummy said you had some questions.'

Rebwar moved some magazines off the sofa and sat down. 'Yes.' He got out his small notepad from his black leather coat. 'It's about your brother...' He waited for her reaction.

She held her forehead and said. 'Yeah, yeah,' Her eyes welled up. 'I'm sorry.'

'Sorry, I—'

'No, no, mummy warned me. Oh!' She breathed in and sniffed. 'Just doesn't get easier, does it?'

'Did he—?'

'Fancy something stronger?'

He shook his head.

She grabbed a plastic flask from the shelf. 'He was the light and soul of this fucked up family. I know that Nahid is the eldest, but she doesn't care on which side her toast is buttered. Spoilt brat and first-class bitch and... Sorry.' She drank from her flask. 'Why did mummy hire you and who the hell are you?'

Rebwar noticed a change in her tone. As if she had surfaced from a deep dive. 'She's got suspicions about your brother's apparent suicide.'

'It was coming, I mean...' She stopped and stared at him. 'Who are you?'

'Rebwar. And I was a police detective back in Tehran. Why would you say that your mother has doubts about the verdict?'

She laughed. 'Obvious isn't it. I mean, do your fucking job. Or should I say, don't, so you can fleece her.'

'So it was a suicide? No note? No previous attempt or calls for help? And it was a shock. But not to you?'

'They didn't care about him like I did.' She looked out

into the garden with the children playing. 'You can't count on their opinions. He just paid their bills and lifestyle.'

Rebwar got up and walked over to a shelf by the television, which had a series of family pictures. He picked one of her with Izah. They were sitting in a restaurant, cheering with their filled wineglasses to the camera.

'I'd graduated from art school and he invited me for a meal.' She grabbed the frame off him and put it back. 'He cared.' The kids screamed outside and she went over to door and shouted to them to keep it quiet. She held her temples and rubbed them.

'You OK?' Rebwar moved over to her.

'You sit there. How many more questions?'

'If this is not a good time, I can come back.'

'I rather not. This is all a farce.' And she went over to grab her flask to take a drink from it.

Rebwar got up and grabbed her flask from her, to which she gave a shriek. He held her off, unscrewed the cap, went over to the door and emptied its contents onto the patio.

'That... that was... That.'

Alcohol fumes drifted into the open door. 'A running theme. Now, tell me... where were you on Friday the 16th of November?'

Sarah fell to her knees and sobbed into her hands. The children stopped playing and looked over at them. He went over to Sarah and was about to put his hand on his shoulder when she pushed it away. He didn't know if she was acting or actually upset.

'How would I know?'

'Look, Sarah, I will come back and ask again. I am going to find out what happened. With or without your help. So where were you when your brother hanged himself?'

She stood up, wiped her tears away and waved the kids

on. It was as if they had seen this before. 'I was at the Wild-wood with some friends. A birthday party.'

'Who was there? Husband? Family?'

'Fuck sake, Oh,' and she held her forehead and paced the room. 'Ex-husband, yeah.'

'Names?'

'Dakota' and she looked up. 'He's my ex and Lisa and Billy...' She looked down at the floor. 'Some others... Are you going to talk to my ex-husband?'

Rebwar wrote the names. 'Yes. And you went home?'

'I can't remember. It's all a blank.'

'Pictures? Facebook?'

She squinted her eyes at him as if she was trying to focus. 'Sure, but... can I do this another day? I've got to bring back the kids. And shop.'

'It's not over.'

'With what authority? You're just a fucking investigator. No. Fuck off and leave us alone. My friends won't have it either. And I don't care what mum is going to say. OK?'

Rebwar took a breath and realised that whatever she was on, it was starting to wear off. He was going to try to find another tack to get her to talk. But at that moment he couldn't think of a motive she would have. From the pictures she had of Izah, they clearly loved each other.

ELEVEN

Rebwar had parked his Prius at the Epping Golf Course and was looking around for Dr Kalvin Roe's car registration. After a few minutes, he found a blue Mercedes. He'd never been to a gold club and this was a novel experience for him. Not that he was planning to play. It wasn't a popular game back in Iran and he'd had to look it up as he had never met anyone who'd played it, although there was a thirteen-hole course back in the capital. From the standard of the cars, it was a rich man's sport. The clubhouse was a large, wooden, barn-like building, which wasn't what he had expected. Raj had explained to him that golf was played on large open fields. He wasn't expecting to find Dr Roe around, as his secretary had told him he played in the morning with his friends. Rebwar tried not to look too out of place but, from the outfits around him, this would be difficult. He expected to be confronted at some point.

He found a map on a board giving an overview of the course with its eighteen holes. He hadn't thought this plan through. He wanted to confront Dr Roe and embarrass him in front of his friends. Also gauge his reaction. But how was he going to find him? There were multiple playing fields. He spotted people using buggies to get around. There was a shed with a couple of them parked up. He waited for a moment where they were unattended. He picked one that still had a key in its ignition, mounted it and silently drove off. He lit a cigarette and set off for the first hole, taking the approach of going through the course in numerical order. The sun was shining and there was a sheen of dew over the green drives. He passed a group of men walking along the course. They glanced at him and carried on with their conversation.

Rebwar was looking for a portly, ginger-haired man. As he carried on driving along the course, He realised it was going to be harder than he had expected, as nearly all the players wore caps and ported similar gear. Steering with one hand and lighting another cigarette with the other, the buggy veered off the path and slipped sideways on the wet grass. Players shouted and jeered. He carried on, leaving a muddy trail behind him. By the fifth hole he found a group of golfers that were about to start. One of them fitted Dr Roe's description. He stopped the vehicle and watched them. The three men across him. Rebwar walked over to them, ready to fire off his questions.

A short man in a branded tracksuit cut off his approach. 'Hey mate, you lost or something?' he said angrily, brandishing a driving iron.

Rebwar walked past him towards Dr Roe. His stare making him turn away.

'Hey! Mate, I'm talking to you. Mate?'

Rebwar carried on and stepped right up to Dr Roe, making sure he was feeling uncomfortable.

He took a couple of steps back and said, 'And you are?'

'Dr Kalvin Roe?'

'What is your business?' Dr Roe said nervously swallowing.

'Hey, mate,' said the short man. 'I was talking to you. You're interrupting our game.'

'Izah Sasani's post-mortem,' said Rebwar. 'You did it?' He pointed at the doctor.

Dr Roe held up his hand to the angry man to hold off. The third man was holding his phone, ready to call for help. 'What about it?'

'I need to have a word.'

'I have office hours.'

'I am investigating for Jaleh Sasani.'

Dr Roe's face dropped and his posture stiffened.

'About his suicide. I need to know if it was one.'

'Well, huh, yeah, I... I did do it, yes.'

The other two men approached the doctor sensing his unease.

'Guys, I've got this. It's... business. Jock...' He went over to him. 'Listen, I'll be right back.'

'You sure mate? Because...' And he looked over to Rebwar, still holding his club. 'You just shout.'

Rebwar breathed in, clenched his teeth and looked over to Dr Roe. 'Like to see the post-mortem report.'

The other two men went over to the tee-off.

'She's got it.'

'What made you say it was suicide?'

Dr Roe crossed his arms and twisted his head. 'The evidence. Read the report. Frankly, you're wasting my time. Mr?'

'Rebwar,' He took out his notebook. 'What if it was made to look like a suicide?'

A large frown appeared on Roe's face. 'No, no. Impossible. What makes you say that?'

'Izah didn't leave a note—'

Dr Roe laughed. 'What? This isn't The Bill. Call yourself a detective?'

Rebwar stepped up to him. 'Did someone pay you?'

'What? Are you seriously insinuating that this is a cover-up? You do know who the Sasanis are?' He grabbed his golf caddy.

'He was killed in a secluded wood. The police came in the morning. When were you called?'

'Look... er... Rebwar, it's a closed case. The coroner's verdict was suicide. If you have an issue with that, then go through the proper legal channels.' He took the handle of his caddy and went over to his mates.

'Dr Roe, he was murdered.'

Roe stopped and looked up. 'No, you're not listening. Give it up and move on. I know it's not what Mrs Sasani wanted to hear. But its closed. Understand?' His two friends had teed off and looked over to him.

Rebwar reached for another cigarette and lit it. He was going to have to dig a little deeper into Roe's story but, for today, that was all he was going to get from him. He had made his point.

TWELVE

The grey sky contrasted with the dark bare trees that swayed in the wind. Brown and red dried leaves swirled around the clearing where Rebwar stood. He zipped his leather coat up to his neck. This was where Izah Sasani had hanged himself, deep in Epping Forest. Geraldine had worked her police magic and got him the police report and the post-mortem. He walked around the edges of the tree line, trying to make sense of the entire scene. It had taken him a good thirty minutes to get to this point. He looked at the photos that had been taken on the day they had found Izah. There was a large thick oak tree that had an overhanging branch. Somehow, he had tied a rope to it and hanged himself from it. Rebwar had seen his fair share of hangings. It was the regime's favourite capital punishment. Then there were all the unfortunates using a rope to end their sorry lives. But not everyone got it right; there was an art to it. If you jumped off a bridge and it was too high, you would decapitate yourself. Not high enough and you would slowly suffocate. The sweet spot was for your neck to break.

From the picture, Izah's body was more than ten feet

above, just out of reach and there was a good six feet of rope, which meant if he had jumped off the thick branch, his head would have come off. He would have to ask a doctor to calculate it, taking into account Izah's weight and the drop. But, from the cases he had seen back in Iran, this one would have ended up in a decapitation, even if Izah had slowly lowered himself from the branch. And why would you do that? Suicide was meant to be quick, not a torture. Otherwise, there was the chance he would change his mind. Also, something Rebwar had seen from some lucky survivors, although most ended up with life-changing injuries. There was no ladder found, so Izah must have climbed up the tree. In the middle of the branch Rebwar could see signs of where the rope had dug into the wood and taken off the bark.

According to the report, he had been found on the morning of Saturday the 17th of November by a dog walker. He'd been dead for twelve hours. And he had died of suffocation, which meant that somehow, he managed to lower himself. Another possibility was that Izah had swung from the trunk side of the tree. Again, it was a lot of trouble to prove something that made no sense. It was an odd choice for Izah to come here. Why? Rebwar couldn't make sense of it. No one had mentioned his love of the outdoors or some occult belief in forests or gods. Not that Rebwar had pushed about Izah's beliefs. He carried on looking around the clearing with its moss-covered fallen trees and piles of crunched-up leaves. There were no signs of a struggle. And of the people they had interviewed, no one had spotted his car or anyone else's. If there had been foul play, they had chosen this place for a reason. It was perfect for staging a suicide.

But how had they done it without leaving evidence and

why? Rebwar carried on walking around, hoping to find something. Had Izah come here of his own free will? Or was this a place he had come to as a teenager? Rebwar had come across empty beer cans, cigarettes and condoms on his way over here. He had plenty of ideas, but he had to find evidence.

THIRTEEN

A barista foamed up a metal jug full of steam and it sounded as if there was going to be an imminent explosion as the pitch of the machine kept rising. Individual conversations either rose in volume or stopped. Rebwar sipped his tea as he observed the scene. He was in a small independently branded coffee shop in the docklands. Of course he'd been here before; his ex-wife had been hiding in an apartment just around the corner. Bijan had been keeping his mistress in a fancy loft in a newly built luxury block. Rebwar had found out that Bijan had been buying gifts from Dinah's shop and sending them to her, so he followed the trail and found Musa and Hourieh camping up. It brought back mixed emotions of betrayal and relief. She'd had an affair with an old acquaintance, Dr Gul, who had been found dead down in a sewer. The whole sorry affair stank, in more ways than one, and Rebwar had to pick up the pieces. He was still trying to forgive Hourieh.

'Hi. You were at the funeral?'

Rebwar snapped out of his reverie to see Elisabeth Knowles. She looked very glamorous in her brightly coloured scarf and large designer sunglasses. She undid her pink woollen jacket to reveal a figure-hugging dress. He couldn't help but stare at her pierced nipples. She caught his gaze and he looked down quickly, embarrassed.

She lifted her glasses and gave him a cheeky smile. 'Are you Dinah's current squeeze?'

It took a few awkward seconds for him to say yes. He had been rumbled and had been hoping to surprise her with a question. He processed the idea of him being a transient lover. What did people think of Dinah? Liz pointed to the free seat opposite him. He nodded and smiled.

'You know I just looove her boutique, sooo avant garde and sexy. Looove to have one of her numbers. Sure you can't get me one?'

Rebwar was still trying to regain his composure as her long slender fingers tiptoed over his hand. It gave him goose-bumps over his exposed forearms.

'Mmm, I can see why Dinah took you to the funeral.' And she gave a quiet murmur as if she was pretending to be a cat. 'I like sharing...'

He moved into his chair, trying to find a comfortable position and put her ideas out of his consciousness. But she moved forward, making sure her dress tightened over her slim body, leaving little to the imagination.

'Oh those, slinky silk dresses. You know best not to wear anything underneath them. It's like...'

The barista made another latte and filled the small shop with a high-pitched whine. Which felt strangely apt given what Rebwar was going through. 'Miss Knowles, I've got some questions about your boyfriend.'

Her smile vanished as quickly as it had appeared. She grabbed her sunglasses and slid them down, only to take them off. 'What about Izah?'

'Do you think it was a suicide or a murder, like his mother?'

She let out a long sigh and pulled her coat over her body. 'You know, I fancy a drink?'

Rebwar looked over at the chalkboard above the coffee machine. 'Espresso?'

'Think I might need something stronger.' She shook her head and stared out of the window.

'Miss—'

'Liz. Call me Liz, please. Why are you digging all this up? Jaleh won't give it up. It was a tragic suicide. It was going to happen. OK?'

'What makes you say that?'

She shrugged her shoulders. 'Look at the family, I mean, what a bunch of privileged arrogant twats. He was different. He had a vision and a future.'

Her eyes welled up. She found a tissue and mopped them before a drop could upset her perfect makeup.

'So why commit suicide? Was it an accident? Cry for help gone wrong?' which he didn't believe, as he would have never chosen such a secluded spot.

'Maybe.' She stood up, looked at him and smiled. 'Sure you can't get me that evening silk dress? It'll be the talk of the town. My Insta lot will set fire to it.'

'Fire?'

She laughed. 'Pass on the message? Mr Rebwar.' And she picked up her designer branded handbag and walked out of the coffee shop.

He watched her as she made her way down the street, grabbed his coat and went after her.

FOURTEEN

Rebwar kept his distance from Liz. He was curious about where she was going. He couldn't work her out. Either she was on drugs or had some character disorder. She kept stopping and either checking herself with her phone or taking selfies. It was something he didn't understand even if had been told countless times by Musa or even Dinah. It did help him to track people down. She arrived at a large glassed high rise that faced onto the Thames. She made her way into the large imposing reception, where she waved at a man behind a desk. From the addresses on the wall, it was a mixed-use building with businesses and flats. He walked in and checked at which floor the lift stopped that Liz had taken. It was the twentieth.

Some people walked out of a lift, and Rebwar tried to get into it. But the man at the reception walked over and stopped him.

'Sorry, sir but you need a guest pass if you are going to visit.'

He played for time by checking his phone. 'Yes, Liz

forgot her...' He searched his pockets. 'I'd rather not say. What flat is she in?'

'Sorry, sir, but I need you to fill in this form and will need to contact the person. You are visiting?'

'Liz... Elisabeth Knowles.'

He nodded, picked up the receiver, and dialled some numbers. Rebwar looked at the guest book and scanned the names. There had been no guests visiting her today.

'There's no one there. Can I leave a message or you can leave whatever it is with me?' He gave Rebwar a fake smile.

He returned the insult and picked out a cigarette out of the box. The man gave him a stare. He lit the cigarette and walked out of the building. In the quiet back streets, he spotted the CCTV covering each corner. He stubbed his cigarette, and a door opened next to him. A man wearing a hi-vis jacket walked out. Rebwar took out his pack of cigarettes and went up to him to offer him one. He was a thin man with dark skin. He took one and they lit up. 'Have a favour to ask you.'

'Sorry?'

'I want to surprise an old friend of mine. It's his birthday. You mind if you let me in? He did it to me last week. Nearly caught me with my pants down.' He winked at the man. 'If you know what I mean.'

'For real?'

'Lucky it wasn't his Mrs.' Rebwar let this thought sit with him.

'Nah, you taking...,' to which he smiled. 'Nearly got me, man. But you... aren't you?'

'Like to...' He took out a picture of Liz from her social media account. The man's eyes widened. Rebwar flicked a few more photos to which he whistled.

'Out of my league.' And he looked at Rebwar. 'And you're... You must be loaded.'

Rebwar reached out for some cash and gave him two twenty-pound notes. 'I need to get him back.'

The man looked around and waved him in. 'Mate, take pictures.'

Rebwar walked into the bare concrete stairwell. It was the service area; was bare of any fittings and had the odd emergency sign with the usual instructions. He carried on up the stairs and looked up. He now wished that he had taken the lift. But he couldn't risk it, as there probably was a security code or card to get up to that floor. His breathing got more laboured as he carried on up. At the ninth floor, he was desperate for a cigarette. His lungs were burning and he couldn't remember the last time he'd walked that far up stairs. It reminded him of the flat back in Chalk Farm which he'd had with Hourieh and Musa. The council owned it and the lift was in a constant state of disrepair. At least this stairwell didn't have the smell of piss and rotting trash. He had tried to make the living arrangements work, but Hourieh had grander ideas. Being in a safe place wasn't enough. Footsteps echoed down the stairwell. He looked up and down and caught a glimpse of a man in a black mac. A door screeched open and he disappeared inside.

FIFTEEN

After what felt like a climb up a mountain, Rebwar stopped in front of a big red 20 painted on a door. He took a few large breaths before opening it. With his handkerchief, he mopped up his sweaty brow. Now he regretted not taking the lift. Fresh air whistled past the gap as he pushed through the door. The carpeted hallway had a thick blue and black pattern. The walls lined with striped wallpaper and hung with pictures. He checked one out of a London skyline. Then he stood and perused a dozen or more closed doors. How was he going to find the flat? At the end of the hallway, he saw a ray of sunshine shone onto the wall, coming from a door that was slightly ajar. He walked towards it and noticed that it had been forced open. He recognised Miss Knowles' voice coming from inside the flat. It sounded like she was talking to the police. He waited and listened and then pushed the door slowly open.

Liz Knowles was pacing up and down the living room, holding her phone. The large windows dominated the room, which looked out onto the Thames and the City of London.

She spotted him and paused for a moment until there

was the faint sound of a voice on her phone. 'No. Can you come now? Yes, it's an emergency. I think he's here...' Rebwar glanced at the door, wondering if he should make a sharp exit. 'Yes... Yes... Okay... Thank you... He's... Fuck sake get on with it!' And she dropped the call. 'Can't you see! I've been burgled?'

'Did you see him?'

'Of course I didn't. Would I still be here?'

'You've checked that he's not hiding?'

Her face paled by a few shades as she looked fearfully at the half-open doors.

'Stay in the corner and away from the door.' Rebwar grabbed a bronze statue from a cupboard. It was of two abstract figures embracing. It felt cold and heavy. He went into an adjoining room where there was a king-size bed. Nothing had been touched apart from of a couple of wardrobe doors. He carried on into the ensuite bathroom, which again was clear. He made his way across the living room to another bedroom. This one was larger and it was a mess. He had difficulty getting around it. He carried on into the bathroom, which was also littered with clothes and beauty products, then went back into the main room. There was only a closed door remaining. He pointed to it.

'An office...,' said Liz.

Rebwar held up the statue, ready to strike. He pushed onto the door handle and opened the door. It was dark inside. He waited for his eyes to adjust, ready to strike. He felt by the door frame and found the light switch. The lights flickered. He swung out. Before him was a large man. As the strip light tried to stay on, he threw the statue at the body, which clanged like an empty metal drum. It was a suit of armour. Liz rushed in and laughed. With his heart still thumping, Rebwar wasn't seeing the funny side. He checked his watch. He had maybe ten minutes to check the flat for clues.

'Fuck!' Liz rushed in and pulled out the drawers to a large wooden desk. 'Our laptop... and his phone... and...' She held her hair up. 'There was... No... What I am going to do?'

Rebwar went back to the master bedroom where he checked the mirrored sliding wardrobes. Hanging neatly were suits and shirts. He went through their pockets and found a Mercedes car key, which he took. On one of the white shirts was a faded mark on the cuff. He took a picture. On the shelves were different coloured T-shirts. He took more photos.

She walked in and swore. 'They've taken all my dresses and outfits. Dolce & Gabbana, Gucci, Armani... That's what they were here for.'

Rebwar looked around. How could she tell? None of her clothes were hung but laid out on a couch, lounge chair, bed. There were big branded shopping bags filled with more clothes. He only had a couple more minutes. 'Who would do this?'

'Whoever it is, they are going to pay. You know how much has gone?' She took out her phone made a selfie of herself.

Rebwar pulled out a cardboard box from a lower shelf. It took him a few seconds to understand what he was looking at. Some kind of sex toys. He pushed it back and left. He needed to get out of there before he was going to be seen, although with all the CCTV coverage it was only a matter of time before he was going to be brought in for questioning. He had an alibi in the form of Miss Knowles. He took the service stairs and made his way down. Voices travelled up from the lower floors. The distinct radio chatter gave them away. He was going to have to find a way out. The nineteenth floor was identical to the one above and Rebwar made his way to the main lift and called it. It pinged its arrival and the metal door slid open. He could see his reflection in the lift's mirror. He breathed a sigh of relief and then pressed for the basement. Now he had to hope there was no code needed and that no one was going to join him. He pressed the button again. The door closed and opened. Voices in the corridor grew louder. He pressed it again. This time the lift descended. He watched the numbers count down.

As he got to minus one, the lift stopped. The doors slid open and he listened for noises. There were faint sirens but he heard nothing in the garage. He walked out and saw neatly parked cars. Some were covered up. He pressed the key he'd taken. Along the far wall lined up with neatly parked cars, a Mercedes' indicator lights flashed. He went up to it. It was low, angry-looking and had two seats. He'd never been in a sports car. He opened the door. The smell of leather and glue oozed out. He sat down and was hugged in like he was in a cocoon. He looked around for the ignition. A couple of lights pulsed at him. He pressed the start button and the car rumbled to life. He felt nervous about being in someone's pride and joy. It was like taking Miss Knowles on an illicit date. He was sure Jaleh would forgive him. He looked up as if she was there watching him. He put the car into drive and pressed the throttle.

SIXTEEN

Geraldine gulped down the last inch of her pint. She put the empty glass down and felt a light buzz. The dullness of her day began to fade away. There was another full glass of lager waiting for her. It was happy hour at her local and she had taken the two for one offer. Groups of men and women filled the bar. Jokes and laughter drowned out the background music. Geraldine let the atmosphere wash over her. Since meeting that man Farrouk or whatever his real name was, memories had flooded back, the very ones she had run away from. She grabbed the full glass and drank as much as she could, hoping to drown out her feelings, or at least dull them. It had worked before. She closed her eyes and tried to listen to the music. Who was she kidding? She took out her phone and flipped through photos of her ex. She still missed her.

'Need another one?'

There was another pint in front of her. She looked up and time froze. It was only when her body demanded air that she moved. The man sat down in front of her. Highclere, her Plan B contact – a tall, black, scarred, suited and booted man. She had hoped to never see him again. 'What the fuck are you doing here?'

'I could ask you the same question.'

She caught her reflection in his dark mirrored glasses. It made her uneasy and she felt her head spin. She grabbed at the table to steady herself.

'Now, what's Rebwar up to?'

She just shrugged and took another gulp from her pint.

'He's your asset.'

'Oh, fuck right off back to your creepy hole,' she tried to say. 'What have you got for me?'

'Why's he popped up in a robbery?'

Her eyes focused on him. He looked stern, as if waiting for an answer. But she had none to give. 'A what?'

'You heard. Your asset is moonlighting. Heard that he's working as a private hack for some crime syndicate.'

She looked over to the bar, hoping that when she turned back again Hichclere would turn out to have been a figment of her imagination. No such luck. He now looked menacing, even pissed off. 'He's got his life and I've got mine,' she said. 'If you need us, then give us an assignment.'

'He's your responsibility...' He looked at a rowdy bunch of girls downing their cocktails and asking for another round.

She felt herself sway and trying to keep her nervous giggles at bay. It just felt absurd. 'And what are you going to do about it? Heh, I mean, fuck this. Fuck all of you.'

Highclere straightened his striped three-piece suit taking out the unwanted creases as if she had just inflicted them. 'No need for your potty language. Just need to make a call to your sister Rachel... Let's just say she won't be pleased to hear from you...'

Geraldine couldn't remember the last time she had

spoken to Rachel who had texted saying she had been let out of prison. Rachel had been the reason Plan B had coerced her into working for them. She had lied for Rachel when she was a DI. Plan B cut a deal with Geraldine that instead of doing time she would have work for them as well as keeping her desk job but as a demoted DC. Now she wanted out and had walked away from it all. Of course, they were having none of it. 'When is this all going to stop?'

He got his mobile out and checked it. 'When we say so. Now get your house in order. Keep him in that taxicab. All right?'

Geraldine downed the rest of her beer. Her pulse was racing again. If only Rebwar had kept his head down. Now she was going to have to be mother. She looked down at the wooden floor.

'All right?'

She crossed her arms and leaned back into her seat.

Highclere took out a mobile from his inside jacket pocket and put it in front of her. 'Call me as soon as it's cleared up.' He stood up.

Geraldine looked at him and back at the phone. She wanted to throw it at him and tell him where to go. But what was the point?

SEVENTEEN

Rebwar knocked rhythmically on the shiny wooden flat door and then used a key to get in. The apartment was large and furnished with stylish designer sofas. He called out for Dinah. She responded with a hello. He slipped off his shoes and hung his leather jacket. He turned around to be greeted by a warm smile and glass of red wine. She gave him a lingering kiss.

'How was your day?'

'Got a new car...,' he laughed.

'Oh? What was wrong with the old one?'

He went over to the white leather sofa and sat down. 'Nothing. Ever driven one of these?' He pointed to the car's remote on the glass table and watched her swing her hips to him. He still couldn't quite get used to her beauty and had to pinch himself. She bent down, letting her loose tracksuit top reveal her bare flesh. His pulse raced.

She picked up the keys, 'SL AMG, yeah, nice car... What the hell?'

'Shall we go for a drive?'

Dinah took the keys and spun the ring around her index finger. 'Not till you tell me what is going on.'

He leaned back into the deeply padded couch. 'Do you think Izah committed suicide?'

She grabbed her glass of wine off the glass coffee table and sat on the floor, legs crossed. 'Yes, why not?'

'I went to the scene. And you've...' He suddenly realised that she hadn't lived in Iran. His ex, Hourieh, would have seen her fair share of public executions and it was frowned upon not to attend them. 'So he hanged himself from a tree in a forest. He couldn't have done it alone without decapitating himself. Also, I haven't heard of any previous attempts. No note and...'

'What about Farhad? Wasn't that a suicide? And it runs in the family, surely.'

It was a good point, which he hadn't considered. He sipped his wine; it was deep and fruity. 'So you think he did it?'

'Sure. Or you would have found some evidence by now.' She got up, went over to him and sat next to him. She grabbed his hand and massaged it softly.

He nodded, but the niggling feeling was still there. 'I met Liz today...'

Dinah looked at him, her hand revealing his. 'Oh yeah? Why?'

'Wanted to know what she thought of Izah.'

'Oh,' She took his hand again. 'And?'

He pointed at the ceiling. 'Up there with the birds. Afluenter?'

Dinah laughed. 'Influencer. Famous one. Is she OK?'

'No. I mean, yes, she's fine. Taking photos of everything and posting them. Asked if I could get her one of your dresses.'

'Seriously?'

He nodded back. Dinah's eyes rolled back. 'My dresses? Which one?'

'She has to pay. A silk one, she said. Likes the feeling.'

'Was she flirting with you?'

He put a hand on his chest to demonstrate his innocence whilst thinking of Liz's slim figure.

'Well, she can piss right off, that slut. She's like a cat on heat.'

'You think she wasn't faithful to Izah?'

Dinah looked away and then stood up. 'Look... she's ambitious, sexy... wants the world and will do anything to get what she wants.' She carried on into the kitchen.

Murder came into his mind, but he quickly dismissed it. 'You know what the Sasanis do?'

She came back into the room with a red bottle of wine and a plate of snacks. 'What do you mean?'

'That their company is just a cover.' He looked at the Zoolbia, which were deep-fried funnel cakes, but he was in the mood for something more savoury and picked out a rice square-wrapped fig leaf.

'I hear that but...' Dinah gave out a big sigh. 'She's my auntie. I've never seen anything. Heard gossip and...' She looked away.

Rebwar wanted to know what position he was in. He still hadn't got that promised visa from Plan B. Although he hadn't had any problems from the authorities, he felt that was just a matter of time. Even after being in London for over six years, life felt as fragile as a glass bell. 'He passed over his phone and showed her a photo.'

She looked back at him. 'What?'

'On the cuff of the shirt.'

She moved the phone around and pinched the screen.

'Stamp,' she said. 'An event, you know... when you enter a fashion event, they stamp you.' She carried on flicking through the photos and frowned. 'Interesting clothes collection. A bit out there...'

'What, like cattle?'

'You don't get out much. Look, have you thought about a new job?'

'What do you mean?' He wanted to avoid the subject. It was a constant theme. She had wanted him to have a different job from the first day they had met. Even when he was with Hourieh. What did they want? To put him in a safe box?

'Oh, my friend has this security firm. He's always asking me about you. I've set up a meeting.'

Rebwar felt anger rising. Couldn't they leave him alone? He took a deep breath 'What about going for a drive?'

'As long as you go and see him. So... who's is it?'

'Izah's. Sure you haven't been in it?'

Dinah went over to him and straddled his legs. 'What are you saying?' Her breasts brushed over his chest. 'That I like young boys?'

'I needed it to get away from his flat. Did you know he had a flat on the river?'

'No! Is it nice?'

'Rich kid's flat. I'm sure Liz is going to miss it.' He looked over at the car key. 'Ever... you know?'

EIGHTEEN

Rebwar was driving along The Strand. In the back seat was a couple, both dressed for an evening out. The man was in black tie and had been on the phone throughout the ride. The woman had been glued to her mobile screen. She wore a backless evening dress and, with his newfound curiosity about dresses, he was tempted to ask where she had bought it. He'd tried light chitchat, but all he had got back was grunts and nods. His destination was The Savoy Hotel. It was just down a street off the main road. As he turned in, he slammed on his brakes. A black cab faced him. He was irate and slamming his horn. Rebwar excused himself to his passengers, who looked shocked and upset. The cabbie pointed next to him. He couldn't understand why he wanted him to drive on the wrong side of the road. He carried on honking.

'Hey, hey,' said the man in the back seat. 'He wants you to drive on the other side.'

Rebwar honked back. 'No, he's...'

'Look at the signs.'

'What?' Rebwar looked around, trying to understand why everyone was shouting at him.

'It's... Oh! Come on, Pandora.' The man brushed his blonde fringe back and opened his door. 'Darling, let's walk. Come!'

She opened her door and swung out her legs. The cab in front of him revved its engine and the driver wound down his window. A red bald head popped out.

The man waited for his girlfriend to catch up. He shrugged his shoulders at the cabbie, who was now swearing at everyone. The girl was holding her high heels in one hand and the hem of her long flowery dress in the other. A black cab drove by him in the left lane and carried on to the hotel's entrance. The traffic flow was back to front. It didn't make any sense and maybe that's what they were all trying to tell him. As soon as the girl had cleared his car, he made his way down the drive. He waited behind a black cab to finish his fare, wound down his window and lit a cigarette. He tapped on his phone, waiting for his next job. He had just started. Was it going to be one of those evenings? He looked into his rear-view mirror and saw Geraldine. He swung himself around and looked over.

'Got one for me?'

Rebwar looked around. He blinked, took a deep breath and stared at her: The same bomber jacket, white T-shirt, jeans. Like a flashback. He rubbed his eyes, waiting for something. Anything but this. 'Sure, sure.' He reached for another cigarette. 'What's going on?' He passed over a cigarette, which she took.

'You know this is the only road in the UK where you have to drive on the right? I didn't either... Had a visit and they asked about you.'

He held his lighter and flicked it. 'Where did you go?'

'Oh, long story.' The tip of her cigarette sucked in the flame. 'Birdy tells me that you've been moonlighting.'

Rebwar put the car into gear and drove out of The Savoy's drive. 'Got a visa for me?'

Geraldine smiled and put the window down. 'Got some tunes for me?'

'I've got a job—'

'As a PI, I heard. Should I call you Sherlock?'

Rebwar took out a CD from the glove box and slid it into the slot. It was an old mix that Raj had made for him.

'Show me the sights, like the good old days.'

He really wasn't too sure what to think. Glad to see her again, angry for her disappearance, annoyed that she hadn't called him and relieved. But why? He considered her as a friend. Even though technically they weren't. Or that's what Plan B said. 'What do they want?'

'Nothing really, they just asked me to check on you.'

'Check? Like... you check some child?'

She laughed and looked out onto the skyline which she could see from Waterloo Bridge. 'Kind of missed that.'

Rebwar looked out onto the city with its collection of skyscrapers. It was rare that he took time to look out. 'So go... on, what's the bad news?'

'No visa... or money...'

'What's going on?'

'You tell me, mate. Got a visit from our friend, High-clere. He was worried about you.'

Rebwar looked on. 'Where have you been?'

She avoided the question by looking out. 'So what's this robbery you were involved in?'

He shook his head and looked into the mirror, and smiled. 'It wasn't me. I'm still looking for him. And if it's about a Mercedes, I'm just borrowing it.'

'They are looking for you. I'm not here to pry and I don't give a shit what you get up to. But Highclere did make an effort to buy me a drink. Can you tone it down?'

'The music?'

She shook her head.

'The job?'

She nodded.

'Nice tunes. Pub?'

NINETEEN

Rebwar followed his sat nav to a residential road in Carshalton in South London. The area was leafy and had rows of houses set back from the road. He drove along Pine Walk looking for Dr Roe's house number. He'd found his address on the post-mortem report. Even though Dr Roe had expressly told him to make an appointment, Rebwar was going to surprise him again. Without some kind of warrant or power, he wasn't going to talk freely about his findings. He was going to have to resort to more basic techniques. And from the size of the houses, money wasn't an issue or that's what it looked like. This was what middle-class life was like: manicured lawns and tarmac driveways, something that his ex-wife had been yearning for. It left Rebwar cold. The house looked like it had been built in-between two properties, as it was modern, with a black-tiled roof that sloped over the first floor and the rest of the building. It was finished in a creamy white facade in contrast to the neighbouring houses, which were brick with brown tiled roofs. On the left were two garages in front of which he parked.

He stepped out and looked around. Apart from the odd passing car, it was quiet. He went up to the door and rang the doorbell. He waited and looked for his cigarettes. He tried the bell again. He walked over to the window on the right of the house. Shielding his eyes from the reflections, he could see into the living room. It looked clean and bare of clutter. He tried calling Roe, but it only went to voicemail. Had he missed him? He tried the front door, but it was locked. Then went over to the garages. There was an odd murmur coming from the left one. He could smell smoke. It was acrid and he recognised the distinct smell. His heart skipped a beat. He grabbed the handle and pulled it. The large wooden door flung up and smoke billowed out as if he had opened a hot oven. A toxic cloud made him turn away as the hot gases escaped. His eyes stung and he coughed as the car's exhaust burnt his lungs. He tripped and fell on the hard paving stones, rubbed his eyes and saw the red car parked inside.

After a few deep breaths, he stood up, took out a handkerchief and covered his mouth with it. He ran in and opened the driver's car door. A body flopped out and his head hit the concrete floor. Reaching for the keys, Rebwar switched off the engine. He checked the neck for a pulse. There was none. He coughed and tried to pull the man out but he was too heavy. Dr Roe's eyes were wide open and his tongue was sticking out. He took out his phone but hesitated to call as he remembered what Geraldine had told him. He took out some latex gloves and put them on then rubbed the car's door handle with his handkerchief then pushed the body back into the car. His seat belt was done up. He looked around for any other clues and took photos. He closed the garage door and went over to the connecting door.

The house was immaculate. It smelled of fresh paint and there was nothing out of place. It was more of a show home than something homely. But as a doctor and single, this wasn't too suspicious. The kitchen faced the garden and had a conservatory. Rebwar opened the fridge and found some ready meals, beers and some medicine. From the sell-by dates, he had planned the week. Rebwar carried on looking for his possessions. He found a power lead that was still plugged into the wall socket. He took a photo and sent it to Raj with a question mark. In the conservatory was a large dining table that seated eight. At one end was a small stack of envelopes. He took them and put them in his jacket pocket. He went upstairs to the bedroom, where he found an unmade bed. It struck him as odd. The wardrobe door was open and a couple of coat hangers were on the floor. He looked in the laundry basket to find Roe's pyjamas and some shirts.

In the distance, Rebwar heard sirens. He looked out of the window. There was no one around but he wasn't going to take his chance and wait and see. He'd barely made it away last time. He rushed into the bathroom and took pictures of the cupboard, ran downstairs and grabbed the rubbish from under the sink. He opened the latch on the front door and closed it behind him, got into his car and drove off. A fire engine passed him and for a moment he was tempted to turn back. He could join the crowd that was going to gather as the news got out. He felt there was something odd. This was the second time he had walked into a crime scene. Was someone trying to trap him? And a second suicide. A text had arrived from Raj saying laptop. He hadn't seen it earlier.

TWENTY

Rebwar stood outside a large white marquee smoking a cigarette. A bitter wind cut through his jacket and he stepped over to a pool of sunlight. The Sasanis' garden looked immaculate, even though it was bare of any leaves or flowers. Behind him, comforting piano notes mingled with a murmur of a light conversation. He was trying to work out what he was going to tell Jaleh. He was no closer to working out if her son had committed suicide or had been murdered but he had his suspicions, and there was something going on in the Sasani clan. Where there was power and money, conspiracy and corruption weren't far behind. But to get to the truth, he had to upset a few people and that could easily become very dangerous. A woman's hand grabbed his cigarette from him.

'Sorry, I need one.' Jaleh looked glamorous in her navy Chanel suit. An impressive gold necklace gave her an aura of royalty. Diamond rings and golden bracelets flashed and jangled around her. 'Before you disappoint me with your findings, can we talk about something else? I'm not ready for it. I would ask you to find out about Nahid's fiancée, but Jake is on it.'

Rebwar held his immediate thoughts. To say that it had been a surprise was an understatement. He was also sure that she thought he should have found out through interviewing Nahid. 'I can make some discreet enquiries.'

'And you call breaking into Izah's flat and taking his car discreet?'

'Someone got there before me and I was going to ask where I should deliver it to.' Jaleh looked at him as if trying to find out if he was telling her the truth. He suspected that Liz had given a story of what happened at the flat. 'Someone's playing in the shadows. I found Dr Roe dead in his garage. Looked like he had committed suicide.'

She finished the cigarette and flicked it into a bush. 'Let's talk later. Got to get through today without smashing something.' And she walked off back into the marquee.

Rebwar walked to marquee and up to the edge of the wooden floor. There was a stage at one end with a speaker system which was overlooking white cloth tables. They hadn't skimped on anything. A couple of chandeliers lit the inside, which was lined with a white fabric. It was fit for a sultan's desert camp.

'We're sitting on the Fars' table,' said Dinah smiling and looking gorgeous in one of her boutique's signatures dresses. It was one from the silk line and flowed from her neckline to the ground. It had a series of creases that complemented her figure.

Rebwar grabbed her waist and whispered into her ear. 'You'll be the envy of the show. How's the bride to be?'

Dinah smiled and kissed him. 'She got a dress from Muse. Think it's an Eliza & Ethan. Bitch. Never got along with her. Curious about Hakan. Some successful business-man. Did she mention him?'

He took a deep breath and wondered what he had missed when he had visited Nahid's flat. 'No, I thought she was a spinster. Bitter, entitled and spoilt.'

Dinah dragged on her cigarette. 'Well, he's quite a catch, or so I hear.' Rebwar waited for her to carry on. 'Some kind of businessman. Turkish, I think... Come on, let's get a drink.' They went looking for the bar.

Rebwar was still kicking himself and thought that maybe this was a good opportunity to move on. Plan B were surely going to make him pay for his moonlighting, even though he wasn't employed by them or had a clear agree-ment. Maybe it was for the best.

The bar overlooked an ornamental pond and people had gathered around it. Even with the gas heaters around, it still felt bitter. Dinah handed him a glass of champagne. They clinked their glasses and sipped the sweet and prick-ling liquid. He didn't quite get the fuss about champagne but Dinah could polish off a bottle in a night. They watched the guests. Rebwar studying them with a keen eye. Sarah was there with her kids. They were casually dressed, not in keeping with the other guests.

'Didn't her mother teach her anything?' Dinah turned to face the pond.

'Who would murder Izah?' He regretted asking instantly, but he just couldn't give it up.

'Rivals?'

'Who are they?'

Dinah looked out onto beyond the pond into the garden. He could see that it was making her uncomfortable and probably having to find uncomfortable answers. She shrugged her shoulders.

'What about her...,' he said. 'Jaleh?'

She turned to him with a piercing look. 'Her one and only son?'

He took another sip of his champagne. A voice shouted over to the crowd for them to take their seats. He was looking forward to getting some Persian food. Bijan had mentioned that they had flown in a top chef from Paris. He spotted Liz with another man. He looked androgynous and was wearing a skirt.

'That's a nice kilt,' Dinah said.

'Who is that?'

'Oh, come on, a friend, the fashion model, Beaux Gal. Doesn't he or should I say it...?'

Rebwar looked at them both and tried to understand. 'Eunuch?'

'Gender neutral.' And she pointed to the table. 'Outer circle, sure, she had a say...' and she mouthed something that Rebwar thought started with a B.

He scanned the names on the table and didn't recognise any of them. Couples arrived and sat around them. They introduced themselves and Rebwar instantly forgot about them. It took him back to the countless family dos that his ex-wife had made him go to. Angry and sour emotions came rushing back. He could already see their prying eyes on him. Dinah was sitting a couple of seats along.

'Hi, you Iranian?'

Rebwar struggled not to stare at the woman's mouth which was a puzzle of teeth. Her flowery dress barely contained her bulging body. Rebwar just nodded, not wanting to correct her or engage in polite conversation.

'We live a few doors down. My husband, James, is a Chief Superintendent for Epping.' Rebwar's attention suddenly turned and he looked over to him. He was sitting next to Dinah. 'James, James!' the woman shouted over to her husband, trying to get his attention. 'This is...' and she leaned in to read the name card. 'Rebus.'

The man turned and looked at Rebwar. His large, round face and small eyes made him look like a harmless pencil pusher. Dinah leaned in and said something to him.

'That's my girlfriend, Dinah.'

'Oh, I'd marry her quick...' And, for a moment, she stopped herself. 'You know what I mean... We're not getting younger. Got kids, Rebus?'

'Rebwar. One son. Musa.'

'Is he here?'

Rebwar shook his head.

'Oh, ours have flown the nest.' And she made some fluttering motions with her hands. 'You play golf?'

Rebwar finished his glass, trying to find an excuse to leave his seat. 'No, no, not very popular in Iran.' He looked around for a waiter.

'So, Rebus, what do you do?'

'I drive an Uber.' He took out his pack of cigarettes.

'Oh, so you're their driver?'

An announcement came over the speaker, calling them to all be upstanding for the groom and bride to be. People stood up and the piano played a tune for them to walk in. Rebwar watched them. Nahid was veiled in an off-white dress and Hakan Basar in a cream suit. They walked from one end of the marquee to the other. Rebwar fixated on them; something was bugging him. Dinah clapped with the rest.

'Oh, don't they look beautiful?' said the woman with the teeth. 'You know, I thought she would never marry.' And she leaned in. 'I'd heard she was a lesbian.'

TWENTY-ONE

Geraldine arrived at a grey, dented metal door. It was in a dark concrete basement in an urbanist estate called the Sandlings in Haringey, North London. Only a couple of lights lit the discarded, unloved furniture. She knocked and listened for a reaction. All she could hear was a dull electrical buzz. The place had a damp smell that reminded her of her mum's flat in Kent. They weren't happy memories. She half expected to see her mother lying on a couch, drunk out of her mind. She'd have to tiptoe in and try to get to the fridge without disturbing her, but she rarely managed it and this usually ended with an argument. The door opened. Her eyes took a moment to adjust to the darkness inside the room. A smell of tepid air mixed with stale food creeped out.

'Geraldine? How?' Raj's head popped out of the threshold and looked down the hallway. 'Alone?' She took a step into the room. Raj held his chest and looked a little pale.

'I need to have a word,' she said. 'Mind if I come in?'

'Don't you need a warrant?' He glanced behind him.

She took another of couple of steps forward and saw a series of computer monitors and piles of boxes and wires. The place was a mess and she struggled to make sense of it. The only light was from the glowing screens that were dotted around. It was more of a dystopian scene than an office. She tripped over a plastic box. 'Raj, I just need to know what Rebwar is up to.'

'You can't be here...' He watched her trying to navigate her way around. 'How did you find me? Are the police here?'

She tried to find something to sit on but every surface had some kind of electronic plug or discarded fast-food boxes. She realised that she should have at least brought some food as an offering. 'Fancy a coffee or drink?'

'I think you need to leave.'

'Rebwar needs your help.'

Raj stared at her for a moment and then waggled his index finger at her. 'No, no, not falling for that one. He would have called me. No, no.'

'If we don't... Let's just say that you're not going to see him for a long time. Come on Raj, as friends...'

He ran his fingers through his jet-black hair and sat down on an office chair in front of the desks. 'You've compromised me. You get that?'

'How?'

He just rolled his eyes and swivelled around to face the wall of computer monitors, tapped his mouse and looked at them. 'Call him and then I'll talk to you.'

She stepped closer to him. 'Who's he investigating?'

He gave a quick glance at her and returned to his mouse-clicking.

'Fuck's sake, this is serious.' She dialled Rebwar's number.

'Scale of one to ten? Ten being dead.'

His number went to voicemail. Geraldine felt her frustration mount and wanted to swear at Raj, but she knew that would only close down the conversation. 'Quite possibly ten.' Although she really didn't know.

Raj sighed and pointed to a screen. It was an internal police document about the Sasani family and their interests.

She leaned forward and used her arms to prop herself up on the desk. It was from an investigation that had taken place in 2004, when one of their employees, Luke Carlin, had been arrested for trafficking drugs. But the case had been dropped when he died in custody. 'Where did you get this?'

He just shrugged his shoulders.

'And he was going to interview this guy when...' An article flashed up about Dr Roe who had committed suicide. 'What's he investigating?' Another screen lit up and showed another newspaper site with Izah Sasani's death. Geraldine tried to work out why Plan B were so bothered about it. 'And?'

'You tell me. Jaleh Sasani thinks her son's death was suspicious. And Dinah is her niece.'

'Oh, that's a bit close. But...' She still couldn't work out why.

'So, who's coming after us?' Raj reached for his inhaler. 'Do I need to start packing?'

Geraldine paced around the boxes and rubbish. 'Maybe, but...' If they had an asset in there, surely they would have told her. Or was there a business interest? It was odd that the 2004 case was just dropped when they knew about the Sasani clan. Was someone paying to stop Rebwar? Her mind continued to race with ideas.

'So? Do I?' Raj took a hit from his inhaler.

'How did Rebwar seem to you the last time you heard from him?'

'Normal, wanted the usual... like he does. Look, should I be getting worried?' He clicked on his mouse and CCTV images popped up. It was from the surrounding area.

Geraldine showed him a picture of Farrouk Serid. 'Can you find him?'

Raj leaned over and with his thick fingers zoomed in. 'Send it.' He typed on his keyboard. It wasn't long before he found something.

'It's in...' Geraldine tried to work out what language she was looking at but it was all squiggles to her.

'Farsi and...' The text changed to English. 'Looks like he's a dead man. Sure its him?'

She leaned in to see a picture of a man hanging off a crane with an onlooking crowd. 'They do that?'

'A traitor to his country and he was trafficking drugs. Think that was Rebwar's old partner in the police. Heard him mention him.'

She nodded and remembered Rebwar talking about his old police partner. It was the reason he'd had to leave the country when an operation they were on went south. It had been Farrouk's fuckup as he kept reminding her. 'But he's alive. I met him a couple of days ago. You sure?'

Raj carried on clicking and typing on his keyboard. 'Don't have enough resolution to do a Face ID. Fake?'

'No idea.' She scratched her scalp. If Serid was here, there was a trail, but she didn't have access to any mean-ingful database. She was going to have to call in a favour. If Serid had come on a plane or ferry, he was on a camera. 'Good work, Raj. Keep digging. We need to find this man.'

'Should I tell...?'

'Not till we have more.'

TWENTY-TWO

Rebwar was outside the marquee having a smoke. He'd heard enough of the gushing speeches of people congratulating each other. Neither the bride to be nor the groom said much of note. Dinah was still laughing at the policeman's jokes, which had made him nervous, as it was only a matter of time till she said something indiscreet about him. He'd tried to convince her to come and join him for a cigarette, but she had just ignored him. He walked around the perimeter of the tent, trying to get glimpses of Hakan Basar. Where had he come from?

'Saved,' said Jaleh, grabbing his cigarette. 'And I'm supposed to believe all that bullshit?'

'Quite a catch, apparently.'

Jaleh laughed and took another puff of smoke. 'What do you think of him?'

Rebwar looked over at him, the bridegroom laughing and smiling with his guests around him. Nahid looked on, adoring his every move. 'She's under his spell.'

Jaleh turned away and stared out into the garden. 'Come... Let's walk and talk.' Rebwar looked back at the party, which was getting louder by the minute. 'So what's the latest and don't spare me? I can take the truth.'

He looked into the vast garden that seemed to go on into the horizon. Like an infinity pool, the lawn had been subtly raised to blend with the fields in the distance.

'I think your son was murdered. But I don't have any proof.'

She nodded and looked on.

'I have seen my fair share of suicides and this one wasn't possible without it being...' He took a moment to find the right words.

'Say it as it is. You've been around the block.' She exhaled. 'You know what we do.'

'The crime scene doesn't match the post-mortem. And conveniently Dr Roe has committed suicide. I feel there is someone playing us.'

She nodded and looked out onto garden.

'Was Izah happy to take the business over?'

Staring at him, she said, 'I had given him the choice and he could have chosen to have been paid off.'

She looked away. 'So there wasn't a choice.' She crossed her arms and turned to him.

'Who would have murdered him?'

She laughed, and with a stern voice said. 'Mr Inspector, isn't that your job?'

'Rivals? Jealous ex-lover? Family? Looks like Hakan has got an interest...'

She shook her head. 'He's some wannabe businessman. They met at a cosmetic clinic in Turkey. I mean... What the hell would a middle-aged man be doing there? Gold digger!' She stopped by a wooden bench and sat down. 'Now, I'm happy with your verdict. Send me the invoice.'

'There's a traitor in your business.'

She looked up at him. 'Are you telling me how to run my business?' Her face had a menacing edge.

'You've paid me to investigate. And that is my opinion.'

She leaned back with her arms stretched out on the back of the bench. 'Have you ever killed a man?'

Rebwar took a moment to answer. Of course he had, and she knew the answer. It was a test to see where he stood on cold-blooded murder, which he guessed she was having to wrestle with. 'You know the answer.'

'Just teasing you. You're such a proud man. Remind me of my grandfather. He was from Tehran. Ran the Venti cafe. Sure you've heard of it.'

Rebwar knew exactly the one: A favourite haunt for the police. He'd always been suspicious of the place and had avoided it, which was probably another reason he had to run. If he had played the game and got himself some allies, he could have greased a few palms. But he well knew that he would have been a dispensable footsoldier. He nodded.

'Better get back before people gossip.' And she stood up and walked to the marquee.

Rebwar headed for his seat at the back. He could see that Dinah was giggling away like a teenager. It wasn't going to be long till he'd have to take her home.

'Rebus, oh you missed the show.' He looked around, expecting to see something different. 'Your wife. She's such a hoot. Never seen my husband have so much fun. We must have you over.'

He sat down and drank the rest of his glass of champagne.

TWENTY-THREE

A light rain sprinkled Rebwar's face as he lit up, dragged on the cigarette and leaned back on his parked car. Since having a series of complaints and threats from Uber, he had decided to smoke outside. It still bothered him, but he still needed the taxi money. The divorce had taken a large chunk of his income. He also resented that Hourieh wasn't giving him a straight answer on what she earned. She had also threatened him with her spilling the beans on his moonlighting. He looked at posh people passing him by. Hyde Park was busy with joggers, horse riders, cyclists and tourists. It was a pretty spot and gave him a taste of the countryside. And his last outing out of town had been with Geraldine when they were chasing down what they thought was Plan B. He hadn't had the time to enjoy it. A few of his passengers had recommended him some places to visit, even though there had been some controversies on how those grand mansions had been financed. It made him laugh at how obsessed people were with history, especially if it wasn't to their own perception of it.

His phone buzzed and informed him of a job. He

stubbed out his cigarette, and he accepted it. He got into his car and drove off.

Whilst waiting for a traffic light to turn green, he got a call from a withheld number. His pulse picked up and his hand trembled as he reached for the phone's screen. He waited for the caller to announce themself.

'Can I speak to Rebwar?'

'Speaking.'

'Hayden speaking. We have a job for you.'

His immediate reaction was to say no. But he was still curious and Musa had recently got a job with them. And Hayden wasn't the type to say no to. 'OK, what is it?'

'We have a parcel that needs to be delivered.'

He wanted to tell Hayden to just order a courier, but obviously this was something they wanted him to do. 'And?'

'I'm sending a text to your phone. Follow the instructions.' And the call ended.

Rebwar waited for the text. He reluctantly cancelled his pickup; it was going to be another black mark to his tarnished record. It had been sold as a job where you had control over your hours, but really they just wanted to you to work all the hours in the day. All the other drivers he had met grumbled about their fees being squeezed. The text pinged and he read it. Drive 2 bus stop park on road flash lights 3x.

He arrived at the location they had sent him and followed their instructions. He rolled down his window and lit a calming cigarette as he looked around him and waited for something to happen. An Asian man knocked on the passenger window and Rebwar unlocked the car. The man opened the door, left a small cardboard package on the seat and closed the door. In his door mirror, Rebwar watched the man saunter away. Another text arrived and he opened it. There was an address and short instructions on how to deliver the box. He picked it up. It was light and about the size of a four-pack of tinned beans. He wanted to shake it but decided against it. It still intrigued him. It didn't have a label or any markings. Not a bomb nor money. A watch maybe, or some diamond-encrusted necklace. His sat nav came back with a Persian art gallery. He set off for Chelsea.

After over an hour's drive, he turned into Old Church Street, which was a narrow and flanked with double yellow lines. He passed a mix of boutique shops and expensive apartments. On his left was a dark-bricked building with large panes of glass. It looked both old and modern. He mounted the curb so as not to block traffic. In the shop window were a series of grey stone sculptures. Above it, the sign read: Hossein's Persian Antiquities. As Rebwar walked in, the door chimed. The walls were lined with large rugs and the odd painting. A large man with a comb-over greeted him. He wore a light brown suit with a flowery shirt and red cravat. He glanced outside at Rebwar's car. Rebwar handed the package over to him. He stared at it and turned it over, looking for a label. 'What is this?'

'Just delivering it.'

He looked confused. 'Amanda, have you ordered this?' He held the box up.

A tall, pretty brunette appeared from around the back corner of the shop. 'What is it?' The man shrugged. She walked over and looked at the package. 'Who is it from?'

'I'm just the messenger,' said Rebwar 'Open it.'

The woman flicked her shiny hair off her face. 'But who sent you?'

Rebwar shrugged. He was losing his patience with them. 'Cash job.'

'Yes, but who sent you?' She handed the box back to him.

He took a step away from them. 'It's a delivery and I can't take it back.'

'Vahid, this is not mine.' With one hand on her forehead, she said 'I have no idea what this is about.'

The man took the anonymous brown box and reached inside his jacket pocket for his reading glasses. His breathing became heavier as he inspected it. 'Was it a man who gave you this? Describe him?'

Rebwar's body tensed up and he felt weighed down with weariness. 'Look...' He held his hands out to them. 'I'm just the courier. I just deliver, nothing else.'

'So who's your employer?' Vahid grumbled. 'There must be—'

Rebwar grabbed the box back off him. 'I'll open it myself.'

'Wait, wait, Mister! It's not yours to open.' Vahid took the box back again.

'Can you show us some ID,' said the woman.

Rebwar hesitated for a moment and took out his wallet from his back pocket. The man walked over to a long, ornate wooden table that had a collection of small statues. He showed her Rebwar's driving licence and she took a photo with her phone.

Vahid, holding his chest, took a couple of steps back.

'What is it?' said the woman.

He grabbed the box and went over to Rebwar. 'Just a messenger?' And turned to the woman. 'Who is he?'

'Mohamed...' She checked the picture on her phone. '... Sulamann.' Her mouth dropped open as she looked into the open package and then she covered her face with both hands.

Rebwar saw an eyeball stare back at him from the box. It was packed in place with bloodied bubble wrap. His immediate thought was an eye for an eye. Had Jaleh made her move? But who were these people? He looked over at the street, preparing for his exit.

Vahid took out his mobile. 'Mr Sulamann, wait.' And he spoke in Persian as he talked to someone on the phone.

Rebwar pretended not to understand and turned to the woman. 'I have nothing to do with this. Sure there is no business card...?' He grabbed the box.

Vahid was talking to a man called Lanny and asking him to come over. Someone was looking for revenge on their family. Rebwar had enough of them and walked out to his car. Vahid shouted after him.

TWENTY-FOUR

Geraldine was walking down Edgware Road taking in a mix of sweet and fragrant smells coming from the Arabian supermarkets that lined the street down to Hyde Park. Outside them were shelves with ugly, exotic-looking fruit. Their spikes and rectangular-shaped skins made her walk around the displays. Men chatted to each other in guttural tones. Oriental music spilled out from passing cars and restaurants. As she had been told by Rebwar, she was in mini Cairo. Seeing women wearing the hijab did not sit well with her. Why did men have to dictate what they should wear? A couple of women passed her with only their piercing eyes on show. It made her giggle as to her they looked like some Dalek-like sci-fi characters from another planet. Most of her colleagues would have cracked a few inappropriate jokes but it was a free a country. She crossed a side street to get to the Shishawi. It had been a long time since she'd visited Rebwar's local. It hadn't changed. The exterior tables had patio heaters above them, keeping the shisha smokers warm. On the walls were loud, colourful graphic posters with slogans saying, 'Bye bye Dubai', and 'Bye bye Qatar.'

She sat down at one of the free tables. They had installed a radiator in-between the table's legs. It catered to its tropical clientele. She reached for an ashtray and dragged it over.

'Shish?' said a man with a thick grey moustache.

Geraldine looked over at the table in front of her, where a large man drew on a pipe. It reminded her of her youth and her dope-smoking friends. She had tried it and it had made her sick.

He pointed to the shish. 'We have strawberry, mojito, blueberry ice flavours, a—'

'Cappuccino... No, I'll have a beer. What have you got on tap?'

'Sorry, no alcohol. Have soft drinks or flavoured teas,' He looked around him. 'Or coffee.'

By this time Geraldine would have walked away, but she was here for a reason. She took a breath. 'I'll have the cappuccino with extra chocolate sprinkles.' When her server had walked off to another table, she leaned back on the green backed chair and looked out onto the busy road. Streetlights had come on and the mood had changed. There was an edge to it. She lit her cigarette and fidgeted with her cigarette pack. She felt out of place and a person of interest, but she ignored them as best she could.

'Looking for me?' Rebwar approached her.

The relief made her smile. 'Where the hell have you been?'

'Hello. Nice to see you, too.' He nodded to the waiter as if there was some secret code for his order. 'You come to give me news or a visa?'

'No.' She watched him light up. 'Need to know what you've been up to.'

'Nothing. Still looking for the killer.'

That didn't surprise her as he was like a dog with a bone, but she was surprised that she was missing her old job. Something she hadn't expected.

'You still in contact with your ex?' he said.

She froze as memories of Beckie came flooding back. They were still painful and hadn't dulled with time. She still missed her. 'Not really. Why?'

'Need info on that doctor that...' Rebwar made some air quotes which made her smile. 'Did the post-mortem on Izah.'

The waiter brought her coffee and Rebwar's drink. 'Thought there... Never mind.' She grabbed her cup and took a sip to distract her meandering thoughts.

'Inshallah,' said Rebwar, to which Berker nodded and walked off. 'The doctor was in someone's pocket.' Rebwar took a sip of his dark amber drink.

Geraldine nodded reluctantly, thinking about where she could get a pint.

'My client is taking her own revenge, eye for an eye. But I haven't found the killer.'

'Revenge on who?'

Rebwar leaned back and looked around him. 'Some rival.'

She felt her frustration rise again. She had to have something to take back to Highclere, especially if she wanted to negotiate a new job out of them. 'Any ideas?'

'It's a viper's nest. Each one is worse than the other. They could have all done it. There are two daughters, one's a hippy and the other a drugged-up lazy princess. Izah was the heir to the empire. And they call themselves the House of Suren.'

She waited for him to explain.

'Oh, some ancient fairy tale from the past. Old Persian history... I didn't go to school, remember?'

She did, and he'd been a street kid before being enlisted into the army for the Iran-Iraq war. 'There's Google,' She took out her phone.

'There's someone playing them. There's a Jake Hayden. He's their security man. Ex-Army, I think, and he has Jaleh's ear. Then there's some shady businessman called Hakan Basar who's going to marry Nahid the lazy princess... and, yes, he's got motive. He's from Turkey, I think, and no connections here.'

'That's your man for sure.'

Rebwar shook his head. 'He'd be playing with fire. Why? How's he going to pull off a takeover of the family? Hayden maybe. Rivals more likely, which is why Jaleh is making a move.'

'On who?' to which Rebwar shrugged and she realised she wouldn't get much more. 'You sure you want the job?'

'Tell me about Farrouk.'

She sipped her coffee and thought back. It had been so out of the blue. 'Creepy and scary. Smokes Marlboro Golds no, a rip-off brand. Mehr?'

Rebwar lit up and drew in. 'Mehr, Iranian brand. SAVAK. They've been hanging around me like flies. And Farrouk's dead.' He exhaled.

'And?'

'Saw a picture of him hanging off a crane. Some state agent smoking Mehr came here to show it to me.'

'You're right, it's on the internet. Raj found it and I saw the picture... Sends his greetings.' Rebwar gave her a surprised look. 'So who's the guy I met? Think he's involved in all this?'

Rebwar shrugged. 'And my visa? Have you asked Plan B?'

'Look, I need to give them something. Sounds like you want out of the job. Choose a name and be done with it. Take the money and run.'

He shook his head. 'Musa is working for them.'

Geraldine let it sink in. 'What?'

'Dinah is Jaleh's niece.'

'Oh...' She grabbed another cigarette.

TWENTY-FIVE

The Ockenden Manor Spa was a couple of hours' drive from London in the heart of Surrey. Rebwar stared at the stone main building, which was attached to a couple of other houses. A moment of doubt crept in: he'd got a text from Berker giving him Bijan's location, but Rebwar had expected a large English mansion with an imposing drive. This was more like a wing and with some outhouses. He walked around the manicured garden, which had empty tables and wrapped-up parasols. Behind them there was a long brick wall with a modern terracotta-coloured building. He headed towards it. Since he'd delivered the package to the art gallery, he'd been hearing rumours that there were people looking for him. He had been expecting it, but no one was giving him any information about whom. It was as if he was a leper. Bijan wasn't taking his calls or visits. Jaleh had gone quiet. Dinah didn't want to talk about it and changed the subject. He skirted the wall to arrive at the path that led up into the block building.

It was a maze of rectangular shapes. The distinct smell of chlorine filled his nostrils. He was getting close. What had Jaleh set off? Rebwar was like a pawn in a chess game, sitting in the middle of the board surrounded by pieces waiting to make their move. And he wasn't going to wait. As he got to the end of the passage, he saw a big glass building within it. He tried to make sense of it. Inside was a large swimming pool that was connected to the exterior one. Puffs of condensation escaped out of the opening. People in white robes lounged around on sofas and recliners. He carried on walking towards the patio area. There was no sign of Bijan. He lit a cigarette and walked around the guests.

'Sir, can I help?' The man wore a white overcoat with the hotel's name embroidered on it. His arm stretched out as if he was trying either to guide him out or grab him. The guests looked at Rebwar with an air of disgust. He saw a trail of mud on the large clean paving stones.

'Yes.' Rebwar stamped his shoe to try to loosen the mud.

'Sir, this way.'

Rebwar stepped back. 'I have an urgent message for His Excellency, General Achmoud. I need to deliver it in person.'

'Sir, yes, sure.' The man kept looking down at Rebwar's shoes, trying to dance around him and corral him towards some stairs.

'It's urgent and I need to see him now, otherwise I'll have to count the chickens.' He crossed his arms. He could see another two men approaching him and the guests were sitting up.

'Please, follow me. We will call for Mr...'

'No,' Rebwar saw Katarena step out of the indoor swimming pool, her bikini not leaving much to anyone's imagination. He'd had run into her when Hourieh had been hiding at her apartment in Canary Wharf. He walked towards the glass building.

'Sir... sir, you can't go there. Sir?' The man hopped over to him as if he was walking on hot coals.

Rebwar threw his cigarette on the floor and pushed the door. But it didn't move. He tried again. Reflected in the glass were two men rushing over to him. He pulled, and it flew open to slam against a rubber stopper. The noise travelled and startled the guests inside the spa. A warm, scented breeze hit him. With her arms, Katarena covered the bikini top that barely contained her large breasts and stared at him in shock. 'Where is Bijan?' he said, and walked towards her.

'Sir,' said the man in the white coat. 'You can't go in there...' and he tried to grab Rebwar's leather jacket, which slipped out of his grasp.

'Rebwar! He here,' said Katarena, 'but this private area.' She turned to confront him on the wet floor.

He grabbed a towel and passed it over to her and grabbed her arm. 'Take me to him.' He squeezed her upper arm, 'Understand?'

Her glacial blue eyes looked at him and she nodded. The three men stood wondering what to do, waiting for an instruction or a moment to make a move. She moved towards the end of the pool area. People stopped their reading, lounging or activities and stared at them.

'Heard from Hourieh?' She looked back at him. 'Don't answer that.' They walked up some circular steps up to the next level. She pointed at a closed door.

'Knock,' he said. She walked over to it and knocked. Behind him were the three men still hanging around like some kids waiting for their roll call. She waited for a reply. 'Harder.' She knocked again. The men rushed over to a suited man who was making his way up the stairs. Rebwar opened the door and walked in. A Thai woman was massaging Bijan. Rebwar closed the door and locked it.

'What you doing?' said the petite woman.

Bijan, face down, groaned.

'*Sartip*,[1]' said Rebwar. 'I'm sorry to disturb you.'

Bijan turned around. '*Sarbaz*[2], what is this?'

Rebwar searched for his wallet and took out a couple of notes. He grabbed the woman's hand and placed them in her palm. Then he opened the door and pushed her out. He locked it and went over to Bijan.

'Who's dead?'

'No one, sir, I need—' There was a knock at the door. 'Who's after me?'

'*Sarbaz*, I...' Bijan reached for Rebwar's hand. 'Come, help me. You idiot.' There was another knock. 'Tell them to go away. No, get Katarena in here and go to the bar. You are impossible. If I didn't know you, I would have you court marshalled and shot.'

Rebwar smiled, feeling the old general's anger and backbone return.

TWENTY-SIX

Bijan was sitting on an outdoor sofa wearing a thick white dressing gown. Rebwar faced him, gently warmed by a gas patio heater. They overlooked the indoor and outdoor pool. On the low table was a pot of tea and two glasses of whisky. Rebwar grabbed one and leaned over to clink the other.

'Have mine,' Bijan looked around him and whispered. 'If you can't see those bullies, pass it over.'

'Sir, why haven't you returned my calls?'

Bijan looked up and waved with one hand. 'Made Katerena my secretary. And I've been hearing that you're a wanted man. Dangerous, they have said.'

Rebwar lit up. 'That's never stopped you.'

'Quick, what do you want?'

'Who's looking for me? Farrouk?' And he passed over the whisky glass.

Bijan took a massive gulp and waited for the burn to pass. 'Sasanis. You've been working for them.' He shook his head. 'Why work with a bunch of gangsters? You should know better.'

This was rich coming from Bijan. But he saw himself as

more of a corrupt official, which was the norm. 'Tell me about the House of Suren.'

Bijan laughed and took another gulp of his drink. 'Foolish history. They think they can buy history and heritage. Means nothing, just horseshit. Who do they think they are fooling? No one. As if they were part of the seven houses that founded Persia.'

'House of Zik?'

Bijan shook his head. 'They are all at it. Maybe I should join them. Ignore all of it.'

'Who are they?'

'Who?'

'House of Zik?' Rebwar noticed how the old man was fading. He just waved him away. He waved to the waiter and asked him for some biscuits and more whisky.

'Do you remember the counterattack? It was marvellous and you should have seen their faces.' He laughed and coughed. 'Bunch of cowards.'

Rebwar checked his watch. Bijan had gone off into his faded memories of the Iran-Iraq war. If Rebwar was going to get anything out of him, he was going to have to endure his distorted nostalgia. Rebwar had grown tired of his glorified tales. He also didn't want to drag out his own painful memories of the war. He nodded and let Bijan ramble. Watched the sun fade in and out from the large white clouds passing by. 'Sir, what art did you buy from the Mohsen?'

'Bought some delightful pieces from them. That fountain, from an oasis garden. It was from Fars Province. Clever bunch. What did you do to upset them?'

Rebwar tried to work out if he had told them who he was. All they had was a fake name. 'Just delivered a package. It was from the Sasani... and eye.'

Bijan tutted and straightened himself. 'What in the world possessed you to do that?'

'I was just the messenger.' Rebwar stood up and pointed at Bijan. 'Someone's playing the Sasanis.'

'Sit, sit, it's not your business. Mohsen are old friends and did good business with them. Farhad Sasani and Vahid Mohsen were old friends. Came over here together. Long old story, but let them fight over what they want. Don't get involved in the old stories. Nonsense, that's all they are. Like little children crying over the broken toys.'

Rebwar lit another cigarette. 'Farrouk?'

'Dead. You saw the pictures. What else is there to say?'

'But he called me. Or are they looking for me?'

Bijan leaned on the chair and looked out on the pool. 'These seven houses are all nonsense. What are they trying to achieve? Seems important to them.'

'What I heard is that they are trying to create a syndicate. Like the mafia. Just one with a Persian flavour. But this is an old story. Nothing came out of it. It died with Farhad.'

'My dear, your medication,' said Katarena, now wearing a one-piece white suit. It had a thin black belt around her narrow waist. 'What have said about drinking? And you have an appointment with Dr Khan. Come, come!'

'Woman, I'm having a meeting with my old friend here.' He lifted his glass. 'And it's medicinal. And who?'

She stood there with her hands on her hips, looking at them. 'Dr Khan. And enough of this stupid talk. I am looking after you. Like the doctor said. And this Rebwar... I know who you are. A driver. You have taken enough time to talk. You must to leave.'

Rebwar got up.

'*Sarbaz*[1], sit, sit. It is an order. Woman, I am having a meeting.'

105

She stepped in-between them. 'No, he need medication. And visiting time finished. Understand Mr Rebwar. Otherwise will get security and police.'

He wanted to stick up for his old friend, Bijan, but he didn't want to make another scene as he was going to lose. 'What did you tell the Mohsen?'

'They know nothing,' said Bijan, looking for a man called Mohamed. I told them to visit a mosque. But—'

'Please leave now,' said Katarena. 'Next time make an appointment. You are not welcome here.' She waved over some men who had been standing by a glass door.

He got the message and went over to Bijan to say goodbye. '*Sartip*[2], sir, a pleasure. And if there is anything, call me. I am at your service.'

'Brave man, I'll see you soon. Won't we, my love? Invite the family over. How is Hourieh?'

Rebwar just nodded, realising how Bijan was struggling with his memory. He'd visibly aged since he last saw him. He just hoped that he hadn't dropped him into the lion's lair. But she could just as easily sell him down the river. And he knew that his ex and she were still good friends. He had to keep an eye on Bijan. He made his way out to the car park. It was a matter of time till Mohsen found him. He had to come up with some kind of plan to get ahead of them, both families, before the feud spilled out of control. He made a call to his son, Musa.

TWENTY-SEVEN

The sat nav was telling him to go down a concrete drive lined with shrubs and short trees. The hum of light aircraft engines filled the air. Discarded rubbish dotted the long grass verges. Rebwar took a moment before driving on. He was following the coordinates that he'd taken from Musa's phone. He had a present in a plastic bag on the front seat. This was a surprise visit. He knew that Musa had told him expressly not to 'pop by' but his fatherly instinct got the better of him. And anyway, he still was looking for Izah's killer – or that's what he told himself.

He followed the track till he got to some warehouses. Their corrugated roofs had moss on them and green and brown flakes of paint clung to the walls. A couple of old trucks were losing the battle against nature with shrubs growing through their rusting panels. A van drove past him, its engine revving out. There was a main yard where trucks and vans parked, all lined up to the large open doors. People milled around, loading and unloading boxes. He found a parking space and rolled up his window, reached for the shopping bag and stepped out. He looked around him.

There had been no security barriers or guards, which surprised him. It was as if they had nothing to hide.

He made his way to one of the buildings. 'Looking for my son, Musa,' he said to a man operating a forklift.

He took off his ear defenders. 'What'd say?'

'My son, Musa! Have you seen him?'

'He lost?'

Rebwar shook his head and pointed to the ground.

'He works here.'

The man just shrugged, put his ear defenders back on and revved the machine.

Rebwar carried on walking around the yard, looking around till someone called him. It was a big black man in an ill-fitting dirty blue overall. 'What are you doing here?' His dark eyes stared down at Rebwar.

'I'm here for my son, Musa.'

The man scratched his large chin. His knuckles were raw and bruised and he had what looked like a bruise on his neck as if he had been in a fight. 'Have you called him?'

Rebwar showed him his bag. 'It's a surprise.' He smiled at the man.

The man sighed, 'What's he do?'

Rebwar wasn't too sure, but he guessed. 'Loading?'

'Right, mate, call him and ask him to meet you. Here. And I'll wait.'

Rebwar reached for his phone and tried the number. It went to voicemail. 'Where's the reception?'

The man's laugh was loud and looked like he was about to run out of breath. He stopped at last and said, 'Nice one. Think you need to leave. Understand me?' He stepped up to Rewar.

He could smell the man's sweat and the peppermint from his gum. He turned and walked on with the feeling of the man's shadow over him. He peered in the large doors, hoping to spot his son, as well as making notes on what he was seeing. There were varying types of boxes: cardboard ones with the company logo and telephone number and white polystyrene ones. The smell of metal and fish clashed with a rotting undertone. Some trucks were refrigerated and others weren't. As he passed the last warehouse, he heard a voice.

'Dad?'

He looked behind him and saw Musa dressed in a white overall and a hairnet. He looked so grown-up. His boy, who locked himself in his room and played computer games. 'Son?'

'What are you doing here?'

'Oh, just drove by and...' He passed over the crumpled-up bag. The large black man still hung around in the background.

Musa looked wary and as if he was trying to keep himself calm. He looked in the bag and took out a football jersey. His eyes lit up. It was a Hazard, the number ten of Chelsea. 'Wow, cool...' Then he looked around. 'You want something?'

The answer was yes, but it waited. 'I just wanted to say sorry for the last time. You know...'

A forklift stopped behind them and a man shouted to Musa. 'Mate, what's going on?' He had a stern look to him, receding hairline, dark stubble and tattoos on his arms. He pointed to Rebwar. 'Who's he?' There was a stamp on his arm, a clenched fist emoji, similar to the partial print he'd found on Izah's shirt.

'I'm his father. Come to give him a present. I start my shift in an hour.'

'Well, we're not paying him to have family reunions.'

Musa was still looking at his shirt. 'A Chelsea pansie. If I'd known, I would have given you a job with the darkies. Millwall, mate, that's the real deal...'

Musa's face fell and he looked down. For a moment, Rebwar wanted to step in, but there wasn't much he could do. Pushing names would just make him a target and upset him. Violence would lose him his job and make a stir with the Sasanis. And he had no idea where this man stood in the company.

The man laughed and shook Rebwar's hand. 'I'm Craig. You've got a good man there. I'm only taking the proverbial piss. Look at your faces.' He carried on laughing. 'Got yous, hey? Nice, nice. Wish my old man had bought me stuff. Just got a clip round the ear and fuck off. So what's you deal?'

Rebwar took out his pack of cigarettes and offered them. 'Uber driver.'

He took one. 'I'll know who to call next time I'm ten down and stumbling into posts. Nice, nice. Not local, are you?'

'Iran, but we liked it here.'

He laughed. 'Bit cold though. Hey, I'll let him out early. Get some quality time. That's what the Mrs keeps telling me. Look Mus, if you want to ever see real football, I'll take you to a Millwall match.'

'I can go home?'

Craig dragged on his cigarette. 'That look, man! Yeah, of course. I've got it. All in. Look after yourselves, right? And offer stands. And no, not going to Chelsea game. Fuck right off.' He got back on the forklift. As Craig's shirt lifted, Rebwar noticed a knife holster around his waist.

'I can give you a lift.'

'I've got my scooter, thanks..'

'Drink?'

Musa looked back with a shocked face. 'I'm... You alright?'

They walked over to his car. 'What's the emoji stamp on his arm?'

Musa shrugged his shoulder.

'They treat you alright?'

'What? And you're going to beat them up? It's a job.'

He wanted to grill Musa further and ask if he'd seen anything suspicious or off. But he had to leave that for Musa to offer otherwise he might just go back into his teenage shell.

TWENTY-EIGHT

Rebwar stood in a lit corridor: white walls, a scuffed light blue floor, with double doors leading to medical departments. He thought that if there was a hell, this certainly led to it. Checking his text again and trying to match up one of the endless signs, he was sure he had passed all the wards and that all he was doing was going in circles. Anxious and not wanting further to embarrass himself, he carried on, trying out his luck – which he needed. Not that he believed in a God or charms, but he wasn't far from asking. He normally laughed at Dinah's little trinkets and odd superstitions. He passed a ward lined with beds. The furthest one had a family around it, and the mood was sombre: heads were down, tissues wiped, tears and arms comforted each other. None of them were familiar to him, so he carried on, wishing that he'd wake up. Like Geraldine, he was now missing working for Plan B – something that he'd never expected to feel. But, like they said, the grass was not always greener. Even for their threats and lies, there was an order and logic to it. Not that it made sense to him. Here he was on his own. And having Dinah had just scrambled all the emotions into a sweet and sour dish. He couldn't make head nor tail of where she stood in this case.

He found himself at a dead end and had two doors to choose from. A lift door opened behind him and a bed came out. There was Kamal, his old friend and business partner. They had split the lease on the car, helped each other when in need. He couldn't have made enough to feed his family. Kamal hadn't agreed to share a taxi. They had met at the Shishawi. Kamal was a Pakistani and former security guard. They had shared bread and got to know each other's families. Kamal was one of the few people Rebwar trusted.

Half of Kamal's face was covered with white bandage and his left hand hung suspended. Metal bars stuck out of his arm like scaffolding. His eye dawdled between Rebwar and the nurse. Like he had one of those clown-popping eye frames. Rebwar looked over to the man pushing the bed. 'Is he...'

'Are you a relative?'

'His partner...' and he left it uncompleted, not really noticing what they thought it meant until it was a little too late.

'He's on medication. He'll be all right. Just needs rest.'

'Kamal... Kamal, who did this?'

Kamal's lips moved but he just grunted and wheezed back.

'What happened?' He asked the two nurses, who just shrugged back. Rebwar followed them down the corridor till they took him into a ward. He called the number that had texted him.

'What did you do?'

'Begun, sorry... it should have been me. They were looking for me. I am going to make them pay. Understand?'

Begun, Kamal's wife stood there anger spilling out of

her intense stare. 'I don't want to see you again. You keep away from Kamal! You understand me? I have reported you to the police. You and all your schemes. Taking us for fools. Now listen to me. You are going to pay us off. No, we are going to sue you. Get that? Yes, sue you.'

It was senseless to try to answer back or try to calm her. The friendship had broken. He had his suspicions about who could have done this but he needed proof. Whoever did it was going to pay. Eye for an eye. Is that what they were looking for? And he felt a chill go through him. He grabbed one of the nurses. 'His eye? Does he still have it?'

She shook her head.

TWENTY-NINE

Rebwar got to Dinah's boutique just off King's Road. It was just past closing time and he knocked on the glass door. Three long dresses were on display. He took little notice of them. Normally, he would imagine how Dinah would look in them. His mind was elsewhere, finding it hard to concentrate. He'd been there before; his first taste was in the war as a conscript. He was never the same after that, his carefree outlook destroyed like all those kids blown up next to him. Then came those police cases that were too horrific to report. Even though people said you got used to dead bodies, the truth was you never did that and you just coped. Now he was trying to cope. Dinah's outline came towards the door. the light from the back door drawing her curves. As she unlocked it, her smile brought a warmth to his cold pain.

'Hey...' She reached up and grabbed him to give him a huge hug then took his hand and turned. He followed her to the back office. It was filled with cardboard boxes and wheeled garments. She dragged one of the chairs out.

'Coffee?' As she noticed his face, she reached for a bottle and some glasses.

'They assaulted Kamal.' He sat down.

'They?' She filled both glasses.

Rebwar gave out a big sigh. 'The Mohsen or House of Zik as they call themselves.'

'May they burn in their graves. Those dogs.' She downed a mouthful of the red wine. 'How is he?'

Rebwar just shook his head and clenched his fists. 'They took his eye! What kind of savages are they?'

Dinah covered her open mouth. 'No! Oh, the dirty animals! Why?' He knew, but he couldn't make himself say it. 'Do you know?' She grabbed his hands. 'My love, you know this will be avenged. They are not going to get away with this.'

'What am I doing in this city? This is no better than back home.' And he pointed to some wall. 'Is it? It's got out of hand. They had no proof. He's innocent. Kamal was just trying to make money for his family, like we all do.' He took a sip of his wine, hoping it would dull the pain.

She looked into his eyes. 'Jaleh will sort this mess out, I promise you, and Kamal will be compensated. You will see. Everything will be right. She always sorts things out. Peacemaker, she is.'

He tried to make sense of what she was saying. Jaleh and her lot were probably just as bad. He reached for his cigarettes and offered one to her.

'She started all this.'

She inhaled and whilst holding the burning cigarette, rested her arm on her hip. 'Why would she do that? Makes no sense.'

'Business. All business.'

'No, I know my aunt. Always been fair and direct. If

there was a reason to pick a fight with these sons of bitches and pretentious Ziks, well that's what she did.'

He got up and poured himself another glass. 'And that's what happened. There is no excuse. Kamal nearly died and it should have been me. What would you have said then? He walked to the back wall, wanting to kick some of the boxes out of the way.

'It wasn't. And if that's what Jaleh wants, as a Sasani, I have to respect her wishes. She has run the family well.'

How could he not have seen it? It was there in front of his face. She was part of the whole mess and he was in it too – as if he'd never left Iran. It was still here tugging him down. 'I warned her against it. They didn't kill Izah.'

'You sure? You said yourself that there was no proof. Of some Machiavelli trying to corrupt her. Sure it's not you?' She walked off to an open box and took out a dress.

'There is, I know. I just haven't found him. I think she's taking an opportunity. Business.' He rubbed his chin and leaned against the wall, trying to think of what to do next. He needed help to defuse the escalating situation. He looked over, watching Dinah unpack and hang the new items. Checking them for any defects. Was it all in front of him? He hadn't noticed anything: no odd deliveries or people he didn't know. He wanted to look around. 'Izah was your cousin?' She looked over her glasses to him with no sign of an emotion. 'How was he?'

She carried on hanging the new collection. 'Bright boy. Liked his fashion and his football. Chelsea, like you.' She looked up at the ceiling. 'You know, when I came over, I caught him wearing his sister's clothes.' She nodded and tapped her head. 'I didn't forget that. Funny guy. Such a loss.'

'Exactly, so who would kill him?'

'The families made enemies. There was always security when I went to one of their birthday parties. We knew.'

He sat down and lit another cigarette which he passed over to Dinah. So... she knew well about their business but chose to keep it from him. 'And the other cousins? You don't seem to get along that well. I mean... first I've heard of them.'

'Spoilt bitches.' She drew hard on her cigarette and exhaled. 'I didn't have much in common with them. I was older than them and they still looked down on me. Bullied Izah badly. They were sent to boarding schools. But kill Izah? Why? They got their own way anyway.'

He crossed his legs and stretched out his hands. 'Yeah, but he was going to take over the family business. Sure, he would have to cut them off?'

'Oh?' Dinah held a small, folded piece of paper. 'Lost this?' She went over to him. 'Numbers? See mine's on it. Who are the others?'

Rebwar took it from her. 'Emergency numbers in case I lose my phone. You never know. Thanks.'

'Who loses his phone?'

He stubbed out his cigarette. 'You never told me about your parents.'

'Not much to say.' She laid a long silky dress in front of her and looked at herself in the mirror. She must have caught his stare, to which she smiled. 'Mum died in Tehran and Dad couldn't cope so, we moved here. He worked himself into an early grave and I'm now alone. The end.' She took the dress and walked behind some boxes.

He filled up his glass. 'But he was a good man?'

'Had his struggles with drink but...'

It went quiet and he got up and walked over to her. She stepped out wearing the silk dress and turned around. It was backless. He grabbed her and pulled her in. She gave a little giggle, turned her head and kissed him. He could feel her warm body against his. The material was light and smooth and as he slid his hand around her to feel her skin, she gave a little protest as he undid her dress. It dropped to the floor, and she turned around to reach for and undo his trousers. He felt unguarded, vulnerable, but at ease with her.

THIRTY

The footbridge split the North Dock in two and Geraldine was leaning on its rails. She had just arrived at West India Quay in the Docklands to meet Highclere. As usual, she was early and was taking in the sights. It was a sunny day and the tall glass skyscrapers that surrounded her beamed with reflections. She was a bit of a sucker for big buildings. Maybe it was because her father had been a bricklayer. She reached for her phone to take pictures and remembered her ex, Beckie. One Canada Square, with its distinct pyramid roof was still the king among the office buildings, but they had built a series of new towers around the wharves and it didn't dominate as it used to. She chose one of the pictures to send to Beckie. She added that she missed her and needed to ask her a professional question – and followed with a few kisses. It made her sigh and remember the good times they had. She headed off to the top corner of North Dock.

There was a large statue in front of an old, converted brick warehouse. Geraldine sat on the low ledge below it and waited. She had a view of water and the surrounding buildings, all old wharves that used to serve the basin and now were businesses or expensive flats.

'Why this place?'

She looked up to see Highclere in his immaculate tweed suit. 'Thought of changing scenes. And...' She pointed at the statue above her.

He looked at it. 'And?'

'Robert Milligan, Scottish slave owner who built the West India Docks.'

'Are you having a laugh?' His black skin glistened in the sunlight. He took off his sunglasses to reveal his scar. 'Really?'

'Just showing you some history and, yes, making a point about our situations.'

Highclere turned around and walked a few steps. 'Save it.' He checked his large watch. 'Ten.'

'Where were we?' He looked at her with a sour look but she knew she had to go in punching and keep him off balance. 'OK, I've got a proposition...'

'You're supposed to be reporting to me. So?' He checked his watch again. 'Get on with it.'

Geraldine got up and faced him. 'We can take down two gangs,' She held up two fingers. 'Rebwar's working for one of them... The Sasanis. But you know all this.'

Highclere's head tilted as if he was losing patience.

'Wait, wait... So he's in there and they have just declared a turf battle with their rivals, the Mohsen or House of Zik. Now we can let them spill blood all over London or stop it.' Looking at Highclere's scarred and torn limbs, he probably wasn't one for empathy for Kamal's troubles. He crossed his arms and sucked on his cheeks. 'But I want back in.' To which he just laughed. 'Nice one! No, no. It does not work like that.' Geraldine looked back at the statue. 'Don't,

I've got the history not you...' He took a deep breath like he was trying to not lose his rag. 'You report to me and that's it. Get it?' He pointed with his large finger. 'Now you were supposed to clean your house. Not make a dog's dinner out of it.'

'I want back in. My old job is as a detective. I've paid my dues. Look, we can ping-pong this all day. But pass it on to your superiors. I'm owed this. I've seen you guys come and go. And it's time for a change. I'm giving you this. And if you play your cards right, you can get your dues.' She reached for her pack of cigarettes and noticed that he had clocked them. She offered him one.

He froze for a moment. 'Why?'

'Why? Because I want back in.'

Highclere walked off towards the footbridge with Geraldine following. 'I don't know who has that authority.' She kept walking with him. 'I'm just a pawn. And you're supposed to report to me. End of.'

'You know that Canary Wharf was built by a Canadian.'

Highclere just carried on walking.

'Thatcher let him down, and he went broke.'

He checked his watch again. 'Why should they care about a bunch of Iranian gangsters?'

'They don't. But there's nothing to lose. What are you in for?'

'Come on, you know the score. No personal questions. Now shut his case down and get him back in that taxi.'

Geraldine jogged ahead and turned around. 'OK, let's see, you took a bribe.' She looked for a reaction. 'Robbed, too obvious, yeah, fraud.'

He looked away and shook his head.

'Close though. Affair?'

'Will you stop with that?'

She could feel that he was intrigued and had authority issues. For all his tough act there was a soft side to him. 'Give me a week and see where this goes. Oh, and his taxi got cremated. Think about it. You might get a promotion. If you don't ask, you don't get.'

He stopped by the bridge. 'A week. And if you haven't come up with something by then you're... history. Get it?'

To which she just nodded and he walked off over the footbridge. She had no idea how that went. But she had seeded the idea and maybe it would lead to something. Her phone buzzed. It was her ex. She took a deep breath. 'Hey!'

'Hey, you... messaged.'

Geraldine's hand trembled and she felt a rush. 'Yeah, yeah, I'm... you know...'

'Nice hearing you. What have you been up to?'

'Oh, you know, this and that. But you OK?' Beckie had been an addict, and this had caused the end of their relationship.

'Yeah, clean and working again. You had a question.'

Geraldine could tell from Beckie's voice that she was full of fresh energy and sounded relaxed. 'I've been looking for some info. He's called Dr Roe.'

'Never heard of him. But I can ask around.'

Geraldine looked over the dock to see Highclere disappear down a side street. 'Oh, that would be great. Discreetly, as you know he's deceased.'

'Oh! Right, anything else I should know about that?'

'No, just... just a favour.' She kicked a pebble into the basin.

'So you seeing someone?'

She watched the concentric circles grow and fade. 'No.' She giggled a bit. 'You?' The question gave her goosebumps.

'Yes.'

She swallowed. 'Oh, and?'

'Seeing a married man.'

Geraldine tried to hide her disappointment. Had Beckie just called to make her angry or to make a point?

'But you know... I'll ask around for Dr Roe. Nice chatting to you. Bye...'

And Geraldine only managed to mouth a bye before she hung up. Geraldine was left feeling as if she had been played. She walked on trying to work out how to break the news to Rebwar – or rather the lack of. They needed Plan B to step in before they both got themselves on the wrong side of those murderers.

THIRTY-ONE

Hampstead Heath was a place Rebwar had never visited, even though he had lived up in Chalk Farm. It was a piece of managed English countryside in North London that had ponds where you could swim, picnic areas, wildlife sanctuaries and a large mansion on the north side and where you could easily get lost on the unmarked paths.

Raj had called him to meet up there. He had given no reason why; it was usually a fast-food joint. Rebwar was a little worried about Raj's brief messages. He paid for his parked car and went off looking for him. At first, he had given him three words to get him to the location, but he lost the will to live when Raj tried to explain that he needed a special app. So Raj had sent him a GPS location so he could follow the blue dot on his phone. There were couples with prams, dog walkers, and families out and about. At the mixed bathing pond, someone was swimming. It made him shiver as it was cold, and he zipped his coat. The coordinates took him deeper into the forest. The drone of the traffic was gradually replaced with the snap of twigs breaking, the odd bird song, and someone calling out for their dog. He had to manage the muddy path so as not to slip.

The direction took him off the track and down a path covered with dried leaves and shrubs. He pushed them out of the way as they rebounded into him. Weaving and ducking, he fought through the undergrowth. Where was this place? His foot slipped and he grabbed a branch that cracked. He fell and swore. Finding a thicker, sturdier branch, he pulled himself back up. He had let go of his mobile and there was no sign of it around his feet. He pushed the dried leaves around, trying to find it. He heard a laugh. It was Raj. 'What is this place?' Rebwar said.

'Hi, uncle. Cool, hey? No one should find us here.'

'Is that what those three words mean?' Asked Rebwar.

'Yeah, something like that... if you—'

He tried to push back some holly bushes which stung him in return. '*Madar Ghaba!*[1] What are we hiding from?'

'I was trying to explain this location app. It—'

'And where is my phone?'

'Shh, I'm calling it.' They both listened out. A broken branch vibrated and Raj reached for it. Something moved and he gave out a high-pitched scream. Something scurried off into some bushes.

Rebwar grabbed his phone, which was next to the branch. 'What's going on?'

Raj had sat down and was holding his chest. 'What was that?'

Rebwar shrugged, 'Nothing. Have you got something?'

'Uncle, I nearly died there. And yes, I have. Jeez. What's up with you?'

Rebwar felt on edge and all this hadn't helped at all. 'Sorry. Been a tough few days.' He took out his pack of cigarettes. 'And I can smoke here?'

Raj nodded, having got his breath back. 'There is something you are going to want to see.' He reached into his bag
for his laptop. He opened it and typed to unlock it and
clicked a few times. He waved Rebwar over.

'What is that?'

Raj smiled and covered his mouth. 'Gay porn.'

'And? You—'

Raj lifted his finger. 'This is from a cloud storage
account that I managed to crack open. It's Izah's and I think
this is his boyfriend.' He showed Rebwar a picture of a smiling, speckled man, ginger-haired with a nose piercing.

'Who is he?'

'No idea. Couldn't find him on any of the socials or
image recognition. They had some... interesting ideas.' And
he flicked through some more pictures.

Rebwar tried to work out what he was seeing. He had
seen these types of pictures before. Back in Iran, there were
plenty of people trying out their dark fantasies. And they
were vulnerable to blackmail. Was this why Izah was
killed? And who knew about it? 'Can you send me the
pictures?'

Raj looked up at him.

'It's evidence, you fool. You haven't answered my question. Why here?'

'Thanks to your friend, my place is burnt. And no, not
burnt, burnt. You know she found me. So I'm couch surfing.
Got one?'

Rebwar shook his head. 'Watch your back.'

'Uncle, you can't just say that. And? From who?'

Rebwar looked around, checking if anyone was near.
'The Mohsen and the Sasani are at war. Or House of Suren
and House of Zik.'

'Why?'

'Izah, and a turf war.' Rebwar kept the news of Kamal from him so as not to freak Raj so out. 'So, I need to find out who killed Izah before it really gets out of hand.'

'And Plan B?'

'Silence.' This was a slight lie, as they had told him to stop working with Jaleh. 'You going to be OK?'

'If you don't get me into more trouble.'

'What about that Hakan Basar?'

Raj nodded and tapped into his computer. 'Yep, here... a businessman based in Turkey. Looks like he imports products from China and sells them off for a profit. Barbecues, tables, flags... anything that makes him a few quid.'

'Where's he from?'

'Fuck knows. Sorry, but he's a mystery. There's not much out there in Turkey. He has no social profile of his own, only appearing in Nahid's. Have you talked to him?'

Rebwar shook his head. 'I've called him and nothing. I need to find him. 'Has he got an address?' Raj typed into his computer. 'You have internet?' He showed him his phone.

'Not much here... You're going to follow him.'

THIRTY-TWO

Music banged out of the car's speakers and it rattled the windows. Rebwar desperately tried to turn it down by pushing, twisting and finally stabbing at random buttons in the car. In desperation, he switched the car off to have a minute of silence and contemplation. He'd just picked up a car from JZ. a friend of Kamal's who had agreed to help him out. Rebwar wanted to make things right and was now taking shifts to pay for Kamal's expenses. But this was a new car, not the usual Prius but some other brand. He reached for his reading glasses and studied the odd symbols on the buttons. His phone vibrated and he checked it. It was Musa sharing a location with him. It was quickly followed by another text: he was going to a fight club with his workmates. Was he gloating that he'd made new friends? Sure his mum wouldn't approve of that. He signed off with a fist emoji. That got Rebwar's attention and he clicked on the link. His son had enabled his phone to be tracked. He was on the move. Rebwar zoomed out of the map and saw that it was an hour north of where he was.

He switched the car on again and music filled his ears. After hitting a few more buttons, he found a dial on the steering wheel that turned the music down. He placed his phone on its stand and drove off. His mind was racing. If only Plan B had his back! He dialled Geraldine's number.

'The fist symbol... I know what it is. Or my son has—'

'Yeah... one sec...' A few muffled sounds and footsteps before she came back to say. 'Go on.'

'It's a fight club and he's going there. Now. And I'm following him.'

'Great, great, we'll then see where it leads.'

Rebwar wanted to hear some kind of reassurance. His son was going into the lion's lair. 'Any news from the meeting?'

'Oh, that. Yeah... I didn't get to ask about your visa. And you know, Highclere is a dick.'

'Did they agree? Did they?'

'You all right?' He tried not to sound desperate.

He wanted to say no, but what was she going to do? Call for the police. Having a family going after you was different from a bunch of criminals. It felt personal, and they had no objections to killing a loved one. And with Jaleh and Musa, he was neck-deep with them. He had seen it happen all too often with his police colleagues. Selling their souls for some pocket money not knowing it was a web of endless string that just kept unravelling. And one day you were all wrapped up and hanging like a string puppet. He wasn't far off. 'Yeah, just trying to drive and talk.' Geraldine gave a little laugh, with which he joined in, realising what he had just said. 'We found photos of Izah's boyfriend.'

'Oh, right, he kept that quiet. You got a name?'

'No, but he could have been blackmailed. Can you chat

to his girlfriend?' He had to repeat himself as she greeted someone.

'Sorry, in a meeting,' at which he laughed as he heard pub-like conversations.

'You paying me for this?'

A car flashed his lights and as it overtook him the driver honked its horn. 'Aa o fut pe mata.'

'Sorry?'

'Couple of beers... I'll send the details.' And he hung up knowing that it would provoke her. He saw a series of texts from Musa. He veered off the road as he tried to read them. Musa had arrived and was going into a barn to place a bet. He wanted to know if he had any fatherly advice. Rebwar shook his head. What could he say? He had brawled and betted as soon as he could count. He pressed on. Street-lights had given way to bare trees, pavements and houses to ditches and dark fields. His headlights picked up cats' eyes and roadkill which, for some reason, upset him. Maybe it was their innocence or their helplessness. He turned onto a small track with a weathered sign overgrown with ivy. The car bounced over the muddy potholes. By a gate was a man trying to keep warm by blowing into his hands. He wore a baseball hat that hid his eyes. He walked up to Rebwar's approaching car. He searched for a window switch.

'Nice night for a few rounds.' His smile faded as he saw Rebwar.

Rebwar pointed ahead to where the cars were parked up. He noticed the man's large and bruised face and hands. He also had a snake tattoo that spiralled around his neck with its head appearing just behind his ear. Rebwar opened his door just enough for him to say, 'Come for the match.' He waited for him to say something. With his two hands, he pretended to box the steering wheel, to which the man just folded his arms. He could hear cheering and whistling ahead of him. The man shook his head and pointed to the path behind him. Rebwar checked Musa's messages. 'My son invited me... Works for Craig Parish.'

The man reached for his mobile and made a call. They waited for an answer, but none came. He signalled for Rebwar to step out, which he did, and regretted not replacing his baseball bat in the replacement car. He didn't know JZ that well to know if he had packed any safeguards. His shoes sunk into the mud and the man made him put his arms up. The man began frisking him, squeezing his arms and working his way down to his shoes. As he got to his pockets, he reached in and took his wallet and penknife, which he kept. When he finished, he handed Rebwar his wallet and nodded for him to head in. The penknife had been a birthday gift from his son and it was inscribed with Best Dad. He weighed his options: make a scene and get himself turfed off; leave it and have to tell Musa he'd lost it; or take the man on. But that last option was going to end in one of two ways: he'd get knocked out or he'd have to fight dirty and risk killing him. Or perhaps he could try him out with a bribe, but that was going to be a fine balance between not insulting him and buying his knife back at an extortionate rate.

'Don't lose it.'

The man smirked.

'It was a present from my son.'

'Do I look like I fucking care? Get in before I change my mind.'

Rebwar opened up his wallet and took out his wad of notes. As he flicked them, he watched the man's face. His neck and jaw muscles loosened as he got to the fifth one. At the seventh one, he checked his surroundings. Rebwar passed him the money. Still making sure the coast was clear, he gave Rebwar his penknife.

'If there's any trouble, I'll fucking stab you myself. Get out of my sight.'

THIRTY-THREE

The barn was made of corrugated metal and the loud music bounced off it like an angry caged animal. It augmented the madness of the crowd when mixed with the pungent smells of a farmyard. On the way in, Rebwar came across the unforgettable noise and stench of a pig farm. He'd once been picked to raid and close an illegal sty on the outskirts of Tehran. Even though it was an illegal activity and a sin in the eyes of Islam, they had managed to keep it quiet. It was in the middle of a rubbish dump. The toxic stench had kept most prying eyes away. But he had got the short straw and was in the lead unit. It took hours to arrest all the perpetrators, and they had to chase them through manure. He smelled for days and was the joke of many of his colleagues. It all came back to him now and he was now close to wrenching.

At the door was a big bald man dressed in black and chewing gum. Next to him was a woman wrapped up in a puffa jacket. The man asked Rebwar to raise his arms. He reached for his wallet and he grabbed the man's arm with a vice-like grip. 'Your mate's checked me.'

'Who?'

'The one at the entrance.' He pointed in the direction he had come from.

'I got my job. Come on, both hands up.'

With his free hand, Rebwar grabbed the penknife from his pocket. Then turned to bump into the man and slipped the knife into the jacket pocket. Now facing the woman, he smiled and winked.

'Mate, face me.' And he grabbed him and turned him to pat him down.

'Who's on?'

The man finished and nodded to the woman.

'Twenty, all right?' she said. Rebwar gave her two notes. She took them and presented a stamp. He pulled up his sleeve.

He had his fist bump. The man pushed the door open. The jacket pocket with the penknife was towards the door. If he was going to pickpocket him, he would have to come up with a distraction. But he had already done one and with two, he'd also get a reputation for being tricky. He would have to come back for it.

Industrial floodlights lit the inside, where there was a circular ring made of blue tarpaulin and hay bales. The crowd were cheering and shouting at two men fighting. Wearing only shorts, they hit each other with blunt thuds and their bare knuckles smashed into their sweaty bodies. Rebwar scanned the crowd for familiar faces and Musa. He spotted a bar in a corner and made his way to it. It was a made of a bunch of bales and a long wooden plank. Canned beer and bottles were on offer and Rebwar pointed to a blue-labelled drink.

'Wanna place a bet?' said a pony tailed man next to him.

Rebwar looked over at the fight. 'Who's fighting?'

'Two Gipsies. Pick your colour and I'll...' There was a massive cheer and one of the men went down. 'Get up, you pussy, get up!' the man shouted over to the ring.

'Twenty on the one standing.' Rebwar took a slug of the warm beer.

An announcement came over a megaphone on the winner. 'I can give you nice odds on the next fight,' said the man. The crowd cheered and two topless women posed next to the bloodied victor for a photo. There were whistles and shouts as the two girls wiggled their wares. 'Mate, so we've got—' and he was pushed aside by a hand.

'Look who we have here.' Rebwar turned to see Craig Parish with Musa. Parish swung out his arm and they shook hands. 'Fancy meeting you here. Got an invite?' He looked over at Musa.

'Friend of a friend,' said Rebwar. 'Good fight. Fancy a drink?'

Parish leaned in and whispered in his ear. 'I don't like you, OK? Now if you step out of line, your son will be watching you bleed. Get my drift? And get me a couple of beers.' He stepped back and winked at him.

Rebwar ordered two beers. He wasn't comfortable. What was Parish's game? Perhaps he was a racist and was he trying to provoke him. He passed the cans over. The mob shouted and clapped. Two men stood in the ring. Rebwar was about to say something to Musa when Parish took him away. Musa shrugged and smiled back. Rebwar held himself back from acting on his emotions. It took a few moments to calm himself. He was here to find information, not start another fight. In the opposite corner were some tables with people sitting around them. He walked over and saw that it was cordoned off. As people milled around, he caught a glimpse of Nahid and Sarah. Hayden was standing by them. They all stood and shouted over at the fighters. Rebwar looked over and saw one of the boxers he recognised. It was Izah's boyfriend from the photograph. The megaphone announced their names. 'And now for the headline fight of the night... Layton the Slayer vs Hooker Haw.' He looked over at the cheering sisters and back to the ring. He took another drink of his warm beer. It was disappointing, but he needed something and he wasn't going to step out to smoke. The referee lowered his hand for them to fight. Rebwar tried to get closer to get a better view, to check if he really was that guy in the pictures. The black boxer swung out twice with a wide haymaker, quickly followed by an undercut. They all missed their mark. He was Hooker Haw, tall, heavy and his swollen face gave him an air of menace. Layton the Slayer hopped around his opponent, taking his time. Toned and muscular, he looked more like a model than a prize fighter. From the chants of the crowd, he seemed to be the favourite. His smile gave him a cocky look.

'Who's Layton?' Rebwar asked a man next to him.

'The Slayer. Got my money on him. Pretty boy, but hell of a boxer. Better get your bet in mate. Don't think it's going to last long. Haw is already puffing.'

'Fuck off Gigs,' said another guy who was next to him, pulling up his saggy grey track suit bottoms. 'That's his style. Like a bull, he is. Just watch his jab. He'll be seeing stars.' And he went on to shout his name. The two boxers landed a couple of punches on each other. A jab drew blood on Layton's cheek. Rebwar went looking for his son.

THIRTY-FOUR

Geraldine had just parked her car in the Brent Cross Shopping Centre. She grabbed a dark blue baseball cap from the driver's seat, dropped the sun visor and put on a pair of wraparound sunglasses. In small red writing on the front of the cap was the name of Hayley Kiyoko, a gay icon. She got out and looked around. She crouched a bit until she spotted a woman walking to the exit. She followed, making sure to keep a discreet distance. It had been a while since she had visited the Mall. Rebwar had chosen it as a meeting place and it had ended up with a confrontation. Another Plan B agent had tried to arrest Rebwar and it all unravelled that he'd been playing them all.

It was a classic-style shopping arcade with glass-fronted shops on two floors. On the ground floor were seats and market-style shops. Families and couples milled around carrying branded shopping bags. The glass ceiling made the place airy and inviting. Geraldine stopped by a handcrafted jewellery stand. She smiled at the woman tending the stand who was polishing some rings. Geraldine looked over at a clothes shop and, in the window's reflection, she saw

Beckie. She was checking her own reflection. Making sure that Beckie didn't spot her, Geraldine moved to get a better look. She looked as beautiful as the first time she had seen her: the smooth olive skin, those marble eyes, that sexy mouth.

'Can I interest you in this lovely gem? Handcrafted and a unique piece.'

Geraldine turned to the woman on the jewellery stand. Her hand stretched out holding a gold ring with a cluster of multicoloured stones in the middle.

'Nice,' said Geraldine. 'It's got all the colours of the rainbow.' The woman nodded and smiled. Her cap had given it away. Beckie was on the move.

'Can I come back for that?' said Geraldine.

'I'll need a deposit to secure it.'

'Yeah, right.' Geraldine kept an eye on Beckie as she carried on walking. 'Sorry, nice, nice.' She lost sight of Beckie as she disappeared behind the escalators. 'I'll be back, thanks.' She went after Beckie. Trying not to push or barge the lethargic shoppers, she weaved frantically around them. If she ran, it would attract the attention of the security guards and Beckie. She took bigger strides, scanning for Beckie's long flowing brown hair and light grey polo neck jumper. She passed the set of escalators that were in the middle section of the shopping centre. Her eyes scanned the groups of people; none of them were Beckie. She kept moving, trying to find another angle. A Marks & Spencer store was in front of her. She remembered that Beckie often bought her underwear from there. She sighed, dreading seeing her. Even though she couldn't stop thinking about her. Why had she decided to contact her? Like an alcoholic returning to a bar, she walked into the store.

On the ground floor was the food hall, and she headed

for the escalator to the first floor where the women's department was. She drummed her fingers on the moving handrail as she ascended. Then moved through the racks of clothes. Beckie went towards the back of the store. She took a left and saw her again. Geraldine stopped and hid behind some flowery dresses. Beckie was in the lingerie section, her hand feeling the texture of a soft bra. Geraldine felt an urge and paused a moment to let it pass. Then she edged closer, hugging the rows of garments, pretending to be interested. Their gazes locked and they both froze. Geraldine swallowed nervously, lost for words and action.

Beckie walked up to her. 'You've got a nerve. are you doing?' Geraldine checked her cap and sunglasses, which had slid down her nose. 'Have you been following me?'

Geraldine tried to say something. Beckie's gaze was locked onto her eyes. 'God, you're such a bitch. How did you find me?' Beckie gave out a frustrated grunt. 'Oh talk, come on! What the hell are you doing here?'

'Babes, I was looking for you.'

Beckie stepped back and looked away. 'Babes, I thought I had made it clear. I don't want to see you again. Ever.'

'But you were—'

'I was playing with you. Like you always did. How does that feel?'

Geraldine moved in closer, trying to smell or tell if she was taking drugs again. She grabbed Beckie's hand and tried to push up her jumper sleeve.

'Is that what you want to see?' Beckie pulled them up herself. 'Have a look! No. I'm clean. Disappointed? Thought you had one over me?'

'What's happened to you?'

'Security!' shouted Beckie; she grabbed Geraldine's arm.

'What are you doing? Let go.'

'She's harassing me! Get her off me! Security!'

Geraldine rotated her arm to get herself out of Beckie's grip. Beckie pushed her, which caught her off guard and she fell into a display table. The mannequin fell off and crashed on the floor, its component parts coming off. Customers came over to look at what was happening. Geraldine tried to get up but was pushed back down. She tried to keep herself from losing her calm. A security guard arrived.

'She's tried to drop me.' Beckie pointed at Geraldine. 'I've been molested. The bitch, arrest her,' and she tried to kick her. The guard pushed, trying to keep Beckie away from Geraldine. 'Don't you touch me! No, no.'

Geraldine got up and walked off, hearing Beckie shout over to her. Not looking back, she just gave her the finger. The security guard asked her to come back, but she kept walking.

'That's right, bitch!' shouted Beckie. 'Just walk off. That's all your good at. Hey?'

Geraldine was sitting on a bench in the main mall cooling down and trying to think. She was convinced that Beckie was taking something. She's seen her psychotic episodes before. What was she getting herself into? She just couldn't help but feel sorry for her. She sipped her cup of coffee.

THIRTY-FIVE

The two boxers were in a hold, both bleeding, sweaty and their chests pumping for air. The referee tried to break them up. Hooker Haw head-butted Layton, who gave out a raging scream. He's stepped back and, in quick succession, jabbed Haw twice. On seeing an opportunity, Layton went for an uppercut. Haw had lost his balance and stumbled back towards the hay bales and Layton missed his next two shots. It gave Haw a few seconds to find his balance again, and he hopped around, avoiding the next set of moves. The crowd shouted over to Layton to finish him.

Rebwar tried to find Musa. He'd seen enough and wanted to disappear before someone made a move against him. He slipped out of the main bunch that had huddled around the ring. He saw Parish snorting some cocaine next to a large tractor. Musa was there with a bunch of mates. Parish spotted Rebwar and smiled as he wiped the white powder off his nose. Then he grabbed Musa by his shoulder and offered him some of the product, looking behind him and smiling at Rebwar. Rebwar tensed up and walked over to him. The other boys turned to face him, making themselves taller and threatening. There were four of them and of varying sizes. All had probably seen their fair share of street fighting. So had, Rebwar of course, but it had been a while since he had brawled. He faced off to Parish.

'Fuck off, old man,' said Parish. 'He can make his own mind up. Right?' Rebwar's fists tightened. Parish turned to Musa. 'Go on, it'll perk you up.' He smiled. 'No harm in it. You should try it, might help the old man too.' To which Rebwar punched him just below his rib cage and stepped on his foot. Parish put out his palm to the boys as he tried to regain his breath. He laughed. 'Is that all you've got?' The boys moved in. 'Guys, I've got this.'

Rebwar hadn't gone for a knock-out blow, as the boys would have piled into him. It was better to give him a run for his money. He noticed some money being exchanged between some people around him. Musa shouted over to him to stop.

Parish reached for his belt and drew out a knife. 'Told ya, I'd be making you bleed, pig.'

'Pig?'

Parish nodded.

Rebwar kicked the ground and hay and dirt spattered into Parish's face. He ran over to a makeshift table, smashed his beer bottle and grabbed the tablecloth. He wrapped the cloth around his left hand. Spitting and swearing, Parish lunged for him. With his left arm, Rebwar deflected his knife away from him then smashed the shards of the bottle into Parish's thigh and he let him tumble onto the ground. More men gathered around, making a circle around them, shouting and encouraging them to fight. A young man helped Parish to his feet. A bloody patch was spreading over his jeans. He hobbled over to Rebwar, swiping his knife. Somebody pushed Rebwar towards Parish. The knife cut into the arm of his jacket. Rebwar held his arms. The blade had pierced the leather. Parish stabbed again. Rebwar held him with both hands. Parish forced the blade closer to Rebwar's chest. Both of them trembled. Their muscles scrambling for that extra inch. The crowd roared and screamed for Parish to which he raged and swore. He flinched and screamed in pain. Rebwar had no idea why but he let him go sprawling back. Rebwar pushed him and let him go. Musa stood there with a crowbar. He had smashed it into Parish's wound. Before Rebwar could move, raining blows forced him to the ground. He curled up to protect himself as boots and fists struck home. It only stopped when sirens rung out over them. Rebwar peeked through his fingers to see running legs and falling bodies. He moved behind a straw bale and looked for Musa. He glimpsed his boy; he was trying to get to him between running bodies.

Rebwar felt the growing pain from his beating. Pulses of sharp stings hit him as he tried to stand up. Grabbing a bale, he hauled himself up. Blue lights buzzed the inside of the barn. The MC on the megaphone had been replaced with a barking voice. He tried to ignore it and go after Musa but he was no longer there. He looked around. Dark uniformed police filled the barn. Holding semi-automatic guns and wearing helmets and bulletproof armour, they moved in sequence. It wasn't long before Rebwar was back on the floor and being handcuffed. When he asked where his son was, they just barked commands. He reluctantly nodded, as if he understood them. He asked again, only to be lifted off the ground and pushed towards the barn door. A couple of shots rang out, and they made him lie down again. From what he could tell, they were coming from outside. He just hoped Musa wasn't involved. A car's engine revved and kept going. But the sound didn't fade away as he had expected. After a couple more shots, the car's engine stopped. Raised hands appeared from the darkness in front of him. An officer grabbed him and pushed him towards a waiting van. Rebwar sat down on one of the two bench seats. Opposite him was Layton, shirtless, caked in dried blood and his face swollen. Rebwar reckoned that his pain was a little less than his. He smiled, trying to get his attention. 'You won that.'

Layton just grunted and looked away. A man further down in the van began shouting over at the officers. With his handcuffed hands, Rebwar leaned in. 'I'm investigating Izah's murder.'

THIRTY-SIX

The van bumped around like a child's doll being dragged from a bike. With their handcuffed hands behind their backs, it was a challenge to stay seated. There were no windows to see out of and, apart from a small dim light, it was as dark as a cave. They swore at each other as some landed on each other's laps. Finally, the van found a road and it speeded up.

A big man by the back door shouted over to Rebwar. 'You're that pig!' Rebwar didn't recognise him from Parish's little gang. 'You called it in,' he shouted pointing and yelling to the other men. 'He's a traitor! He's a copper!' And he stood up and tried to make his way over to him. Layton got up and stood in front of him. 'Out of my way.' The big man snarled. 'He's got to pay, hear me? Not having a snitch here!'

The other men looked over at Rebwar. Layton glanced at him too then turned and head-butted the man, who flew back into the side panel and slumped down out cold.

'Hey, what's going on?' came a voice through the thin metal panel in front.

Layton shouted into the bulkhead, 'It's all right! Someone just slipped.' The men looked away. Layton sat back down and looked over to Rebwar. 'Talk.'

'Your... friend... he was murdered. Who? I don't know.'

'My boyfriend?' Layton said. Heads turned, which Layton stared down.

'Yes, boyfriend. Why was it a secret?'

Layten looked up. 'His family wouldn't... have appreciated us.'

'Did Liz know?'

He nodded. 'She encouraged us. So who killed him?'

'What was he doing in a forest?'

'No effing idea. But I thought he was having some kind of affair.' He hung his head down.

'There was something. He was keeping something quiet from us. Even Liz was suspicious.'

'What about?' Rebwar leaned in. 'One of the Sasanis?'

Layton snorted. 'Really? Why? He was the prodigal son. You're not really a copper?'

Rebwar wondered if he had something on him: bad smell... walk... look? He just shook his head and leaned back on the cold metal of the van. 'Could he have committed suicide?'

Layton gave him a cold hard stare of which a rival boxer would recognise as a challenge.

'What were the Sasani sisters doing there? Bit suspicious.'

'They like it,' Layton smiled and shook his head. 'Love to see Jaleh's face when she hears.'

'So who organises the fights?' Layton looked around him and motioned to the front of the van. Rebwar held himself back from saying the police? 'Who, exactly?'

Layton just shrugged. He looked at Rebwar as if trying

to work out if he was testing him, to see if he was a police informant like the others thought.

The van slowed down and it came to a stop. Murmured voices reverberated through the thin metal panels of the vehicle. Everyone looked at each other, wondering what was coming next. The back doors opened and a bunch of police officers waited for them, batons at the ready. Some even wore helmets.

'What's wrong with him?' said one of them pointing at the big man that Layton had floored. No one reacted and the officer went over to him and slapped his face. 'Hey, wakey, wakey,' He prodded him with his baton. Another officer moved him over and checked the big man's pulse. He waved over for some help and they offloaded him. 'What are you a bunch of idiots looking at? Come on, get out!'

Layton leaned over to Rebwar. 'Listen, Can't see forest. That's what I found written on his hand.'

Rebwar was about to ask him what he meant when an officer shouted for him to get out of the van. Once outside they were made to form a line. Rebwar noticed that the big man had regained consciousness and a medical crew went over to help him. They were in a walled backyard in some police station somewhere not too far from the farm. Flood-lights lit the patrol cars and other parked vehicles. It wasn't long before Rebwar found himself in a cell. They processed him at the reception where he had been asked some basic questions. He asked if he could see his son, Musa. They largely ignored his pleas till he got angry. And then they whisked him off to a holding area. He got up and banged on the door. 'I'm an Uber driver and I'm looking for my son. Can I speak to someone? Hello?'

No answer came.

THIRTY-SEVEN

The sun was beating down on the dusty street and Rebwar had noticed the puddles had dried out. The old woman opposite had emptied her bucket into the road and just missed him. He'd given her a few swear words and his friends had laughed. He regularly got chased around for his foul comments, but, since this entertained his mates, he would go out of his way to find someone to insult.

Now he sat on the step of the empty house that his little gang had made their temporary home. Being the youngest, he had to keep a lookout. He scuffed the dirt up, with his feet making some random shapes. Whilst scouring the tip, he'd found a magazine and seen how rich people made sandcastles on beaches. It had fascinated him: the idea of a vast ocean and beaches.

A couple of car engines sounded at the end of the road, but he took little notice of them. But then at man whistled. Rebwar stood up and called out to his sleeping mates. 'Police!'

A few grunts came back, telling him to leave them be. It had been a long night, scavenging from the streets. He *shouted again and got no response. The door to the old lady's house slammed open and a stream of policemen came out. Like a long snake, it wove across the street towards him. And he ran into the house, shouting.*

Heading for the back door, he felt a thud and then fell to the ground. Then, a police baton clanged on the concrete, just missing him. He tried to get up but two policemen grabbed him. They kicked him with their boots till he found a corner to hide in. They didn't bother with handcuffs, just tied Rebwar and his mates up with rope or wire and hauled them outside. The neighbourhood came out to look at what all the fuss was about. The police made them walk to the station, shouting at them. People took out their anger on them by spitting, throwing stinking rubbish, stones and old shoes. Rebwar had seen and been there before: when there was too much trouble, the police would round them up to show they actually were doing something and then they had to give them money. From whatever they'd stolen or found, half had to be 'gifted' or that what's they called it. Some days they didn't have enough to eat; today was one of them.

In the cell, they were made to stand, a mix of gang members and vagrants. The room stank of human suffering. There was a small oval window above them. It barely provided light, let alone fresh air, twenty, maybe thirty men and boys, all of them huddling in groups.

Rebwar's bruises became black and swollen. His mate had the worst injury: blood was still oozing out of his wound, a cut from a fall. They knew it needed washing but there was no water. They tried to cover it up so the flies wouldn't make a meal of him. Rebwar had lost a few friends that way. In the summer, the heat made everything worse and it was mid-July. Tempers were short as were the opportunities for escape.

A guard came in with a long stick and an angry look. Everyone tried to blend into the old stone walls. Carved in them were stories of old, like a library for an unwanted generation. Rebwar had carved his name. The man waved his black shiny stick as if he was in a circus with wild animals. His snake-like eyes seemed to be searching for someone as he slowly made his way around the room. Some men shook with fear, others kneeled and prayed. As he passed Rebwar, he stopped, knelt down and grabbed his hand. The grip hurt him but he kept his pain to himself. Whispers followed his exit.

The door shut behind him and he was taken down some dark corridors, passing closed doors and stale air. Another guard waited by an open metal door. They pushed him inside a small cell with a curved ceiling and no window. There was a metal bed with an old mattress, and a bucket in a corner. The door shut and everything went black.

———

Rebwar woke up to find himself on a plastic foam mattress. Bright off-white walls and a solitary light in the middle of the ceiling. A white toilet with an integrated sink was in one corner. He rubbed sleep from his face. Looked at his watch and it was three in the morning. He got up and went back to hitting the metal door. He shouted Musa's name and asked for someone to see him. He paced around the room and lay down again to calm his frayed nerves. He couldn't stop worrying about Musa. Why hadn't they given him some information? The slot on the door slid open and a tray with some water appeared. Rebwar stood and went over. 'Hey! Where's my son?' The tray nudged forward a bit, demanding his attention. He took it and the metal plate slid shut. He banged it. 'I want to know where my son Musa is! I demand...' He sighed and drank the water. Then he lay back down and closed his eyes.

———

The door opened. A man came in to put a blindfold on him. He protested by lashing out, but another man came and tied his hands. He shouted his best filthy words to make his protest heard. The door closed again and he waited. He shivered because of the damp air. The rusty hinges squealed and slow footsteps came towards him. A heavy weight next to him made him jump.

'Hello,' *The deep, soft voice was reassuring, even friendly.*

'Who are you?' *said Rebwar.*

'That is not important. What is your name?'

'Rebwar.'

'Strong name. How old are you?'

'Ten.'

The man got up and walked in front of him. His smell was distinct: a flowery perfume mixed with incense. He sat on the other side of him. 'You like chocolate?'

'Yes.'

'Sir.' *And he slapped him.* 'If you want some, you are going to do what I ask you. It's simple. Don't be afraid. It's fun. For both of us.'

Rebwar leaned back, sensing that something was off. 'What?' *He felt the man's hand settle on his skinny leg.*

'Something between us.'

———

Rebwar lashed out.

'Wow! Steady there!'

His eyes focused on a man wearing a uniform. He rubbed his eyes and wiped the sweat from his brow.

The uniformed men looked at him and moved closer. 'You all right? You were mumbling stuff and stirring. Bad dream?'

Rebwar held his foggy head. 'Yes, old stories. You have found my son?'

He shook his head. 'But I'm taking you out of here.'

'Where?'

'Come on, I'll tell you on the way. Quick, quick.'

The man stepped out of the cell and looked to see if the coast was clear.

'Who are you?' asked Rebwar.

'PC Clive Sheppard.'

THIRTY-EIGHT

The car was speeding down along a dual carriageway. Rebwar had seen signs to London, so guessed they were heading towards the capital. PC Clive Sheppard was holding the steering wheel with his right hand and had a small revolver in the right. It was one he'd never seen before, had a white grip and looked like a retro cowboy gun. He had taken Rebwar out of the police station by the garage exit. With very little fuss, which had made Rebwar suspicious.

'Can I call my son?'

'Sorry. Orders. There's some gum in that glove box.'

Rebwar reached out for it, but it was locked. Sheppard just shrugged, as he would have to stop the car to unlock it. 'Can I borrow your phone?'

Sheppard turned his head to face him. 'Mate, I was supposed to put you in the boot. I'm just soft and let you sit here, son.'

'Who?'

'You're running out of credit.' Sheppard pointed at the road and him with his gun. 'Just enjoy the journey. Hey?'

Rebwar spotted a hint of madness in him. 'Clive, what was your sin?'

He laughed and banged the wheel. 'I should have put you in the back. Sinned! Can't make it up. You religious or something?'

'I came here.'

'Well, that'll teach you. Lucky should have sent you back.'

'Did they catch you?'

He shook the loaded gun like it was his index finger. 'Not falling for that. You tell and I tell?' He snorted. 'Not born yesterday.'

'PC. So they kept you in the force. Sergeant... What were you? Detective or? Divorced.' And he pointed to his ringless hand. 'Had a family, house and you got greedy. Close?'

Clive fidgeted as he carried on looking at the road. Moved his head from side to side. 'Enough!' He held the gun at Rebwar's head. 'Yeah?' He pushed the cold barrel deeper into his temple. 'I'm...' He cocked the gun's hammer. 'Just shut up.'

Rebwar saw his eyes flicker. The man had killed before. He wasn't shy in pushing the limits. He also now wondered who he was working for? The Sasanis, the Mohsen, or someone else? There was a real possibility that someone wanted him dead. And Sheppard was capable of that, if that was his real name. He hadn't noticed anyone else in the police station greet him with his name. It was nods and ordinary greetings.

'Got a son?'

Sheppard pushed the gun harder into his temple.

'Nephew, family?'

'Shut it! What's it to you? Hey, just a turban-wearing

terrorist. Hey?' He lowered his gun and carried on driving.

'Did you see my son?'

He looked ahead and shook his head. Rebwar sensed he had hit a nerve, but he was in an emotional minefield.

'One call?'

Sheppard rubbed his chin with his loaded gun.

'I need to know...'

He pointed the gun at him again. 'Shut up.' He ground his teeth. 'Let me think.' He blinked furiously. 'I...I...'

Rebwar grabbed the seatbelt fastener and unclipped Sheppard. And with his other hand, he went for the gun. Sheppard let go of the steering wheel, grabbed Rebwar's neck and pushed him hard towards the glove box. Rebwar punched Sheppard's groin and his face contorted then a flash blinded them. The driver's window exploded into shards of flying glass. Noise reverberated and rung in Rebwar's ears. The car's tyres screeched and it violently changed direction. A fist impacted Rebwar's chin and whipped his head around. The sound of metal screeching mixed with the smell of burning metal. Sparks flew, and the car spun. Both were thrown like lifeless dummies before the air bags exploded into their faces, thrusting them back into their seats. The vehicle jolted, banged and rolled. Sheppard disappeared through the broken window. The car flopped right side up and steam gushed out from the hood. His ears still ringing, Rebwar whaled as if it was his first breath. He banged on the door, but it was stuck. He undid his seatbelt and pushed out the broken windscreen with his feet. After escaping the hissing car, he stumbled around and looked at the scene.

The car was crumpled up like a paper ball. Pieces of bodywork were scattered all the way back to the road. They had narrowly missed hitting a couple of trees in a field.

Rebwar stumbled back, wanting to take a moment, but then he saw the still body of Sheppard. He looked at an extremely awkward angle but Rebwar didn't stop to think about it. Instead, he checked for a pulse, but found none. Then he went through Sheppard's pockets and found his wallet and mobile. Tapped the screen. It was locked, and he grabbed Sheppard's right hand only to find half of it was missing, including the index finger. Rebwar swore. The phone gave him the option to call the emergency services. He declined; he couldn't go back there. He switched on the torch on the phone and searched the undergrowth for Sheppard's finger. The light caught the shine of the gun. He picked it up and rubbed the mud off it. It was a Ruger Vaquero. It felt balanced and well made, not the kind of knock-off replica that was popular with gangs. He slipped it behind his belt.

A van stopped on the hard shoulder and a man stepped out. Rebwar found the remains of Sheppard's hand. He put the index finger on the phone's scanner. It kept asking for a four-digit code. The van reversed and lit the scene with its headlights. Rebwar dropped the hand and shielded his eyes.

'You all right?'

Rebwar waved back and nodded. A car stopped behind the van. It was getting busy and the emergency services were probably not far behind. More people gathered around the crash site and Rebwar slipped into the darkness by pushing his way into the bare bushes. He had to get away as quickly as he could, before they realised he was missing. The ground was wet and boggy. His breath condensed as he fought his way through hedges and fences. Sirens and flashing blue lights lit the roadside verge, which he kept to his left. He concluded that if he followed the road they had been on, it would lead him to London.

THIRTY-NINE

He was crossing a sea of nettles. The wind had picked up and was blowing across the empty fields to his left. His face and hands were numb and the rough ground made it hard not to trip or fall. Each step was heavier than the last. Traffic had picked up again, and he guessed they had cleared the accident. He was still keeping off the verges of the road as he didn't want to be seen. He was hoping a town would come into view. The large clouds had hidden the half moon. The thought of getting into a warm car made him stop to rethink his options; he had to find a place to shelter and think clearly, and not in a cell or in someone's basement. Who was looking for him and had been willing to break him out of a jail? That involved some deep pockets and corruption, the sort the Sasanis or the Mohsen could organise as well as Plan B. Each scenario invited its own questions and possibilities. He didn't think Plan B would go to all the trouble of getting him out of a police station. It left a trail they would have to cover up and there were easier ways for them to summon him: if that was what they wanted to do.

The gun bothered him and the way Sheppard dealt with it. The Mohsen was his bet. They had been after him and his arrest was a good opportunity. If they had a man in the right place, why not? It seemed as if they had planned to dispose of him. Why did Sheppard mention the boot? For an assassin, his game was off. Why talk to your victim and use him to keep you company? Odd and slightly comical. The Sasanis could also have ordered it. All he could think of was Parish and his dislike of him. Had he somehow convinced them he was the inside man? Or had they interrogated Musa? He tried to keep calm at the idea that his poor boy was in harm's way.

A light flashed in the distance. The branches swayed in the wind, making it hard to see what it belonged to. A couple of lights appeared as he moved towards it. He couldn't work it out. There was no clear outline of a roof or chimney. Some kind of flag fluttered above. This was curious; you always lowered them at dusk.

As he closed in, cars' headlights lit what turned out to be a container. It was blue, white and red and a painted sign read Penny's Cafe. Rebwar approached from behind so that no car would see him arrive. There were some solitary-looking lights around the metal box that seemed to be more for decoration than practical use. There were some windows cut out of the metal walls. He used his phone's torch to light the inside. There were some tables and a counter. He walked around it, trying to find a back door. He stumbled on a hard metal object, which clanged. Next to it was a door. A padlock hung under the door lever. He shone his torch, looking for what he'd walked into. It was a small gas canister. It was half-empty and he picked it up. With the lip at the bottom, he hit the lock. After a couple of hard knocks, it gave way, screws ripped out of the wooddden frame. He pushed the door open. It felt warm out of the bitter wind. His steps echoed inside the empty box. There were written menus, posters of corgi dogs, a couple of English flags and a poster of a black boxer. Rebwar took a seat by one table and felt himself sag like an unwound spring. He felt like a sack of lead. The pain was going to come next.

———

A prod woke him and his eyes focused slowly on a woman.

'Yeah, he's awake... what? No, don't think so.' She was poking him with the end of a mop. And holding a phone to her ear. 'You all right, love?'

Rebwar tried to straighten himself, but the wooden stick was digging into his ribs. He forced a breath to say, 'Where am I?'

'In my caff. You just come off the boat?' She listened to the voice on the phone. 'Of course, I can ask him. I had a few of them last week.'

'No, no, just an Uber driver.' His eyes were now adjusting to the bright strip lights.

'Oh, so you're a bit early, love. And why did you break in?' Still brandishing her mop, she looked around. 'And where's your car?' Rebwar tried to move and find a more comfortable position. 'You just stay there. Till I know what is going on. You're going nowhere.' She spoke into the phone. 'No, don't call the police, not just yet.'

He raised his arms and showed him his palms. 'No police. Let me explain.'

'Ethel, he's going to explain...' And slowly and a little louder, as if she was talking to a child, she said, 'What's your name? Your name.' And with her phone, she pointed to him.

'Rebwar, I need a phone.' And he reached for his pocket.

She shook her head. 'No, no, where are you from?'

'Live in London, I have a driving licence.'

'He said London.' And she looked at him with a confused look. 'You're not one of Micky's boys. Or C17... you're a bit old for them or county lines... Wait, wait it's OK, he's all right... oh shut up Ethel,' she smiled looking down embarrassed by whatever had been said by her friend.

He reached for his wallet and remembered it was Sheppard's. His belongings were still at the station. He showed her some money and hoped she wasn't going to ask for his ID.

'I'm looking for my son. Up in the farm. Boxing match. You know?'

She nodded.

'I need to make a call?'

She stepped back slowly, still maintaining the mop pointing at him. 'All right... I'll call back. Yeah, in ten.' And she ended the call. 'Mr Rebwar, why should I trust you?'

He put a couple of twenty-pound notes on the table. 'Can I get a coffee?'

'I'm not looking for money and don't want trouble. Ten and I'm calling. OK?'

He nodded.

'If I don't call my friend in...' She looked at her watch. 'Nine minutes. She's calling the coppers. Right?'

Rebwar took the phone, which was unlocked. 'Thank you, I didn't get your name.'

'Carol.' She walked off to the counter.

He searched in the small rectangular pockets of his jeans and got out a folded piece of paper. The handwritten phone numbers were on the list. He had to make a choice.

In normal circumstances, he would have called all the numbers and asked for Musa's whereabouts. But he didn't want to sow panic and set alarms off and then have the police looking for Musa. He had to convince himself that Musa was a grown-up and could take care of himself. It was hard, and he struggled with the idea. So calling Hourieh was out of the question and if he was there, she'd be calling him anyway. Dinah was also a liability as she could easily give him away to the Sasanis. He wasn't going to call Bijan; for all he knew, he could be in the Mohsens' camp and Katarena was protecting him like a golden goose that was going to pass away. Geraldine was also out of the question as Sheppard could have been Plan B. Till he had an idea, he had to keep his distance. But maybe he was worrying about nothing. He dialled Musa's mobile.

FORTY

The phone went straight to voicemail and he hesitated in leaving a message. He quickly dialled another number and hoped that Raj would pick up. Carol had switched the lights on and was prepping the roadside cafe for business. The call went to voicemail, but he dialled again. On the third attempt, it picked up, and before Raj could answer, Rebwar said, 'Raj, listen, I've only got a few minutes.'

'Sure, what's wrong and whose number is this?'

'Not to worry, I need you to subtly ask around for Musa.'

'What's happened to him?'

'Raj, listen... no panic. I need you to be calm and focused. He might be in custody or...' He didn't want to tell him what he thought. 'So call Geraldine and Hourieh but just say that you've got something for him or a question. They can't be suspicious as I can't have them call the police.'

There're was a big sigh and Raj said, 'Uncle, you're making me sweat. Are the Sasanis after us? What about Dinah?'

Rebwar checked the wall clock. 'Raj, be careful. I'll call back.' He dropped the call. He got up and went over to Carol to hand the phone back. She nodded and took it back. 'Find your son?'

Rebwar shook his head. 'You've been to the boxing fights?'

Carol looked over at the boxing poster. 'Been invited but never had the courage. You ask a lot of questions for an Uber driver.' She sized him up. 'You some kind of snoop?' She crossed her arms. 'And what happened to you?'

He put a ten-pound note on the counter. 'Can I get a coffee? Long story.'

She took the money, went over to the kettle and turned it on. Faced him as it boiled.

'It was raided and I had my son with me.'

'I knew it. See, I told them I wouldn't go. Bloody right I was.'

'Who organises it?'

'Questions, questions. You're full of them. Sure you aren't police? I've got a nose. My ex was one and—' The kettle stopped and she made his coffee.

Rebwar took a pack of sweets. A big artic lorry pulled up on the lay-by and its engine noise rattled through the metal container. 'Was he involved?'

'Look, Mr Rebwar, you take your coffee and be on your way. I've had enough of the law for a lifetime.'

He took his coffee and left the change for her. A phone vibrated in his pocket and he remembered that he still had Sheppard's mobile. He stepped outside to pick it up.

'Mate, where the fuck are you?' said a male voice.

Rebwar waited for a few seconds. 'He was in an accident.'

'Who's this?'

'Rebwar.'

There was silence and then some mumbling. 'What happened?'

'Who's talking?'

Another man's voice came on. 'Come to the warehouse. We're waiting.' And he ended the call.

Obviously, it was the Sasanis but did they have Musa too? He had to get there, but he'd just run out of goodwill in the cafe. He sipped his coffee and tried to work out a plan. How could he face Jaleh and her crew and what did they want?

FORTY-ONE

The breeze banged the loose metal panels on the warehouse. With no rhythm it made the atmosphere tense. As if Jaleh had planned it. She stood planted in front of Rebwar holding Sheppard's gun and wearing a white trouser suit and a black blouse. Her gold jewellery was on display and picking up the spotlights that lit her crew. They stood in a circle around the chair where Rebwar sat with his hands tied behind his back. He had hitchhiked and taxied over to their shipping facility where Musa worked. He had guessed right. There had been a welcoming committee, and they had searched and restrained him. Not much was said. And his questions about Musa were still unanswered. He wasn't there, which slightly worried him.

'Where's Musa?' he asked again.

Jaleh's high heels echoed on the concrete floor as she walked around him, holding her chin with her hand. Hayden was close by, waiting in his black suit like a guard dog for this mistress to command. 'What were you doing at the fight?'

'Where's Musa?'

'Answer the question!' Hayden shouted.

'I want to know where my son is.'

Hayden walked over to Rebwar before being stopped by Jaleh's dismissive hand gesture. He halted and looked a little disappointed at not getting the chance to have a go at Rebwar. Jaleh clicked her fingers and out of the shadows hobbled Craig Parish.

'Have you got my son?'

Parish showed him the penknife that he'd misplaced in the bouncer's pocket and never got a chance to pickpocket back. Parish smiled, his face still bruised from the fight.

'My son gave that to me.'

He pulled the blade out. 'I told you.'

'Enough!' said Jaleh. 'Craig, tell him what you said.'

'He's the traitor.' Parish pointed at him. 'He's a copper. Your son told me that you work for them. Some plan or something, he said. That's why the old bill came round for a visit ain't it. Got you.'

Rebwar just shook his head. Looked around him, hoping to see Musa. 'If you touched one hair.'

Parish went right up to him and laughed. 'And what?'

Hayden motioned for one of his thugs to pull Parish back. He protested but gave in.

'Where is he?' Rebwar said again.

Jaleh walked up and waved the gun at him. 'Rebwar, is this true?'

'I didn't call the police. You knew I was a detective. It takes weeks to organise a raid. Your mole failed you, that's what happened. Now where is Musa?'

She walked around him looking about, contemplating what he had just said.

'Can I get a cigarette?'

'So why is everyone saying they saw you call the police?'

She looked over at one of the men and instructed him to get some cigarettes. 'I pay them.'

'Exactly. Yes men. Did you know your son had a boyfriend?'

One of the men presented an open pack of cigarettes and she took one for herself and placed another in Rebwar's mouth. 'Who said that?' The man flicked a Zippo lighter and she lit her cigarette.

'He told me.' Rebwar drew in the flame into the cigarette, taking in the soothing smoke. 'He was one of the fighters.'

'A lie! He would have told me. He was my boy and we had no secrets.' She turned away. 'And I would have known. I'm his... was his mother.'

'Ask your daughters. They were at the match.' Around her, a couple of faces tensed up and looked down.

'Nonsense.' She looked around at her gang and stared into their blank faces.

Hayden stepped in. 'They asked to be there. It was Izah who wanted them there. He instructed me strictly not to say anything. They asked me.'

'And you thought that this wasn't something I should know about? And I had to find out like this? In front of them? Humiliating me. Do you take me for a fool?'

'Sorry Mrs Sasani. But I had it all under control. I was there making sure it was all—'

'And then it wasn't. Was it? Where are they?'

'Home. Nothing to worry about.'

'And my son?' said Rebwar.

Parish shouted. 'Such a broken rec—'

'Yes, where is he?' said Jaleh.

There was a moment of silence as they all looked at each other, waiting for someone to say something.

'And? anyone? He was there.'

Rebwar tried to get up, but the zip ties stopped him. 'Ask Parish. He took him there. You invited him. What happened?'

Jaleh looked over at him, waiting for an answer.

'Well, he hit me and then the fuzz came in. We had to get out of Dodge.' He rubbed his head. 'Still hurts.'

'Did you look for him?' To which he just shrugged. Jaleh squeezed the bridge of her nose. 'If Rebwar, here, didn't call the police, who the hell tipped them off?'

Rebwar flicked his head for Jaleh to come over and she did. 'You've got a traitor in your organisation.'

She walked towards Hayden. 'Get me the Chief Super now! And call me when he's here.' She went over to Parish and said something to him that Rebwar couldn't hear.

Parish hobbled over to Rebwar. 'Sorry mate, I was wrong. No hard feelings...' He put his hand out for Rebwar to shake, but he couldn't and Parish reversed awkwardly away.

'Get him a beer or something,' said Hayden. 'But he stays here till we sort this mess out.'

Jaleh looked over at Rebwar. 'And find his son.' The door slammed behind her. All eyes turned to him like those of a pack of wolves.

FORTY-TWO

The panels still banged away and echoed in the dark warehouse. Smoke swirled around a small table. Rebwar held a set of cards and a can of beer. Cardboard boxes made a makeshift table where he sat with three others. Hayden had left to do what Jaleh had asked him to do, or so he presumed. They had left the others to guard him. In the middle of the table was a small pile of money with a couple of rings and a watch. It had been a while since Rebwar had played poker. He was more of a dominoes man. He couldn't say he was up, but he wasn't down either. Sheppard's money had come in handy. He'd also sized them up. Parish had the idea for the game. Apart from hating Rebwar for what he guessed was a racist reason. Parish was a bitter, twice-divorced, alcoholic middle-aged man in midlife crisis. He recently got a tattoo of a swift, said it reminded him of his getaway skills. Then there was Al, the one with the crew cut. He'd been in the marines and had been discharged after being blown up in Afghanistan. And finally, Noah, the youngest, who said he had chatted to Musa and liked him. He was originally from the West Indies.

'So who killed Izah?' said Noah.

Parish shushed him. 'He killed himself, didn't he, I mean, he did. I could see it in his eyes. Seen it. I know...' He looked down, clearly having some kind of flashback.

'So why's the boss got a bee in her bonnet about it? Hey?' Noah said, putting a card down and picking another one. 'Hey? Mr PI over there? What's the story?'

'Did you guys know Izah?' said Rebwar.

Parish took a card and raised the stakes by putting a couple more notes on the table. 'There were rumours. I didn't believe them. Nice guy. Talked the talk. You know... looked like the boss.'

'Rubbed a few people the wrong way,' said Al. 'Had to... well, it's done.' And he put his cards down and lit a cigarette.

Rebwar looked at his odds. He was missing a king to get a flush. Parish looked like he had some kind of suit. He kept raising as he picked up cards but there was a lack of confidence for something high. Noah was a little harder to read, as he was a natural bluffer and could go either way. There was about a grand on the table and for Noah, that was big. There was ambition in his style and he was obviously not too shy to ask questions. Rebwar picked a card and it was an ace. He was still waiting for the right card and Parish was soon going to call it.

'Was Izah making a deal behind Jaleh's back?' Rebwar asked.

Parish picked a card and his eyes darted around the table.

Al leaned back. 'It was the Mohsen family.'

'Why?'

Al blew out his cheeks. 'Why not? Is there a bad time for war? No.'

Noah knocked on the table for a pass.

'Hakan is an odd one,' said Rebwar, getting blank looks back. 'Turkish guy... Nahid's fiancée... know him?'

Parish smiled. 'The delight. Too sweet and powdery for me.' They laughed.

'Didn't have you down for a bum shagger,' said Al. 'Each to their own. Fucking hate Turkish delight. It's from your part of the world, hey?'

'We have similar delights.' Rebwar took a card and got a king of hearts and he had spades. He was trying his luck.

'Bet you do,' said Parish. 'Heard about you a lot.'

'Nahid's a catch.'

They all smirked.

'Priceless,' Noah showed him some pictures of Liz Knowles from her Instagram account. 'Now she's smoking.' He whistled and showed them to the others too.

'She used Izah,' Rebwar said. 'She knew about Ben. She might have done it.'

The three of them said no way.

'But I remember that huge argument they had,' said Parish. 'You know the one?' He looked at the other two. 'She wanted something expensive and he refused. In the yard. Some ticket to a show in Vegas. Remember? Al, you remember?' He looked at him blankly.

'He had his Merc and she had that Stanley knife. Didn't she cut him before you took it off her?' And he clicked his fingers. 'When was that?'

'She had a temper,' said Al. 'Highly strung. It blew over.'

A door opened and Hayden walked in with Chief Super James McKintosh behind him. Rebwar had only exchanged a few words with him at the engagement party. In his dark blue uniform, he looked very different. He still had his merry face but there was no smile. The three men stood up.

Hayden said, 'Fuck's sake, clean up.'

'Where's Jaleh?' McKintosh held his cap under his left arm and checked the time. 'What's so bloody urgent? We've got an officer down.' And he looked over to Rebwar and stopped for a moment.

Rebwar looked back.

'Jake, come on, what's going on? Is it about that raid?'

Jaleh appeared from some stacked boxes that were behind them. 'Yes, who ordered it?'

McKintosh's hot sweaty face shone off the lights. 'It wasn't me. Came from above. No idea, I only got to know this morning.' He pointed at Rebwar. 'And what's he doing here?'

'Apparently, he called it in,' said Jaleh.

'What do you want me to do about it?'

'Sort it.'

McKintosh looked at Jaleh, not knowing what to say.

She brought out Sheppard's gun and put it on Rebwar's temple. 'Is this your man?'

Feeling the cold barrel, he glanced up at Jaleh, trying to work out what she was trying to really find out.

'Jaleh, come on, I can understand that you're upset. If I had heard, you would have known.' He wiped his brow. 'And no, I don't know who he is. Never seen him in my life.'

Jaleh pulled the pistol's hammer back. 'I remember you two chatting at my daughter's engagement party. Now it's since then the shit has hit the fan. Coincidence? Or?'

Rebwar tensed up, feeling that she wasn't playing. Was he still regarded as the mole?

McKintosh took a closer look at Rebwar. 'Oh, now that you mention it. Your niece... her boyfriend... He was a detective and drives an Uber.' He looked at Jaleh who kept staring at him. 'What else do you want me to say?' She pointed the gun at him and he raised his hands. 'Jaleh... now... think about this. We've got a good thing going here. Don't we?'

She stepped up to him. 'Did you kill Izah?'

'No, why would I? And it was suicide. Wasn't it?'

She looked over to Rebwar. 'He doesn't think so. Suspicious. And what happened to the pathologist? Dr Roe?'

McKintosh's eyes darted around, waiting for an answer. 'You tell me.'

'Suicide? Are you working for the Mohsens?'

'Come on, this is getting out of hand. Why would I do that? I'm risking enough being here and with all of you. Look, whatever the problem is, I'm sure I can help. Think about—'

Rebwar questioned what he'd just seen flash in front of him. A déjà vu of McKintosh's head with a third eye and a puff of red mist behind his skull. The flash and echoing bang only registered as McKintosh's body folded onto the concrete floor.

FORTY-THREE

The big Mercedes limo sped down the motorway. The heavily tinted windows and interior lighting made it hard to see out. Rebwar sat next to Jaleh, both in plush leather sofa-like seats in the back. Facing him was Hayden, wearing gloves and holding the Ruger Vaquero revolver that Jaleh had just used. Up front, Parish drove the limo.

'Where are we going?' said Rebwar.

'Never mind that.' Jaleh pointed to the gun. 'I have plans.' She nodded to Hayden, who passed the gun to Rebwar. 'Take it and hold it.' He did as he was told. Hayden took it back and put it into a clear bag. 'Insurance.' She reached for her phone, tapped in a code and brought up the image of an overweight middle-aged man, with a trimmed beard, and large golden framed glasses. 'This is Lanny Mohsen. You are going to plant that gun on him. Where and how, I don't care, but it has to be done by tomorrow.'

Hayden passed the plastic bag back to Rebwar.

'But...' He stopped himself as there was no point in discussing the reasons behind it. 'I don't think that policeman was the traitor.'

Jaleh reached into the centre console between the two seats. She flipped a lid and an illuminated fridge presented itself. Between a couple of handguns and cash were some water bottles. She offered one to Rebwar, who declined. 'He was past his sell-by date.' She checked the bottle before opening it.

Rebwar put the gun away in the inner pocket of his jacket. 'Can I suggest that we meet with the Mohsens?'

'That's a stupid idea,' said Hayden.

Jaleh held her palm up and took a moment to reflect. 'Tell me more.'

'If I can be so...'

'Out of order,' said Hayden.

'Honest, you're making a business move on the House of Zik, aka Mohsen. Before it gets too hot and attracts the attention of the police or the section that you won't be able to pay off, why not consolidate a deal with them? And then slowly and subtly make your restructuring of the organisation.'

Jaleh leaned back and smiled. She looked over at Hayden who was waiting for her lead. 'I'm now doubting your pitiful sob story about being a humble Iranian detective. But just how would you convince them to meet?'

Hayden shook his head and adjusted his seatbelt. 'That's nothing new.'

'But you've got a situation and, like you, they know that they have a lot to lose. And your son...' Rebwar speculating. 'He met with them before he was killed. Ben told me.' Jaleh squeezed the now empty plastic bottle, cracking and collapsing it into a flat outline. 'At least let me find your son's killer.'

'You're not trying to pull one?' Hayden rubbed the back of his neck. 'What about your son? Because like Jaleh said, I don't buy your bullshit stories. Because I've not found a traitor and you seem to be convinced that there is one. I'd say the lady doth protest too much.'

'Jaleh vouched for you,' said Rebwar to Hayden.

'Boys, let's not have a pissing contest.' She turned to Hayden. 'Off, I know you've... fuck sake I don't need to explain myself.' She looked out of the window, putting her hand up to shield the reflections. 'Hayden, if we would have taken your advice at face value, we'd all be either dead or in jail.' She twisted herself to face Rebwar. 'What do you propose?'

'A pact of some sort.' Rebwar felt out of his depth. 'I'm just the messenger and they want me dead. Any news on my son?'

Jaleh smiled and rubbed Rebwar's hand affectionately. 'You're a good man. I can see what my niece sees in you. After this, I would love to have you on board. Let's have a cigarette.'

Rebwar reached for them. 'I had my lighter taken.' No one offered. They looked for a car lighter, but there wasn't one.

'Tell the driver to stop at a shop and get a lighter,' said Jaleh. After a couple of roads, the limo stopped. 'Rebwar, you're going to have to set this meeting up. I can't. Needs to come from you. Tell them that we want to talk about the noble houses and make an alliance. Embellish it... making glorious history... leaving a lasting legacy. Speak to their egos. Understand?'

Rebwar nodded.

'Add some Persian nonsense. I'm sure Dinah will help you.' She looked at his clothes. 'And get her to choose an outfit. Something business-like.'

'What about a gift?' said Hayden.

Jaleh nodded. 'Good. See he can bring something to the high table. What?'

'The gun.'

Jaleh closed her eyes. 'And that is disappointing. No.' She tapped her long, manicured nails on the car's leather armrest. 'We need some antiquity to represent the union.' Parish slid the door and handed over a lighter that he had just bought at a corner shop. 'Get a bottle of fizz, I need to think.' Jaleh added as she leaned into the flame of the lighter.

Rebwar lit his cigarette and waited for an idea. His knowledge of culture was limited to things he had stolen as a kid or what Bijan had shown off to him. The tat that his wife had made him buy was a little crass. Cheap trinkets would be an insult. But he was sure Dinah could help. 'I can call Dinah?'

'You know, all this has made me hungry,' said Jaleh. 'Let's have dinner. And I'll keep this gun as insurance.' And she put the Ruger Vaquero revolver in the car's centre console.

FORTY-FOUR

The warm yellow glow of the setting sun caught the rusting piles of crushed cars. Highclere had sent Geraldine a location pin to her phone. It was on the outskirts of London by Mill Hill, a piece of derelict land next to the M1 motorway. The groan of passing traffic added to the gloom of discarded metal and unruly thorn bushes. Avoiding the orange-stained puddles and large cranes, she made her way deeper into the compound, expecting to see some movement or hear a beep from a moving machine. Nothing came and no one showed up to confront her.

After passing piles of plastic and tyres, she saw a row of parked cars. Some were clean; others had accident damage. At the end of the line of vehicles, next to some trees was a caravan. In front of it was a lounger with a table and empty cans of beer. Still looking around for any sign of life, she made her way to the trees. The place gave her the creeps. Death and decay were everywhere. The caravan door opened and Highclere squeezed out. It was a strange relief to see a familiar though unusually unwelcome face. He wore a dark pinstriped suit and sunglasses. In the circumstances, more fancy dress than a statement of rank. He held the door open as if it was a portal to some plush office.

The smell of incense caught her out. Inside it was a temple to some hippie culture. Batik cloths hung from the covered windows. Wind chimes jingled as she made her way to the back of the caravan. Sitting on a sofa was a big man in a black and yellow tie-dyed T-shirt and jeans. She noticed a large Bowie-style knife sheathed on his belt. As he got up to greet her, his big beard swayed. 'Aspen. Take a seat.'

Geraldine moved some newspapers from the couch opposite and sunk into it. Highclere sat on a wooden stool. 'What's this?' she said.

'Interview,' said Aspen in a deep voice. He grabbed an attaché case, put it on the table and opened it.

'For?' Geraldine had been expecting some kind of spiritual reading.

Aspen put some reading glasses on. 'From what Highclere told me...' He read his notes. 'The House of Suren...' He looked over his glasses. 'You know them?'

'Want back in the force. Want my old job back.'

He nodded and grabbed some peanuts from a bowl. Whilst chewing, he said, 'Can't say... It says here that you've got some intel. Some organised crime in Essex, Epping way. And?'

'Rebwar, my asset, has insider access. And there's an opportunity to stop a turf war and close them down.'

Aspen took another handful of nuts and looked over at Highclere. 'Thoughts?'

Highclere just took off his sunglasses and cleaned them with his handkerchief. His scarred face not giving anything away.

Aspen scribbled some notes. 'Do you know this man?' he handed over a picture to Geraldine.

She took a closer look but didn't recognise the balding man. 'Never seen him.'

'Where's your asset now?'

Geraldine wasn't sure herself and had left some messages on his phone. But to get what she wanted, which was her old job back, she needed to reassure them. 'Working for them.'

Highclere cleared his throat. 'You know he was in custody?'

'Was?' She played for time. It probably explained the radio silence. She tried not to act surprised and checked her phone. Raj had left a voicemail.

'It happened just after your man left the station.' Aspen said.

'What happened?'

'You tell us,' said Highclere.

Aspen brought out more pictures from his case. 'This is what happened.'

Geraldine checked the photos, which were of a crashed car and a body. It was the same man she had just seen in the picture. Her hands trembled as she flicked to the next picture, expecting to see Rebwar's body. 'You told us to keep out.' She got to the last picture, which was of a couple of bullet casings. 'What's this got to do with me?'

'We think your asset is involved.' Aspen collected the pictures back from the table. 'We need to talk to him.'

'He's your asset. That's why you wanted us to keep away.'

Aspen and Highclere said nothing and remained stone-faced.

'OK, but I want back in.' Not that she was certain that she was ever out. 'What's going on?'

Highclere and Aspen looked at each other, as if they were agreeing on something between them. Aspen gave out a large sigh. 'Fuck's sake. If my mother knew.'

'Oh, shut it. Go on,' said Highclere. 'You sure you had a mother?'

'We've been keeping an eye on them for a few months,' said Aspen. 'And... now lost our intel. We need it back.' He leaned in. 'This is what we propose. A meeting with...' He looked over to Highclere.

'Rebwar.'

'Yeah, him. We're going to make sure he's right for it. We'll contact you.'

Geraldine wanted to add terms and conditions but she had little to bargain with.

Highclere raised his arm, 'Hang on... What is he doing for them?'

'He's investigating Jaleh Sasani's son's suicide.'

'Right, and what's the verdict?'

She decided to be economic with the facts, as she needed their attention and still didn't trust them. 'Looks like it was a murder.'

'Who?' said Aspen.

'Still at large.'

'What's the proof?' said Highclere. 'There must be something. Where is the report?'

'There isn't one. We were told to stop. Remember?'

Highclere clenched his jaw. 'That's not the point. We need a full report with all the details and names. By tomorrow.'

'Can I get an advance?'

'No.' Highclere got up and straightened his suit and shirt. 'You know the drill.'

Aspen was still making notes as Geraldine reached out to say goodbye. Highclere motioned with his head for her to leave. They were keeping it strictly above board. What she really wanted to ask them was where Rebwar was, but that would have been another mark against her.

She left the rickety caravan. Outside it was dark and cold. She found her phone and checked the voicemail. It was Raj asking her if she had talked to Musa. She wondered why he would ask her.

FORTY-FIVE

The limo stopped in front of the Nobu restaurant just off Park Lane. Rebwar had dropped some clients off there but had never been himself. It was out of his budget and he would have rather spent his hard-earned money on a holiday, if he'd ever had any. Everything went to his family. The door slid open and Hayden stepped out, checking the area. He gave the all-clear and Jaleh went over to the main door, which was being held open by a doorman.

Rebwar followed her in, taking in the atmosphere. A staircase led up to the main area. It had a minimalist decor: sharp lines and white walls with basic wooden furniture. They ended up in one of the function rooms, which was a little plusher with a carpet and same framed black and white photographs. It was also out of public view.

Dinah was sitting and waiting with a glass of wine. She smiled and stood up. He was glad to see her but there was now a lingering feeling of mistrust. Were they now all in this? She went over to Jaleh, kissed her cheek and thanked her for inviting her. She came over to Rebwar and kissed him and lingered for a moment. He took in her sweet perfume and lost himself in her dark eyes. She wore a colourful, flowing dress with some simple jewellery. He guessed she didn't want to compete with Jaleh.

He whispered in her ear. 'You're looking as hot as a Persian princess.' She smiled and looked down. He grabbed her waist, feeling her soft dress. 'Have you heard from Musa?'

She shook her head.

'Come, you two love birds, take a seat,' said Jaleh, 'I'm famished.' She poured herself a large glass of wine and made them sit opposite her. 'I've invited a few friends.' She checked her phone.

Rebwar sat down and asked Dinah if he could borrow her phone to call Musa. He was quietly panicking. He hadn't yet heard from him. Before reaching for her black and gold designer handbag, she asked him where his phone was. She said that she had left some messages on it. He lied and said he had lost it, although the last time he'd seen it was at the police station. He was sure that at some point, they were going to look for him. The number went to voice-mail after he dialled Musa. He left a brief message. He didn't dare to call Hourieh, but he was sure she'd get to him soon enough.

Dinah grabbed one of his hands. 'Everything all right?'

'Yeah, fine...' He kept himself from revealing his instincts, which were to try every number and drive to look for Musa. He grabbed a glass of wine, clinked it and drank a large gulp. The door opened and Jaleh stood up to greet Nahid and Hakan Basar. They both looked glamorous and made quite an entrance. Behind them was Sarah, also dressed up, which surprised him as the impression he had of her was more of a flower child. 'Have I missed something?' he said to Dinah.

'It's *Shabé yaldā*[1] .'

It was a festival that he had occasionally celebrated. The longest night of the year was observed in Iran as a gathering for family and friends. He looked around and saw that they had put out plates of food and drinks. Not the traditional specialities that he loved, but a Sasani version. Bright colours and exotic smells made up for the lack of authenticity. Basar and Nahid came over to say hello.

'You're the Uber driver?' Basar wore his suit jacket over his shoulders. 'Might need a lift later on.' He laughed.

Rebwar noticed that he and Nahid both had bloodshot eyes and manic stares; they were on something that made them quite obnoxious and he was looking for his excuses to leave.

'Jaleh forgot to mention you would be here,' said Nahid. 'Did Mister Columbo have any more probing questions?' The pair of them laughed.

'He's going to be in charge of security.' Dinah said as Rebwar shook hands with Basar. 'Back in the country?'

'Yes, yes, been very busy with some important deals. Everyone wants a piece of the pie.'

'What's your job?' said Rebwar, noting Basar's shaking hands.

Basar took out a business card and handed it over to him.

Rebwar took a quick look before putting it away in his jeans pocket. 'Import, Export?'

'Yes, any product you might need. Like Amazon, but in bulk.'

Dinah grabbed a tray of food from the table next to them and offered it to Basar. 'So where did you two meet?'

'In Turkey,' said Basar. 'We were both on holidays.'

'Oh, so modest,' said Nahid. 'We were having some

186

work done. You know.' And she winked at Dinah. 'Got an amazing surgeon. Even Basar got a few touches. And you know.'

'Oh, I see, see.' And Dinah turned to Rebwar. 'What do you think, my love? What should I get done?'

With a mouthful of canapé, Rebwar tried to reply. It was something delicate yet chewy. He tried to swallow it as quickly as he could. It left a sweet and sour taste. 'Nothing. Your natural beauty is enough.'

'Yeah, but there's always room for improvement,' said Basar. 'I was thinking about it.' And looked down at her boobs. 'What do you think, Nahid?'

Nahid laughed. 'You won't be able to stop flaunting them.' She grabbed Dinah's hand. 'Back soon.' And they went off.

'You were in the police?' asked Basar.

'Yes.'

'And you have a son... Musa? Likes his T-shirts. How is he?'

Rebwar felt a little chill. Basar's delivery and look had a sinister tone to it. 'Who told you?'

'Typical policeman!' He waggled his index finger. 'You have a suspicious nature. Nahid told me. If I may ask, why did Jaleh hire you?'

'I think you know. I did have some questions. Izah, have you met him?'

A waitress in a tight dress came by with a tray of hors d'oeuvres. Basar took one before she could say what they were. Rebwar passed. 'No, never had the honour. So tragic.'

'I have a friend. He's from Anatolia.'

'Oh yes? Nice place. Lovely city.'

Which was a lie, as it was a region that his friend Berker came from.

187

Basar spotted that he was being summoned by his fiancée. 'Excuse me, I am needed.'

'Give me a call for that ride.'

Basar smiled back and walked away. Rebwar filled his glass with some wine and went over to Dinah, who was talking to Sarah, the youngest Sasani daughter.

'Mr Rebwar, nice to see you again. More questions?' She shook his hand softly.

It took him a few seconds to take in her glamour. She was a different person, even her handshake had changed. 'Like boxing?'

She looked at Dinah for a clue. 'Sorry?'

'Boxing. You went to a match.'

'You said boxing? Yes, I have watched some matches. More silly questions.'

'Sorry, he never stops.' Dinah grabbed his arm.

Rebwar looked over at Jaleh. She and Hayden were keeping an eye on him. 'I was there yesterday,' said Rebwar, 'Ben, 'Izah's boyfriend.'

She looked down and felt her head. 'Sorry but I'm feeling dizzy.'

Dinah grabbed Sarah and she dropped into a seat behind her. Jaleh and Nahid came over to help.

'Is she all right?' said Rebwar. He felt a little embarrassed and expected one of them to tell him off.

Jaleh, looked around the tables. 'Pass me a Coke and some sugar.'

Hayden tapped Rebwar's shoulder. 'Mate, what did you ask her?' He stood close to Rebwar, his eyes burning into him.

'It was about yesterday's boxing match. You know.... the one you were at. I had a little ride with Ben, courtesy of the police.'

'What game are you playing at?' Hayden said in a low voice.

Sarah regained consciousness, and they fussed over her. Rebwar moved away from the group. 'I'm still looking for my son,' he said to Hayden. 'Did you see him there?'

'I've put the word out. Sure, he's lying low somewhere. Now back off. You've got a promise to deliver.'

'One more thing, Can't See Forest, does that mean anything to you?'

Hayden looked puzzled, as if was some trick question. 'Not a clue.'

Dinah came over to him. I think you outstayed your welcome. Go and say sorry and have a drink. I can't take you anywhere, can I? This my dear family and you treat them like this.'

He looked at the scene: a normal enough-looking rich family celebrating the longest day. But he had scratched the surface and everything was coming undone. 'Jaleh murdered the chief inspector,' he whispered. 'James McKintosh. The guy you joked with at the party.'

Dinah froze as if struggling to take in what Rebwar had just told her? Her mouth moved, but nothing followed. He grabbed a seat, made her sit down and handed her a drink, which she gulped down. 'Why?'

'He was—'

'No, why did you just tell me that?' She knocked back the rest of the wine. 'I don't believe you. You're mistaken.' And she handed him the empty glass to fill.

FORTY-SIX

Rebwar stepped out of Nobu to have a cigarette and let them chat to each other about their empty lives visiting beauty clinics. Parish was on the roundabout opposite, looking up at the solitary tree that was in the middle. A sports car revved its engine to show off its high-powered engine. Rebwar ignored him by cutting him off and crossing over. The driver responded by giving him the middle finger.

'Got a cigarette?'

'How's the party?' Rebwar simply nodded.

Parish brought out a pack of cigarettes. 'Hazard did his magic.'

'Missed the game.' He lit his cigarette and looked around him. Traffic crawled around them. Between five-star hotels and tall luxury apartment buildings was Hyde Park, which was dark and closed off.

'Still behind Tottenham.'

Not wanting to get into a slagging match and trying not to provoke him, Rebwar changed the subject. 'The card game... What did you have?'

He glanced at Rebwar and shook his head. 'Nah, mate

that's for me to know and you to find out...' He looked down on the pavement whilst dragging on his cigarette.

'Got children?'

'About that... Sorry about Musa, I was being a dick.' Rebwar wondered where he was going with his sudden guilt.

'Good little worker. You should be proud of him. Was going to give him a little present. McDonald's or Burger King.'

'Oh?' Rebwar stretched out his arms, feeling a sharp pain from the accident. 'Last time I asked him it was KFC.'

'How did you get into this?'

Parish grimaced, shook his head then rubbed the back of his neck. 'Got pissed in the local and got into a fight. They picked me off the pavement and offered me a job.'

A blacked-out van screeched to a stop nearby. The side door slid open and two men in balaclavas jumped out to grab Rebwar. They slipped a hood over his head. And all went black.

———

After the initial getaway the van seemed to get into the rhythm that was not dissimilar to driving in London traffic. They had zip-tied his hands and feet and left him lying on the floor of the van. It wasn't too long till the vehicle went down a ramp and there was the distinct clanking sound of a metal shutter being opened. They got him out and undid the zip ties around his ankles. Two men grabbed his arms. He grunted at the pain. They just ignored him and marched him over to an elevator. From the echo and jerky nature, it was a service elevator. As it passed each floor, it gave out a sharp click. He counted twenty-two. The door opened and he was taken to a chair. He tried to find a comfortable position between all his wounds. The adrenaline high had long worn off and now the throbbing pain was coming. Footsteps shuffled and tapped around him. The heat of two lamps hit his face. They took the hood off his head, along with some of his hair, and he gasped. His eyes stung at the bright lights and he looked down, trying to find some shade. They dragged a table over to him and two silhouettes sat in front of him.

'Is your name Rebwar Ghorbani?'

He wasn't in the mood for games and he tried to stand up. From behind came two large hands to push him back into his chair. He looked back to see two men in ski masks. He'd seen those outfits before when he'd been summoned for a Plan B interview.

'Give me a cigarette.' Footsteps approached him and he was given one. It had already been lit for him. 'Nice service.'

'That's a yes, then. We have questions.'

'Who's we?' His eyes had adjusted a bit and could just about make out that one of the men opposite was black and wearing a suit and tie. He guessed that was Highclere, as he fitted Geraldine's description. The other had a ponytail, a large beard and what looked like a colourful T-shirt. Building materials were packed around the bare concrete floors. Through the windows, he could see the lights of the London skyline.

The man with the beard slid some photos on the table and laid them out for Rebwar to see. 'Any of these mean anything to you?'

He leaned in to have a look. They were of the Sasani clan. He nodded. They had been taken at Izah's funeral.

'Tell me if I'm wrong.' He pointed to the first one. 'Jaleh

Sasani.' He carried on: 'Sara Sasani... Nahid Sasani... Dinah Sasani.... Jake Haden.... You.' He went on to point to some other photos that had been taken in other locations. 'Craig Parish, Noah Alba, Alistair Bellingfield, Craig Parish.' Rebwar's cigarette fell onto the floor. 'Untie him.' And one of the hooded men cut the restraints off him.

He rescued his fag. 'Yep, that's the family album.'

Highclere brought out some more pictures. They were of the crash. 'What happened?'

'We had a disagreement.'

'No time to get fresh with us. You killed a man and there will be consequences.'

'It was self-defence. What's all this about?'

'Did someone rat him out?' said the hippie-looking guy.

'I know you, but who are you?' said Rebwar. 'Like to know who I'm talking to.' He still tried to find a comfortable position, wanting a pillow to ease his pain.

Highclere looked at his partner, waiting for him to say something.

'To you, it's Aspen. Now, what happened?'

'He put a gun to my head, but that's not the problem. It's the gang war you've got on your hands. Did your man kill Izah?' This was something he had just thought of. Maybe he had been the inside man who was playing with them.

Aspen scribbled some notes on his pad. 'Why did he put a gun to your head?' Rebwar made a circle with his index finger around his temple. 'Take us through it.'

He was getting bored and angry at having to go back to something he really wanted to forget. 'I need reassurances. Need to know where my son is.'

Highclere leaned in and whispered something to Aspen, to which he stood up and came close to Rebwar, who noticed he was wearing long khaki cargo shorts and flip-flops. He perched himself on the table. 'Mate, I don't think you can start to dictate your terms to us. Prove to me that I can trust you.'

'Is there any consistency in your organisation?' Rebwar held up four digits at him. 'That's how long I've been... doing time for you guys. And you've promised, lied, tricked me, threatened me and for what? The only thing I've got left is my son and he's missing. So shit on your face.'

Aspen got up and walked around him. Rebwar smelled incense. 'What do you want?'

'My son back, a visa, salary and a new car. Oh, another cigarette.'

Aspen stared into his eyes like he was looking for some foreign object. 'Why should we do that?'

Rebwar just shook his head in defiance and dissatisfaction. 'Just send me back. I don't care anymore about all your petty fights and issues. Let them kill each other.'

Highclere got up and joined Aspen, their long shadows drawing abstract shapes on the bare walls and pipes on the ceiling. 'Tell us about this meeting.'

'The Sasanis wanted to know who called the police to their boxing match. They brought in James McKintosh for questioning.'

Aspen went back to the desk and opened an attaché case. He tapped on a tablet. 'Go on.'

'He denied it. Told them it would take weeks to set up a raid. Jaleh shot him.'

Both of them looked up. 'Shot him, wounded him?' said Aspen.

'In the head.'

Highclere stretched out his arms and interlocked his hands to hold the back of his head. Aspen paced some more with his flip-flops smacking the rough concrete floor. 'And you saw it?'

He nodded. 'I've proposed a meeting.'

'With us?' said Highclere.

'With the Mohsens.'

Aspen drummed his fingers on the table and looked over to Highclere, waiting for him to chip in. Nothing came. 'Go on.'

'Well, I need to get to them without getting killed.'

Highclere got up and brought his chair closer to Rebwar. 'Explain to me how you got involved in all this?'

Rebwar tried to find his eyes, which were behind a pair of dark sunglasses. 'I was hired to find out if Jaleh's son committed suicide or was murdered.'

'Took his own life,' said Aspen. 'It's not a sin... Just saying... Go on.'

Rebwar wondered what his actual point was and if they were at some point going to be asked to kill themselves. 'I found that the post-mortem had overlooked some basic physics. And that someone is killing off the witnesses. Someone killed him.'

Aspen brought his seat from behind the table closer to Rebwar. 'OK, Sherlock. So who did it?'

He shrugged.

'Oh, come on, you must have an idea. Pick one. I'd say it was Jaleh. Sounds like a right cold-hearted bitch.' He looked over at Highclere. 'Where would you put your money?' Aspen reached for his wallet and got two twenties out.

Highclere crossed his arms and looked down at his black and shiny shoes. 'Who's the sister's boyfriend?'

'Which one, Sarah? Or Dakota the husband? He's a bit of a spacer. Don't think he could say boo to a goose. Or the Turkish guy?'

'He had a boyfriend,' said Rebwar.

'The Turk? Isn't that normal?'

'Izah. It was Ben Layton.'

Highclere reached into his suit pocket to get a flask. He offered some to Aspen, who took a few gulps. Rebwar declined.

'So?' said Aspen to Highclere.

'Turkish guy.'

'Why? What's he got to benefit? Jaleh wants it all. I mean, look at the turf war she's just unleashed.'

Rebwar stood up and the two masked men rushed over, but Aspen lifted his hand to stop them. 'This isn't a game,' Rebwar said. 'You just going to put up bets or give me a job. Otherwise I'm going to walk out.'

Aspen waved a hand for him to sit down. 'All right, you've got our attention. I can't give you any a job sheet but then you know that.' He went back to his case and brought out some electronic equipment. 'I've got some requirements this time.' He brought the gear onto the table and waved Rebwar closer. 'A wire.'

'You trying to get me killed?'

'Not losing... another asset. And we need proof. You're an ex-copper, right?'

Rebwar rubbed his face. He'd worn recording devices before but they made you nervous. He hated them and had lost too many colleagues to them. 'I want to see my son first.'

Aspen clenched his jaws and looked away. Visibly, they were all getting tired and either needed a drink or a breather. Highclere took the slack and sat down behind the table and tapped into his phone.

'He was last seen at the boxing match.' Rebwar stopped himself from going on and winding himself into a panic. He wasn't sure how long it had been since he had told him to run. It felt like days, but he hadn't slept since getting out of that cell.

Highclere stood up. 'He's OK. At home with your ex. Hourieh?'

Rebwar breathed in and exhaled his relief. He wasn't going to ask to talk to him, as there was going to be a whole argument. And his mind was not in the right space for that. His next chat with Musa would be on his terms.

Aspen passed him the wire. 'I'll let you work out how to put it on.' He pointed out a little switch. 'And here is the on-off button. The rest you can get your handler to deal with. We're done.' He looked over to Highclere, who nodded. 'Now, this didn't happen and I don't know you.' The men in ski masks went over to switch off the lights. Silently in the darkness, they packed up and left. Before he could ask if he could go or where the exit was, Rebwar was left alone in the unfinished building site. He went over to the large windows that overlooked the Thames and tried to make sense of what had just happened.

FORTY-SEVEN

Drizzle swirled around the Shishawi's tables only to be burnt off by the hanging patio heaters. Traffic inched slowly along the wet, shiny tarmac. Rebwar sipped his coffee and let his gaze drift along the street. How was he going to set up the meeting? He didn't know any of the so-called House of Zik. Last time he checked, they were after him. He was also no closer to solving Izah's murder, something that was still dear to him. Izah was a victim in many senses and needed justice, as well as a clearing of the memory of who he was, a man of many facets and secrets.

Berker arrived with his tray covering a branded box that he passed over to Rebwar. 'Put it on the account,' he said. He tore the cellophane off it. It was a phone.

'I've got a tip,' Berker looked at his digital watch. 'It was in half an hour. Pony Soprano.'

Rebwar inserted the sim into the phone. 'Who's he?'

'Wasted. Heard there's a price on your head.'

'Yeah, my friend. You going to cash in?'

He smiled. 'Don't fancy prison food. You said you had a question about Anatolia.'

'There's no city of that name?'

'A region and an old empire. Didn't they teach you that?'

He switched on his new phone. 'No, my school was on the street. Still trying to find out more about this Hakan Basar. Says he's from Turkey, but I've got my doubts. Shady businessman.'

Berker laughed. 'Take your pick. They line this street. Does he owe you money?'

Someone shouted along the street and they both looked over. They were both a little on edge. 'Oh, talking of shady.' And he looked down the road.

Rebwar looked over his shoulder to spot Geraldine. She and Berker and had not really had a good introduction. She thought he was in bad company.

'What will it be for the princess, hot chocolate?'

Expecting an expletive from Geraldine, Rebwar ordered himself another coffee. 'Nice to see you. Come with some gifts?'

'Get me a Coke.' She said to Rebwar and sat next to him. 'Where have you been?'

'Here and there. Got to see your boss. He's a man of few words.'

'How?'

'They kidnapped me in front of Nobu and I was with one of the Sasani's gang. Another fairy story that I am going to have to explain to them. They could have just called. And Berker tells me that I have a price on my head.'

Geraldine looked around her as if there was someone watching them. 'Shouldn't we go?'

'For my stupid sins, I've convinced the Sansanis to set up a meeting with their rivals. And Plan B has asked me to wear a wire. As if I haven't already had a shit day.'

Berker put the Coke and coffee on the table and walked off.

'Got a call from Raj. How's Musa?'

'He's with his mother. Have they contacted you?'

'Not yet,' She sipped her Coke. 'I thought you made a plan with them?'

'Let's say...' He brought out a cigarette and tapped it on the table. 'It's hands off. Asked for the usual terms. And it's pending.' He shook his head, wondering why he was doing all this.

'Right, but what are you hoping to achieve with the meeting?' She got her vape out and sucked on it, releasing a cloud that partially obstructed her.

'Buying time and getting a target off my back. And maybe get some justice.'

'Noble, but...' and she took a moment to think.

Rebwar sipped his coffee, wondering if she was in on it all too or just an observer. He needed her in the team. It had been lonely and hard out in the cold. Raj had done his best, but he too had been spooked.

'They called me in too and I asked them to give my job back... Pending.' And she gave a middle finger to the conversation. 'They asked me to find out what was going on... Guess they got to you before me. What was that car crash about?'

Rebwar cleared his throat, trying to remember what he had told them. 'The short version is that he drew a gun on me.'

'I'll remember that for next time.'

'It was their man on the inside. That's how they found me. Now they need me.'

'Sweet job creation.' She finished her Coke. 'I didn't get

very far with that doctor and the post-mortem. My...' And she looked down. 'Anyway...'

Rebwar spotted a man step out of a white car that had just pulled up. He was making his way to them, wearing sunglasses, and hiding his hands inside the front pocket of a hoodie. Rebwar picked up Geraldine's empty glass and threw it at him. He dodged it and brought out a gun, squeezed the trigger and the hammer clicked. Expecting a flash and bang, Rebwar had pushed the table over. Nothing came. The man panicked and looked at the gun in confusion. He pulled the slide back to reload. Rebwar picked up a chair and swung it at the man's arm. He shot into the pavement. People screamed and ran away. The white car revved its engine and drove off. Seeing his ride fading into the distance, the man ran after it. Rebwar gave chase down the street.

The whizz of a bullet passed by Rebwar's head, followed by a bang. He sought cover behind a parked car. The man stopped by a crossing. Raising his arms and holding them onto his head, he kicked the ground. With his gun, he stopped a passing car and made the driver get out. Rebwar ran towards him and the man tried to shoot, but the gun jammed again. This time, he threw the gun onto the street as he climbed into the car. The car jerked forward and stalled. He seemed to be struggling to drive a manual transmission, desperately trying to find a gear, and the car stalled. Grabbing the gun, Rebwar used the grip to smash through the glass. It exploded just as the man managed to re-start the car, its engine revving to the red line. Rebwar carried on striking into the car, the man's face taking a couple of blows. Rebwar opened the door and grabbed him.

'Who are you? Who sent you? The Mohsens? Hey?' But it was no use. He'd already knocked him out.

Geraldine shouted over to him. 'We need to go!'

He looked behind him and saw a crowd gathering around the crossing. Sirens were growing louder. He ran over to Geraldine and they ran back into the Shishawi. Rebwar had used their back exit before and it would buy them a few minutes of time. As they ran through the kitchens, he threw the gun in a large wheelie bin.

FORTY-EIGHT

A large, wheeled metal bin was being pushed by two men out of a side entrance of Bijan's mansion. The wheels rotated around as if they were emergency amber beacons. Once in position, they stopped and both took a fag break. Rebwar went up to them. 'Busy day in the kitchen?'

Both looked at each other as if one had the answer. They wore white T-shirts and trousers with black clogs. 'Just cleaning up,' said one of them.

'Is Manish in?'

And the man pointed down the drive towards the kitchens. Rebwar nodded his thanks and made his way down to the door. He'd been to Bijan's big house many times but since Katarena had come back into his life he'd been ghosted. Still shaking from the attempted hit, he considered himself lucky. First, that the guy was clearly an amateur and second, that he'd used a recommissioned replica gun, which was a cheap favourite among gangs but notoriously unreliable. Third, they had made a getaway. Now, he had to ask for some help to set up a meeting with the House of Zik. He pushed the door and made his way into the large kitchen with its extensive array of stoves, hanging pans, fridges and clean shiny stainless-steel countertops. The times he'd been there, it had always buzzed with activity. Now it looked sad and empty.

He went through the kitchen and out to the back, where there was an extensive herb garden. Or that is what he was expecting. Manish was sitting on a stool, his portly belly barely being held in by the buttons on his dirty white shirt. His eyes looked bloodshot and tired. He stubbed his cigarette with his clog.

'Manish, good to see you, my friend.' He just grumbled and reached for another cigarette from was behind his ear. The once lush herb garden was now a series of lawns with kitsch sculptures of naked women and animals. 'What happened?'

'The lady of the house. Or should I say bitch?'

Rebwar lit his cigarette. 'I take it she's in?'

Manish just shrugged. He went back into the kitchen and made his way into the main house. It was quiet and the large dining room with its imposing chandelier was all covered up with large white sheets. Only the paintings were on show, which were of old Persian scenes. He wondered if the Mohsens had sold them to him. He carried on onto the main hallway with the marble spiral staircase. There had been a couple of big statues, but now the black and white square tiles were all that was left. He stopped to listen for voices or sounds. None came. He peaked into the lounge, where he'd had so many whiskies and chats. All he could hear was a grandfather clock ticking away in a corner. Bijan's butler had stopped him every time he'd come to visit and he had to trick him to see Bijan. Not this time. It was odd. He carried on looking into the reception room and his study. There was no sign of Bijan.

He checked the mail and the dates were recent and so were the still untouched newspapers. One was from yesterday. He carried on looking. The gardens looked untidy. Small piles of dried leaves had gathered in the corners of the garden. Broken branches littered the long grass. He noticed the conservatory, which extended to the left of the garden. The view into it was obstructed by condensation and overgrown plants. He walked down the hallway to the door. It was locked. He knocked and put his ear on the wooden panel. He bent down to look through the keyhole. There were a lot of pots and flowers. On the floor were some slippers. He tried again to push the door open. It wasn't giving in. He shouted Bijan's name. Nothing. He tried to kick the door down. He reached for his penknife and realised he didn't have it anymore. He made his way out onto the patio and found a small statue of a cat. He found the door to the conservatory, smashed one of the square windows by the handle and he reached in to unlock it.

He rushed in, looking for Bijan. Overgrown plants and the stench of something rotting hit him. Old, crumpled-up rugs covered the sofas and chairs. He found Bijan in a wheelchair, head drooped over his chest and dribble on his smoking jacket. He crouched in front of him, feeling his hands. They were cold. He went to check his neck for a pulse and he stirred, his eyes barely opening. 'Sarbaz[1], my friend, are you OK?'

Bijan looked at him. 'Where am I?'

Rebwar moved him out of the shrubs that surrounded him. 'What's going on?'

'Who are you?'

Rebwar parked him close to a table with a glass of water. Bijan swung out and knocked the glass on the marble floor.

It shattered, spilling its contents. 'Oh, Sartip[2], you are finally here.'

'What do you mean, finally?'

Bijan held his head. 'Maybe I asked...' He looked around and stared at things, as if trying to make sense of them. 'I asked her to leave. Has she?'

'Katarena?' Bijan tried to push the wheels on the chair. In the corner was a glass cabinet. Rebwar went over to it and took one of the crystal decanters and poured two glasses of whisky. He drank one of them and let the liquid burn and tingle. He topped up his glass and went over to Bijan. 'Some medicine, drink.'

He grabbed the glass with both hands and swallowed the amber drink. With his eyes wide open, he said, 'More.'

'Sarbaz, Sir, I need your help. I need to meet the Mohsens.' And he returned to grab the decanter and bring it over.

'You want a picture? It's a good investment.'

Rebwar grabbed a chair and brought it over to Bijan. 'That's what I want them to think. They are after me. They made me deliver them an eye... Remember?'

Bijan nodded. 'I remember, yes. Trouble. Why do you want to see them?'

'I want them to meet both houses and make a truce. Jaleh Sasani has agreed to it. But I need an in.'

Bijan took another swig from his glass. 'Is this whisky?'

Rebwar looked at the decanter and smelled it. He wasn't sure and showed it to him.

'Cognac. Now, you want me to set up a meeting with the houses?'

'No, just the Mohsens and pretend that you want to buy some art from them.'

Bijan looked towards his garden and his eyes focused on something. 'Yes, if that is what you wish.'

'Do you have a gun I could borrow?'

Bijan reached into his trouser pockets and brought out a set of keys. 'In the basement.'

FORTY-NINE

Geraldine had Hakan Basar's address from Rebwar. He'd been staying at his fiancée Nahid's flat, in Sloane Square. Geraldine had waited there for him to leave the flat in the morning and a couple of takeaway coffees later, she was on the move. They were on the District Line going east; she was standing in the carriage with the commuters. Basar was reading a copy of the Metro and sitting comfortably in the middle of the tube, legs spread out and making the passenger next to him squeeze into her seat, a typical male staking out his territory. He wore a camel-hair coat and a dark suit. What surprised her was that the bottoms of his trousers were frayed and dirty, his slip-on shoes were scuffed and their heels were worn down. It didn't really match what Rebwar had described as a successful Turkish businessman. Listening to some music over her headphones, she wondered what he was about. The word chancer came to mind. He'd hit the lottery with the Sasanis.

The question was, what did he really do? She hadn't found an office in the UK. All she had was an address in

Istanbul and, from a quick search on the web, a small shop in the suburbs. He must have woven some kind of magic over the Sasanis. At Whitechapel Station, he stepped out with his suitcase. Something that Geraldine had thought had been out of fashion since the early eighties. She kept a distance, as he seemed a little unsure of where he was going and kept referring to the tube maps. For her, it was second nature. He then took the overground line west. She hadn't been on these new trains and found that if you stood in the middle, you could still see the back or the front; one continuous tube. It mesmerised her to see the train move around like a snake.

At the next stop, Shoreditch High Street, Basar got out. It was a place that she associated with the homes of hipsters and the latest London trends. Again, he consulted a map before setting out onto Bethnal Green Road. It had been a while since she had set foot in that area. She had missed the buzz of seeing new boutique shops and new cuisines. At the crossing with Brick Lane, he took a left. The famous old curry houses were behind her and she caught a few smells of spices. Back in her youth as a PC, she would regularly have curries on Friday nights with the team. They'd get plastered and there would be stakes on who could eat the hottest vindaloo. There were always casualties the next day. At Chambord Street, Basar took a right. Bare trees lined the area of residential houses. Once an affordable area, people had now been priced out by well-to-do city folk.

At Columbia Road he took another right. Famous for its flower market, it looked bare on a regular day. She always loved its walks and its stalls filled with all the flowers of the world. Or that was the way she remembered it. The street was lined with trendy boutique shops selling any old junk that could be washed and polished: old vintage tea sets, plates, clocks. She tried not to be distracted by what was on offer. At Jack Garcia Coffee, he went in. It surprised her. The window was filled with fresh bread loaves of all sizes, cakes and Danish pastries. She went in. A couple of men with beards and tattoos were serving the customers. Basar ordered and, from his lack of hesitation, she decided he'd been here before. It took Geraldine a few minutes to read the coffee menu. Every variation she could think of and more was listed.

She noted that he'd gone out into a side alley where there were some tables. For mid-winter and for a Turk, she thought it was a brave move. She panicked and ordered a latte with oat milk. She had never heard of it and never tried it. To that she added a pecan tart, which the man recommended and gave a little sales pitch, which she instantly forgot. She took her treat outside to find a table within earshot, but far away enough as not to be seen. The patio heaters took the edge off the bitter wind that was channeled down the little alley, which had a regular wooden garden fence on one side and a recently white painted wall on the other. There was a tarpaulin above them to keep some of the heat in. Basar brought out his Metro paper and carried on reading it.

One of the waiters arrived with her coffee. He wore a blue apron and a tight T-shirt and had tattoos all over his arms. 'There you go, latte with oat milk. Haven't seen you around? Where you from?'

A chatty waiter was the last distraction she needed, as well as creating unwanted attention. 'Like the heart.' She pointed to swirl on the cup. 'Thanks. Just passing through.'

'You should come by on market day. It's a sight to see. I'm from NZ and it kind of makes me homesick.'

She turned herself to face away from Basar in case he got nosy. 'Right, been here long?' She really wanted to tell him to bugger off.

'Oh, came over in the summer. Yeah, I know, bad timing, kind of missing my summer. Where are you from?'

There were footsteps behind her; the wooden floor carried the vibrations. 'Oh, from Kent.' She really hadn't thought out a cover story.

'Right, where's that?'

She now really wanted him to go as she heard two men greeting each other. 'You know this pecan tart is... I chose it but really wanted a Danish.'

'Hey, get it all the time. Brett is a hell of a sales guy. Told him he should get a job selling cars. You know that was Bernie Ecclestone's first job.'

'Who?'

'The owner of Formula 1, the little guy.'

She passed him the plate as a hint.

'Right, yeah, well, he was based on Goodge Street. Imagine old cars lining up all down that street.'

She could hear the two men chatting in the background, but she couldn't quite make out what they were saying. She sipped her coffee, which tasted a bit like cardboard. It made her grimace.

'Is it off?'

'Not to my liking. It's...'

'Like wood. That's what my other half tells me. Oh, you should see her face.' And he took it. 'Normal one then?'

She nodded. 'Kent, is that—' His name, 'David!' was shouted out from around the corner. 'Oh, that'll be me chatting. Nice to meet you. Yes, I'm David.' He wanted to shake her hand but with his hands full, he turned and went back. She let out a sigh of relief but now had to subtly try to snoop on the two men. Basar had his back to her and the other man faced him. She swivelled in her chair to see them and instantly recognised the man from one of the photos that Aspen had shown her. He was part of the Sasani clan. She took out her phone and pretended to be looking at some app. From what she could make out, they were deciding when they were going to meet again. Both got up and she raised her phone, ostensibly to make a selfie but using the back camera to take a picture of them.

'You got enough...' The man winked at Basar to which he shook his head.

The man slid something to Basar over the table. It was just out of sight to see exactly what it was but she guessed that it might have been drugs.

'Mate, heard anything about that Rebwar guy?'

'Still sticking his nose where it doesn't belong. What about him?'

'He got picked up by some heavy dudes. Still not sure on who to tell. I mean...' He looked around and put his hand over his mouth. 'Mohsens?'

'If no one is missing him, leave it. Don't mention it. And good.'

They both started getting up from the table and she went into the cafe to get her latte to go. When she came out with it, she looked down the street. They had gone in opposite directions. She followed Basar, who carried on walking up Columbia Road. He took a right and ended up down Baxendale Street, which had two rows of small residential houses. He slowed down and she crossed the road and carried on. Basar made a call. Geraldine passed him. A door opened in front of him. She tried to use the parked car's mirrors to take a look but she couldn't get a good view of who he was meeting. She passed a van and used it as cover. A woman kissed him on the doorstep and then they walked in.

FIFTY

The stone spiral staircase led down to the cellar. Lit with basic light bulbs, it was a contrast to the luxury above and had more in common with a military dungeon. He had been to a few during the war and he'd sworn never again. The place made him shiver. Bijan had told him to open the second-last door. Out of curiosity, he peaked into a couple of them. There were stacks of branded wooden boxes; he guessed wine by their French names. He spotted some of the statues that had been in the main reception. As he got to the penultimate door, he inserted the key into the lock, twisted it a couple of times and pushed it open. It was pitch black and he felt for the light switch. The lights flickered and he got his first glimpses of what was inside. He thought he was back in Iran, in the police basement, where they kept their weapons. He looked back and wanted to shout back at Bijan, asking if this was right. It was an arsenal of weapons enough for a small army. He walked in and took it all in. The weapons were from the late 80s.

AK-47s lined against the wall. There were crates of

rocket-propelled grenades and pistols of various makes. There was an M79 grenade launcher, the same as he had used back in the war. There were grenades, body armour, bayonets and boxes of ammunition. He couldn't believe his eyes. How had Bijan got all this over and who knew about it? You could start a small war with what he had. Rebwar picked up a Persian Mauser or M1310, another relic he had used, a long rifle that dated from the Shah's time. He slid the bolt in and out and aimed as he had on the battlefield. The muscle memory came back so that the rifle was like an extension of him. Voices travelled down the bare walls and he put the rifle back. It was Katarena. She was back. And there was someone else with her. He grabbed a hand grenade and closed the door behind him.

Katarena was surrounded by designer shopping bags and two men in black suits. Rebwar appeared from the cellar and walked over.

'What are you doing here?' She had a stern, angry look.

'Visiting my old friend.'

She pointed to the cellar door. 'What were you doing in there?'

'I needed to return something to the general.' He turned around and walked towards the conservatory.

'Mr Rebwar, I don't want to see you here again. Understand? My husband is very ill and needs rest.'

Rebwar turned around and walked off to the conservatory. He could hear Katarena talking to the two men in exasperated tones that echoed off the high white walls. He went over to Bijan and topped up his glass. 'Impressive collection.'

Bijan looked up and smiled. He pointed his crooked finger at him. 'You never know when a revolution comes around. You have to be ready for the opportunity. Like I was when the Shah returned.'

Rebwar handed the key over to him. 'Got what I needed. Now I'll call them to make a meeting. What do you fancy to buy?'

Katarena's high heels sounded off the walls as she came towards them. 'I told you to leave?' She took the decanter and the half-empty glass off the table. 'Don't you see that he is ill?' She went over to the drinks cabinet to return the whisky.

'I forgot. Pass on my greetings to Hourieh and Musa. Tell them I'll be popping by to see them.'

Katarena came back and grabbed the wheelchair and tried to move it. 'No, have not see them. You should look after wife. No-good husband, she keeps telling me. Bad husband.'

'I bring the...' He stopped himself and tried to shake Bijan's hand but she had undone the brakes and was pushing him out of the conservatory.

'Now, take front door. And call before visit.'

Rebwar watched her tight dress swaying side to side in provocation and then she glanced back to catch him out. She gave him a dirty look. He tried not to laugh and incite a row, which was probably what she was looking for. Instead of taking the exit, he made his way to Bijan's office, where he found the Mohsens' business card. He used the office phone and called the gallery.

A woman's voice picked up. 'Hossein's Persian Antiquities, Amanda speaking.'

'Hi, I'm calling on behalf of Bijan Achmoud. He would like to have a private visit of the gallery.'

'Oh, Mr?'

'Ramin, Mr Achmoud would like to come this afternoon. I know it's last minute but he is a very rich impulsive man.'

'Yes, sure... I will. Just a minute.'

As he waited, Rebwar checked the large wooden desk's drawers. He found a key and a gun. Which he took.

'In an hour?'

FIFTY-ONE

The big black Rolls-Royce came to a nearly silent and smooth stop in front of the antiques gallery. Rebwar put the car into park using the stalk on the steering rack. It had taken him a few goes to get used to the car. The last time he had driven it with Bijan in the back, he'd nearly taken the wings off it. Never again, he'd said.

Amanda, the pretty sales assistant, had already walked out of the shop to greet them in. Rebwar stepped out, checking his pockets, and walked over to her. She no doubt expected him to open the rear door, but he walked past her and into the shop instead. Looking confused, she walked after him. Rebwar glanced in the shop window's reflection to admire the way her pencil skirt moved. Inside were the usual sculptures, paintings and rugs.

'You're...' She looked for the cover name he had previously given.

'Mohamed?'

'Yes,' She looked back at the car, which was parked on a single yellow and in danger of either getting a ticket or towed. 'Mr Achmoud... is he?'

'Are they here?'

Not knowing where to look, her head swivelled between him and the car. 'Yes, sure, I'll call them up.'

'Mr Achmoud doesn't like waiting.' Rebwar looked around the showroom as she made a call.

'Would you like a coffee?'

Rebwar shook his head and found a floor plan for the emergency exits. There was a large back area to the of the shop that he hadn't noticed and seemed out of bounds, as there was only a small discreet door leading to it. With a sign on the front entrance, they had closed the gallery for a private view, which was what he had asked for. Out of the back door came Vahid Mohsen. His comb-over slipping and holding a handkerchief, he came over to Rebwar. Behind him was a tall, thin man with hollow cheeks, his black suit bulging below his armpits. He stopped just behind a column, obstructed from the street view and putting himself in cover.

'Is he here?' Vahid looked over at the parked car. His face had a sweaty sheen to it. Rebwar stood in front of him, testing his mood. Vahid's eyes widened. 'You're the man who brought in the package. Are you working for Mr Achmoud?'

'General Achmoud.' Rebwar crossed his arms.

'Explain yourself. You have a price on your head.'

'About that...' He reached into his pocket.

The man behind the pillar pulled out both of his guns. Both were Heckler and Koch and looked like police issue. 'Just a moment...' Rebwar held one hand up. Mohsen's hands trembled and Amanda had stepped out of view.

'One wrong move and you're toast, mister. Understand?' said the man with the two guns.

Rebwar nodded and slowly took out a hand grenade.

The pin had been taken out and what they couldn't see was that he had used two rubber bands to secure the safety lever. They both stared at him.

'What? What do you want?' Mohsen wiped his brow with a white handkerchief.

'Slowly put the guns down and kick them over.' The man complied. Rebwar picked them up and put them in his leather jacket. 'Both of you, turn around and put your hands behind your back.' He zip-tied them both. 'To chat, can we go out back?'

The two men looked at each other nervously. Mohsen looked over at the car.

'Come on, I am an impatient man.'

They turned around walked towards the back door. As they walked past the desk, Rebwar ripped out the telephone cable. And motioned Amanda to follow them. He followed them down a short, dark corridor to arrive in a storeroom. It had a series of three connected glass ceilings. An old Victorian steel frame held it up. There were tall shelves that had various packed art pieces. Lined up on a long wooden table was a series of identical stone heads. He recognised them from Bijan's collection. Two men in blue overalls were unpacking them. They looked like they were from somewhere in North Africa. 'Where's Lanny?' said Rebwar.

'He's...' Mohsen looked around him. 'He's...'

Amanda stepped in. 'Told me he was going to the bathroom.'

'Point to it.' And she pointed to the back. Rebwar grabbed Mohsen from behind and held his neck with his free arm. He could feel his heavy breathing and whispered in his ear. 'Now, call him, but as you would when you need his attention.'

Mohsen tried to talk, but just only managed to mumble.

'You, Amanda... you ask for him. Tell him he has an urgent call. Rebwar made Mohsen take a few steps back behind a cupboard and told the man to step into the corner, making sure he had eyes on everyone. The two men in blue overalls probably had too much to lose by doing anything stupid. Amanda called out to Lanny.

'Who is it?'

'Oh, a Mr Samuel.'

Rebwar stepped out, holding his brother. 'I'm here to talk.' And he showed him the grenade. Lanny Mohsen was a younger-looking Vahid: thinner, and still with a full head of dark hair. He wore a black polo neck jumper and a blue suit. He stopped and took in the moment, looking around him.

'Not a move,' said Rebwar.

'You want money? Is that it?'

'Brother,' said Vahid. 'He's, he's the Sasani. The eye.'

'Oh, the one with a 10K price on his head.'

Rebwar looked over at the two men to see how they reacted. 'Amanda, who else is here?' He looked over to her.

'No one. Just us.'

'It's Tuesday, is that everyone?' Rebwar turned to the two North African men. 'Hey?'

'Mister, we no see or hear. Just work here.'

'It's Wednesday,' said Vahid.

'Right,' He had purposely got the day wrong to test them. 'And what happens today?'

'The usual, uh, unpacking and customer deliveries,' said Lanny.

'When's the van coming quick, quick?'

Vahid looked up at the big clock that was on one of the walls. 'In an hour.'

'Is this a robbery?' said Lanny.

'No. Amanda... Sit there, and I'm sorry' He pointed to an office chair. She sat down and he zip-tied her to it. He tied up Lanny with his brother both facing in opposite directions. Then he tied up the tall man to a radiator. He put the pin back into the grenade and used one of the guns. 'You two carry on with your work. Sure, your bosses will give you a raise.' He lit up a cigarette. 'Now, I'm here for two things... maybe three.' He sat down in a chair. 'One, cancel the hit. I'm not a Sasani. I'm Rebwar and I'm here to make an offer. So?' And he went over to them.

'We don't know you,' he said.

'Enough to put a hit on me. So?' He cocked the gun, looking to see if there was a round in the chamber; there wasn't. He tutted and looked over at the man. 'You would have lost that draw.' He cocked the gun again to put a round in the chamber. 'So?'

'Yes, yes,' said Vahid.

'And you, Lanny?'

Lanny nodded.

'Out loud for all these lovely people to hear.'

'Yes.'

'OK, now for the *Khoresh e fesenjan*[1] . I have been asked to set up a meeting between you lot and the Sasanis. Yes?'

'What for? To kill us?'

'No, a business opportunity. To discuss a partnership.'

Lanny laughed; Vahid seemed to be working out what his brother was thinking. 'You're joking, right?' said Lanny.

'No, no, Jaleh is asking for a meeting. Instead of killing each other and getting the attention of the SOCA[2]. I'm sure you know who they are? As I'm sure you've had dealings with them. Not easy to pay them off.' Rebwar went up to Lanny and waited for him to react.

'I'm listening.'

'I'll call you with the location and we'll meet.'

'How do we know it's not a trap?' said Vahid.

'You don't. But it's basically your only option, as I know you're on the SOCA's radar.' Rebwar walked over to the stone heads that the two men were unpacking. He looked at one of them. 'What are these?'

The younger-looking man looked nervous and just started at him. The older one said. 'Art.'

Rebwar lightly knocked the top of the stone head with the pistol butt. It made a dull thud as it was made of solid rock. The younger man picked it up and dropped it. It landed with an almighty thud and crack and rolled around. The concrete floor had been damaged. The older man suddenly grabbed Rebwar's second gun from his pocket. He pointed it at Rebwar.

'You don't want to do this,' said Rebwar. 'Give me the gun back. Understand?'

The man's dark eyes darted from one face to another, pointing the gun at whoever he was looking at. 'Man, you give me the gun.'

'Selassi, do as he says, hear me?' said Lanny.

'Listen, where are you from? Ethiopia, Mali? You've handled that gun? No safety, you understand?' Rebwar was trying to work out if he had been in a war zone. His impression was that he hadn't served. Instead of taking it, he should have kept it in his pocket and held it against him. That had been his first mistake. 'Hey, listen, Selassi, no need to do this. Give it to me and leave. OK?' He watched him getting more agitated.

'I won't go after you, OK?'

'Put the gun down!'

'No. Give me the gun.' And he stepped closer to Selassi, trying to provoke him, his calculation being that he would have shot his gun already if he was capable of shooting a human being.

'Back! I will shoot! Yes!' His hands were trembling, and he saw that Rebwar had noticed it so he put the gun to his head.

'Don't do that, no!' Rebwar put his hand out. But he stepped away. He looked over at his co-worker, who was on the floor with his hands over his head. Rebwar suspected that he, too, must have been in a war zone and he was having flashbacks. 'Why do you want to do this? Think about it. You can just go. They won't ask for you.'

Tears started to stream down the man's eyes, and he pulled the trigger. The hammer cocked and released, to no effect. The chamber was empty.

Rebwar grabbed the gun. 'Idiot! Why? Hey?' He felt a sense of relief, breathed deeply. Selassi just collapsed on the floor and Rebwar left him there. 'Go home,' he said.

'You should have—'

'No, not my style. Unlike you two. Now... Yes... I'll leave it for the meeting as a topic.' Rebwar made his way to the exit. 'I'll call.' And he left.

FIFTY-TWO

The Dog House pub was a local for Geraldine, and Rebwar was meeting her there. He was still shook up from visiting the Mohsens and hoped he had made enough of an impression for them to turn up to the meeting. He also had an idea on where to meet, but he had first to work out the logistics. The pub buzzed with people who had just finished work. With lots of bare old wood on show, it had a rustic and authentic feel to it. It was on the corner of a crossroads and the building had a distinct triangular shape, the main door being on the Kennington Lane side. The tall ceiling had been painted in a deep ruby red and they had hung tea and coffee pots, which he hadn't noticed on his last visit. Geraldine sat at the bar chatting to the bar lady. From the laughter, they seemed to know each other.

'Rebs, good to see you. This is Denise. Pub landlady.' She put her hand to cover her mouth and pretended to whisper. 'Remember? She threw us out for being drunk.' She and Denise laughed.

'It was you who was drunk...' Rebwar began.

Geraldine gave him a hug. 'Oh, lighten up, mate.'

He could smell the alcohol and guessed she'd been here for a couple of pints, as she rarely engaged in bodily contact. 'OK, can I have a beer?'

'What'll it be?' Denise held the beer pumps ready to serve.

'Give him the Beavertown,' said Geraldine. 'And two Jägers.'

Rebwar was too tired to protest or even make a decision, and let them get on with it.

'So, what's the crack?'

'Sorry?'

'Oh, you're behind. You need to catch up and quick.' She passed him the pint. 'On my tab.' And she winked to Denise. Who just shook her head. 'What? Are you—'

Rebwar stepped in and handed over his credit card, guessing that Geraldine hadn't worked for a while and had spent what she had.

'Cheers!' She downed about a third of her pint.

Rebwar took as many gulps as he could before he had to breathe. It hit a spot, but his nerves were still on edge as he retrieved his credit card. Rebwar brought out his pack of cigarettes and like a well-oiled routine, she took her pint and, trying to take a straight line, made her way to the exit, bumping into a few chairs on the way.

Outside, they sat on one of the wooden benches, away from the other groups of smokers. The passing cars momentarily lit them. Rebwar reached for his pack of cigarettes and checked his phone. No messages. He had left a few for Musa and Dinah. He wanted some news.

Geraldine took out her vape. 'Oh, fuck it! Pass me one.' They watched the groups of people walking by, letting their moment of silence become a soothing mediation.

'How's it going?' Rebwar wondered if she was celebrating something.

She slumped in a massive sigh. 'My sister is up the duff.'

'Duff?'

She made a large belly shape.

'In jail?'

She wiped her mouth. 'She's out. And she hasn't got the foggiest on who the dad is.' She held her head. 'But, hey! She's family.' And she laughed aimlessly at her fast-diminishing beer glass.

'And the boyfriend?'

She gave out a massive burp that even attracted the attention of other smokers and drinkers around them. 'Zane, the fucking waste of space. In jail.'

'Ah, boy or a girl?'

Geraldine just shrugged and finished her pint. 'Mind if I borrow your card?'

Rebwar gave her his credit card and she just wobbled off back inside the pub. 'Hey, you're going to be an auntie,' to which she gave him two fingers. He unlocked his phone with his thumb and checked for any messages. Then he hovered over Hourieh's number. He still hadn't had the courage to call, reckoning that she would only call if there was bad news or needed money. He wrote a text to Dinah. Was she pissed off with him? Probably. Was he pissed off with her? A little. A beer landed next to his, with some of its content spilling onto the table. He looked up and saw Geraldine drinking.

'So...' She put their pints down. 'What's the news? Oh, I followed your family friend.'

Rebwar looked over to her wondering what she was talking about.

'The Turk. He's an odd one. Likes to go for coffees. He

227

went to a coffee shop on Columbia Road, which took me back. Mum used to take me there...' She drew on her cigarette, taking it in. 'He met up with one of the Sasani lot. Jim?'

'Really?'

'Only managed to get part of the conversation. Something about you getting kidnapped?'

Rebwar sipped his beer. 'That was courtesy of your lot. No one cares...' He checked his phone. 'No one's called.'

'He couldn't quite believe his eyes and I think he confided in Basar. He thought the Sasanis had planned it.'

Rebwar nodded. He now understood why no one was actively looking for him. He felt some of the burden lift from his frame. 'Idiot. What did Hakan say?'

'Something along the lines that it was a good thing?'

He found that puzzling. 'Good? What's his problem? Tell me more.'

'Like I said... oddball. Dresses like a poor man. Worn shoes and frayed trousers. I mean he's engaged to the eldest daughter. He just drifts around like he's got no job. And get this...' She took a large sip of her beer. 'He went to see a prosi after that.'

'Whore? Sure you followed the right guy?'

She showed him the selfie photo she took of them.

He zoomed into the faces. 'What's going on?'

'Loser.' She made an L with her hand and held it on her forehead. 'What do they see in him?'

Rebwar also tried to make sense of it. Basar had been in Turkey getting some plastic surgery and now he was drifting in London. 'I met them.'

Geraldine waited for him to add to his statement.

'The Mohsens. They want to meet.'

'Oh, them. What's the plan?'

He stared into his pint, hoping to find something. 'It's a stupid idea. But, as I said, got them off my back.'

Geraldine held her head, probably remembering the attempt on his life.

'And that wire!'

'I told them not to. Where are you going to meet them?'

'Still working that out. Not sure that anyone cares about Izah anymore. Jaleh is seeing it as a business deal. Dinah is backing her all the way.'

'So, who was behind it? Jaleh? Kill your own son? Sisters?'

'Ben, the boxer boyfriend, said he was keeping something from him. Also, mentioned three words. Can't... see... forest.'

Geraldine scratched her scalp. 'All a bit cryptic. Maybe it is a suicide and Jaleh is just using you to get what she wants. Whatever that might be.'

FIFTY-THREE

Rebwar had parked his car at the Mount Pleasant car park in Epping Forest. The meeting point was at the clearing where Izah had been hung. Loughton Camp was where an old stone age fort had been found, but Rebwar hadn't made any relevant connections as to why Izah had chosen the location.

He was over two hours early and was checking the area for any traces of anyone hiding out or tampering with location. He expected one of the two houses to spring something to get an advantage. Raj had given him three miniature cameras to plant around the clearing. What Plan B had asked him to do was too risky. The other option was easier to deny if someone found one of the devices. He had mapped out a concentric circle that focused on the middle of the clearing.

Both parties had agreed to meet without too much protestation. He had expected them to ask for more concessions and reassurances. It was Jaleh who had kept phoning him. She had wanted to go through the details of the meet. There wasn't a lot to say; just to turn up and talk. Rebwar had taken precautions and was in a ballistic jacket that he had taken from Bijan's arsenal as well as a gun and the hand grenade. He knew that if he had asked them to come unarmed, it would have been ignored anyway and simply caused the first disagreement.

The clearing looked exactly the same as he remembered it. The tree where Izah was found looked ominous and there were still marks where the rope had worn the bark away. He went over to a hollowed-out fallen tree trunk that faced into the clearing. Looking inside, he saw a couple of beams of light dotted along it and he found a suitable sized hole to hide the camera. He covered it with leaves and sticks so that only the small lens was visible, his insurance, he hoped, perhaps providing something he could negotiate with. He checked his watch and found he still had thirty minutes until the meeting, although he expected them to be late. This could well end up in a pissing match or worse, a slaughter. He tried to hold on to his nerves by having another cigarette. He had bought a couple of extra packs. There had also been no messages or calls from Musa or Dinah. He also didn't need more stress. Even though either of them would have eventually calmed him down, he didn't have the time or the energy to take that on.

A break in the cloud cover allowed the sun to shine onto his face. Its warmth was like a hot towel. He closed his eyes, enjoying the fresh winter's air. The initial dampness that had seeped into his clothes had disappeared. A crack caught his attention. He looked around, trying to find its location. He held off from shouting and moved around, peering into the forest. Rows of brown tree trunks were all he could see.

'You're here,' Hayden walked out from the bushes wearing an army camouflage jacket and green trousers.

'Checking on me?' said Rebwar.

Hayden whistled, and Craig and Al revealed their positions by appearing from behind some tree trunks. 'Been here long?'

'Why here?' said Al.

Rebwar moved on to the centre of clearing. 'Is Jaleh here?'

As if on cue she walked out of the woods in a knee-length puffa jacket and stopped at the edge of the mound and looked around. Her face was stone cold, devoid of emotion. 'So this is it.' And she made her way over the dried leaves to the tree. She took a moment to make a prayer it looked like.

The sound of motorbike engines echoed through the forest. Their high-pitched whine inched closer and filled the clearing. Jaleh's men checked their weapons, cocking them and holding them ready. Hayden made Jaleh stand by the tree trunk. Rebwar was surprised by the Mohsens' choice of transport. It wasn't subtle, but it did make an impression. Four off-road bikes appeared from the small dip where a stream ran south. Each one took a separate direction and rode around the clearing. Jaleh's gang drew their guns to show force. After a couple of noisy and disorienting laps, the Mohsens stopped.

The bike opposite Jaleh had Vahid on the pillion seat, from which he dismounted, looking a little unsteady on his feet. Lanny was in-between Rebwar and Jaleh. The other two bikes were parked, looking across from Al and Craig. They weren't quite surrounded, but the Mohsens made their presence felt.

Jaleh stepped forward. 'Welcome. Glad you made it.'

Lanny and Vahid both made their way further into the clearing. Both wore boots and leather jackets. 'Jaleh, your beauty holds you proud,' said Vahid. 'Glad that our two houses have agreed to talk. We offer our condolences in your time of tragedy.' Lanny nodded his agreement.

'Glad you bring it up.' Jaleh pointed to the tree. 'It was here. And...' She took a moment to regain herself. 'And I can't turn back time. I have to move on and turn a page on this.'

Lanny held his silver gun in front of his crotch, pointing it at the ground. 'All right, with all the soul searching,' he said. 'We've all had our share of grief. What are we doing here?' He pointed to the tree with his gun. 'Thinking of hanging someone and getting your retribution?'

Rebwar held onto his grenade, feeling the mood change.

'Lanny...' said Vahid. 'Respect. Sorry, he's—'

'I've got a...' Jaleh looked around her. 'Request.' She moved from under the tree. 'Eye for an eye. Need commitment from your house. A show of dedication to this venture.'

Lanny turned to face his brother. 'Is she taking us for fools? Lay it out and we'll consider. Eye for an eye? You started this. We are owed.'

'We need each other. You have the international distribution—'

'Wait, wait,' said Lanny. 'And him?' He pointed the gun to Rebwar. 'He's what in all this?' And he walked over to him.

'He's mine.' Jaleh waved Rebwar to come over to her side, which he did.

'Well, he's got balls,' Lanny tucked his gun away into his belt. 'And I haven't finished with him. But go on.'

'I want us to grow and create a legacy that is worthy of our legendary history. We make history. So, I say let's put our differences behind us. We have much in common and our businesses would complement each other. What do you say?'

Lanny and Vahid looked at each other as if they were trying to work out their thoughts. They walked over to each other and talked out of earshot.

Jaleh shook her head. 'Too much pride, idiots,' she said to Hayden and Rebwar. 'It is a partnership. A pact.' She picked up two sticks and she snapped them over her leg. 'See, this is weak.' She picked up four sticks and tried to break them. 'Strength in numbers. If you're not going to share, it's going to break.'

'Are you saying we're weak?' said Lanny.

'Like this, yes,' She walked over to them. The men moved their guns in anticipation. 'You know what is needed for us to survive.'

Rebwar tried to move closer to hear what they were saying, but Hayden held him back. He hoped the camera he had hidden was picking up the conversation. They all looked around, checking if anyone was going to spring a surprise. Lanny jerked back, grabbing his gun. Everyone else drew their weapons. Lanny was visibly agitated. Jaleh pointed at the tree. Rebwar tried again to move.

They finished their conversation and Jaleh made her way back through the dead leaves. Rebwar got some cigarettes out. The two brothers were still talking. Rebwar offered Jaleh a cigarette. She took one. 'Deal?' he asked.

'Let's see if they honour my request.' She looked over at Hayden. 'Let's get back.' And she walked up to the small bank.

Rebwar tried to work out what had gone down. They hadn't shaken on anything. The motorbikes started revving engines. Smoke puffed out of the exhausts and the high-pitched sound filled the forest. Al and Craig jogged to catch up with Jaleh and Hayden, making sure no one was coming after them. Rebwar was left asking for answers. The bikes scrambled away from their positions and drove off into the woods. As their sound faded, he heard Jaleh talking to someone on her phone. He couldn't make out what she was saying. He needed to go back to get the cameras but, for the moment, he made his way to his parked car. The blacked-out 4x4 Mercedes drove off with Jaleh. He was going to come back another day. Jaleh had a plan that he wasn't in on. It made him angry and powerless, which is probably exactly what she wanted.

FIFTY-FOUR

The train arrived at Chingford Train station; it was its last stop. The doors opened and Rebwar stepped off the train with drunken passengers. It was late and as the other people stumbled around and sung some football songs, he made his way to the exit. He put his ticket through the machine at the barrier and walked out onto a mini-roundabout that was set off down the main street. A few closed shops and parking spaces were dotted around. The lone lamppost in the centre of the island lit the area with prison-like ferocity. A big, black, off-road Mercedes drove towards Rebwar.

The window rolled down and Hayden said, 'Get in.'

Rebwar complied and hauled himself up into the jacked-up vehicle. Inside, it was plush with dark leather and had a new-car smell to it. Its powerful engine roared and they went off down the road. 'What's so urgent?'

With his eyes fixed on the road, Hayden said, 'You'll see.'

Rebwar had got a call an hour or so before asking him to meet Hayden at the station. He said there was a situation, and he needed to get there as soon as. 'So what is it that you can't say over the phone?'

'We're nearly there.' Hayden floored the accelerator down a minor road that was lined with trees and shrubs. He checked his mirrors and he slowed down to a car park. The entrance was closed off by a small, metal gate. Beside it were some dried-out logs. He positioned the car in front of the logs and gave a sharp stab at the engine. The car's front tyres hopped over the log and he repeated the manoeuvre for the back wheels. He drove across the car park and onto a walkway that ran along a small lake. After a couple of hundred metres, he stopped by a small pontoon. 'Get out.'

Apart from the car's lights, it was pitch black and there was a bitter wind sweeping across the water. Hayden took a rucksack, brought out a flashlight and walked into the undergrowth. He swept the area with his light and slowly went deeper and deeper into the forest. Rebwar followed, not daring to ask. He kept looking for broken branches in case he needed one. He questioned himself about why he had so impulsively agreed to meet and without even asking for a reason. If they were going to dispose of him, he would have brought more men. Or had he been tasked? He let Hayden stay a couple of steps in front.

He stopped and tuned to Rebwar. 'Here.' He looked down.

Rebwar carefully approached the spot where Hayden shone the light. He was expecting a grave. Instead, he saw some legs and then a shredded grey hoodie with dark brown marks. It was Craig. Hayden, who had a gun pointed a gun at Rebwar, asked 'Why?'

'Why?'

'Why did you kill him?'

Rebwar crouched down to have a closer look at the body. He reached for his phone.

'Hey, what are you doing?'

'Phone. Need my phone.' And he took it out and switched on the torch. 'It was a woman.'

'Stop trying to pull my leg. Just tell me why and I'll make it quick.'

Rebwar lifted one of Craig's arms. 'See... defensive wounds.' He showed Hayden the deep cuts in Craig's hands. He checked his watch. It was past eleven. 'And this happened over eight hours ago. I was working. You can check my Uber account.'

'Why eight?'

'No rigor mortis.'

'Right, and why a woman?'

Rebwar pointed to the belt and the zip. 'The belt... look... the tip is on the right.' Hayden checked Craig's belt. Its end was tipped on the left. 'I think he was trying to rape someone.'

'No, too neat.' Hayden held the gun back towards Rebwar. 'You had it in for him. Didn't you two have a fight?'

'Look, it was a crazy attack. Twenty, maybe thirty wounds. And who found him?'

Hayden scratched the back of his neck and hovered over the body. 'Sarah. She was walking her dog.'

His first reaction was to say that it was her. 'When?'

'Who cares? We need to move him.' He opened the rucksack to take out a neatly folded black body bag. 'Come on, before some weirdo comes by.' He laid out the bag next to him and passed him some blue medical gloves.

Rebwar took a few pictures with his phone. He quickly checked around to see if there was anything else that had been left. He could have ripped off some jewellery. Before he could check Craig's pockets, Hayden had emptied them into his rucksack. He was sure that his phone held the answer to who he was meeting. They rolled him over into the bag and zipped it up. They carried him over to the car, where they put him in the back of the Mercedes. Hayden brushed some of the mud off the clean, carpeted interior.

'You're going to have to get rid of it,' Rebwar said.

'Get in.'

FIFTY-FIVE

After making their way out of the park, Hayden drove off in the opposite direction from the way they had come. Rebwar spotted signs for Epping and it wasn't long till they arrived at Jaleh's mansion. The gravel driveway had a couple of fancy cars and an old scruffy white Polo. They got out and Rebwar glanced quickly into the white car. It had discarded sweet wrappers, some children's toys and a dog bed in the back. Inside in the reception room was Jaleh standing with a glass of red wine. She was in a matching flowing black top and trousers.

'So he didn't do it?' she said to Hayden.

'I'll let him explain.'

She walked over to Rebwar and stared at him with her dark eyes. 'Are you going to tell me that the House of Zik was responsible?' And she crossed her arms. 'I'm listening.'

'No.' But it was a thought that had crossed his mind and not knowing what they had agreed made it difficult to know what was going on. 'Only if they sent a female assassin, as it was a crime of passion between a man and a woman.'

She kept staring at him.

'He was stabbed to death. At least twenty times. His trousers were down. He raped the woman.'

Jaleh looked away and held her hand over her face. 'Or tried to. Then he was covered up. But the killer made a mistake... and the belt was like yours.' She looked down at her thin black belt. 'Men wear them the other way round. Like the buttons on blouses.' Her eyes were streaming with tears. 'Hayden said that Sarah found him.'

Jaleh took her wineglass and drank. 'You had a fight with him. What was it over?'

'Musa. He was deliberately making me look like a ball-less man.'

Jaleh walked around the grand room sipping her wine. Large landscape paintings with golden frames dominated the space. Rebwar looked at the oriental-looking sculptures wondering if she had bought them from the Mohsens.

Hayden stepped in and said, 'He was working all afternoon—'

'Shut up.' She turned to Rebwar and pointed her mani-cured index finger at him. 'Are you lying to me?'

'Was it your daughter? That's her car out there.'

Jaleh stood by the large window that faced onto the lit garden.

'Was she having an affair with Craig?' He was putting a theory out there that he had been running though.

With her head bowed, she nodded.

Rebwar now wondered if they had murdered Izah. But he stopped himself from asking, as he didn't have any evidence.

'Sorry, it was me.' Sarah appeared by the door to the hallway in a white jumper and baggy colourful trousers.

Jaleh walked over to her and slapped her. 'You lied to me.' And she slapped her again. 'Why?'

'I didn't know what to do. He just lost it when I said no.' She cried into her hands, and then Jaleh hugged her. 'I wanted him to stop. He was angry, so angry. He wanted us to run away.'

Rebwar was itching to ask more, but he had to bite his lip and not outstay his welcome. Like Dinah, they could turn and protect their own. He hadn't blood ties. He took the opportunity to step out and have a cigarette as they huddled together on a sofa. Out on the front porch, he looked up to the starry sky. Maybe this was a good point to leave. He still hadn't reviewed the video he had left running at the meeting. He needed Raj to access it. Anyway, it didn't really interest him anymore. They did still have the gun that murdered Chief Super McKintosh with his prints on it. Rebwar's phone rang and he saw that it was a with-held number. He picked it up.

'Is this Rebwar?' said a distorted voice.

'Yes.'

'Now, listen to me very carefully. I will not repeat myself; you understand?'

'Who is this?'

'Listen, I have your son. And you will do what I ask, otherwise you won't be seeing him. Have I got your full attention?'

Rebwar's chest tightened as if he was being crushed by a boulder. 'Yes.'

'Now, you are going to kill Jaleh Sasani and bring me her head. You have twenty-four hours. And if you tell anyone or call anyone about this, you will not see your son again.'

'Only if I can speak to my son. I need proof.'

After a moment of silence, the man agreed. Rebwar heard echoing footsteps and then the man telling Musa to say hello and nothing else. 'Dad, Dad—'

Rebwar walked onto the gravel driveway, away from the house. 'Are you OK? Has he harmed you? Hey, what? Musa?'

'He's here, OK?'

Rebwar heard his son shout that he wanted his favourite T-shirt, the one with I'm Not Lazy. on it 'Hey! Is he OK, is he cold, does he need—?'

'Twenty-four hours.' And he hung up.

Rebwar checked his watch; it was just past midnight. He crouched down on the gravel and breathed in to calm and compose himself. Think, think, think.

Jaleh came to the door, looking for him. 'I've had a phone call,' she said. He stood up, shaking, and took out a cigarette. 'You need to pick up a package.'

He felt like telling them to get lost. He looked at her now, asking himself if he should kill her. He could draw her into the garden and then take one of the cars. But he had no weapon, and he didn't know if could just strangle her. Not in cold blood. Like a murderer. No. How was he going to do it?

'Rebwar, did you hear?' She was standing in front him. 'Are you OK? You look white?'

'Oh, just a cold, I think.' He felt his forehead; it was wet with sweat. 'Package?'

'We can get someone else, but they asked for you.'

'They?'

'Mohsens. Sure you all right?'

'I'll be fine. Maybe some water.' He felt his head spin a

little. He crouched down and held onto his knees. 'Long day. Sorry.'

She went back into the house to get some water. Rebwar tried to think straight. What options did he have? Who had Musa? He couldn't make any sense out of it. Mohsens? Why ask for him now? Plan B?

FIFTY-SIX

Traffic was snaked around the London streets, like an interminable nest of vipers. Rebwar had been told to take the big 4x4 Mercedes. Hayden had tried to protest, making quips and comments about Rebwar's driving. He told him that they had moved on from donkeys and asses to cars. It hadn't gone down well; Rebwar wasn't in the mood. He looked into the rear-view mirror. His eyes were bloodshot and he ached from exactly what he couldn't remember. Craig's body was still in the boot festering in the body bag. He'd asked about it but they had all just shrugged as if it was something that had to be taken to the recycling centre.

He admired the finish of the car. All he knew was that it was German and that in the time of the Shah, Mercs were driven by the elite. He'd thrown a few bricks at them when he was living in the streets. Reaching for a cigarette, he looked in vain for the car's cigar lighter. He pulled out his lighter and, with some satisfaction, filled the car with smoke before opening the window. Hayden's precious new car had now been marked. It was a little childish pleasure, but he'd take it.

He contemplated the pain that his poor son must be going through. It was for his son that he came over here and now that was in jeopardy. He didn't dare think what might happen to him. How had they got to him? Only a handful of people knew where he was. It was also only a matter of time till Hourieh called. Maybe she already had, as she didn't have his new number. For the moment he couldn't involve her. She would call the police, the embassy and the Shah if he was still alive.

The sat nav was guiding him back to the Mohsens' gallery. Was it them? He called Geraldine to ask her to meet him after he picked up the package. He hoped that, with her help, he could find a way out of this hell.

Driving onto the pavement and abandoning the car, he walked up to the glass door. It was closed and only a few spots of light lit some of the precious antiques. He knocked on the glass with his knuckles. After a few minutes, a light came on by the door. He noticed a camera above staring at him. He smiled and pointed to the door.

There was somebody behind him. He turned around to see a man holding on to the wall. He had unzipped his trousers.

'Hey!' Rebwar stepped back and the man began peeing on the doorstep. Some men across the street jeered in encouragement. The man smiled and looked up with glee.

The door opened and Arlo pushed the man, who stumbled back till his back hit the car. He slumped down onto the pavement, grumbling and trying to pick himself up. He grabbed Rebwar's jacket and threw a punch, which missed him.

'He's not with me.' But Arlo kicked Rebwar's thigh, which made him buckle down.

'Stop, Arlo, listen!' Lanny was now standing behind Arlo. 'He's a drunk from the pub. Go and get him.'

Rebwar picked himself up from the floor, rubbing his dead leg. 'You know him?'

'He's the local drunk.'

'And you asked for me.' He held onto the shopwindow.

'Arlo, teach him a lesson but away from the cameras.' Arlo dragged the man around the corner of the gallery. 'Sorry, yes. We have a delivery and from your last stunt, we're a little nervous.' He walked into the gallery. 'Who are you?'

Rebwar followed him in. 'I work for the Sasanis,' he said, picking a side, thinking it might keep him from being harmed, his reasoning being that they were trying to negotiate a deal.

'That's not what you said the first time. Was it Rebwar Ghorbani? I've heard that you're a detective. And that Jaleh had brought you in to investigate Izah's suicide, as a mother would. You know, didn't believe the verdict. I'm sure I would, stricken with grief, have acted the same way if I was in her shoes. Is she of sound mind?'

Rebwar looked at Lanny, searching his face for some telltale sign. What did he want from him? Had they kidnaped his son? 'I think he was murdered.'

'What makes you say that?'

'That tree branch was over eight feet high. And if he had jumped off, his head would have not come clean off. No ladder was found or note. The post-mortem had been tampered with and then the doctor conveniently committed suicide.'

Arlo came back in and walked over to the small sink to wash himself. Lanny stood by the till where a brown box was waiting. 'So who did it?'

'Someone who he knew and we didn't.'

'Was it his lover, Ben?' Lanny smiled. 'Gays, sure Izah was two-timing him.'

'Why you say that?'

'Heard it, seen it. They fuck around like rampant rabbits. He wanted to meet me, ask me some business advice and vouch for some guy. You know, sound out if the guy was legit.' He pushed the box over to him. 'Now this is the package.'

'Did you meet him?'

Lanny shook his head.

'Why not?'

'Can't remember. Too busy.'

Rebwar picked up the package. It was heavy. 'It's not a bomb, is it?'

'Now that's heresy. And what do you take us for? Or is that what Mr Achmoud takes us for?'

'What... gangsters? Probably. But he's not much better.' Rebwar was going to add that he also considered him a good friend and it was thanks to him that he was still in the game. But he knew that if they'd felt he was somehow going to betray them, they'd kill him without a second thought.

'Give Jaleh my love. I'm sure she will appreciate the tribute.'

Rebwar went back to the car and put the box on the passenger seat. He itched to find out what was in it. She must have asked for something when they had that hush-hush powwow in the clearing. Drugs? Money? Guns?

FIFTY-SEVEN

The Queen's Arms was a pub just south of Kensington Gardens on Queen's Gate Mews, a dead-end cobbled street with a series of old converted stables. Even for their diminutive size they were very sought after and considered trendy. The cottage-like houses had their backs to larger terraced homes that lined the grand streets of Kensington. Rebwar had parked the car just within eyesight of where he was sitting with Geraldine. With its body bag in the boot, he didn't want to leave it very far in case he had to make a run for it. The pub was set in a corner and was decorated with a waist-high wooden panelling and white walls. Christmas decorations hung off the ceilings and there was a decorated tree in one of the corners. He had brought the box with him and he laid it on the table.

'Let's open it,' said Geraldine.

Rebwar held on to it. 'No.' He drank his beer, which tasted like bitter soda water. 'What are we going to do?' He'd told her about Musa and she had been lost for words. She wanted to call in her colleagues to help them but he had told her to hold off.

'So how long have you got?'

Rebwar checked his watch. It was ten thirty. 'Till they call me.' He took out his phone and called Raj.

'Am I safe?' said Raj.

'I need your help. Urgently.'

'Go on.'

'I've got one of these plastic cards with a video on it. I need to know what the people on it are saying. And you need to come here.'

'But—'

'I'll pay. Cash.'

'Oh, that serious. Right, can you give the location? Got three words... Of course not. Send me a pin or tell me the address.'

Rebwar looked at the bottom of the menu. 'Three words? What do you mean?'

'Uncle, I tried to explain that last time we met. Don't worry about it.' He giggled. 'Some tech, you know? Good for finding exact spots. It's nothing.'

'Wait, wait, so what if I said Park, Obey, Image, is that some kind of file, code, app?'

Raj giggled again. 'Oh, wait...' Rebwar heard some taps on a keyboard.

Geraldine came back with another two pints and a packet of crisps.

'That's in the middle of Epping Forest. What's there?'

'Thanks, thanks. Get a cab and come over now.' Rebwar picked up his beer. 'He did meet someone there.'

'Who do you mean?'

'Izah, he was meeting someone. I'm sure those three words that Ben Layton gave me is the location where he was killed. Now who?'

'How?'

'Raj will explain. But is there a link to Musa?'

'Could we make a fake head? Like that wax lady.'

Rebwar leaned back in his seat. 'Plan B? Would they?'

'Sure. Bit elaborate for them and risky. What if you called the actual cops?' She leaned into the table. 'And those two... Highclere and Aspen they're just hoping for their pensions... But... divorces aren't cheap. Maybe...'

'Mohsens. They want rid of Jaleh. But they...' He looked at the box.

'You think there's a clue?'

'They asked for me.'

Around the bar came Raj, out of breath. He sat on the chair wheezing. 'Wait...' And he took out an inhaler and used it. 'Right. Hi...' He looked around. 'You having me followed?'

Geraldine shook her head. 'Stop being paranoid. Drink?'

'Coke. Pint. Uncle, what's so urgent?' He handed Rebwar a couple of small plastic tiles before searching into his rucksack to bring out his laptop. He cracked his knuckles, inserted one of the cards and noticed the box. 'Amazon delivery?'

'No, it's just a delivery. What's in the files?'

Raj put on his headphones and listened, his face glued to the screen. Geraldine came back with another round of drinks. Rebwar was stacking his drinks, focusing on what do next. He was sure Jaleh would soon call about the package.

'I think it's one of the Sasanis,' said Geraldine. 'What if Izah faked his death? You said the post-mortem was suspect. The funeral? Wasn't an open casket, was it?'

Rebwar rubbed his chin, trying to see how that might fit. 'They run. Make a new life. From what everyone says, he didn't really want to be in business.'

Raj sucked on the straw as he carried on listening.

'Hakan... he was my other horse. But he seems more of a loser and needs the income from the family. And with Craig gone...'

'Guys...' Raj took his headphones off. 'What's in that box?' They both looked at him and then at the box. He turned the laptop and gave the headphones to Geraldine, who listened. 'The woman asked the two guys for a tribute eye for an eye.'

Rebwar shut his eyes, knowing exactly what she was asking for. There was something disturbing in that box. And the pub was not the place to open it. He moved it onto the floor. Geraldine was about to ask him something, but he just looked down and rubbed his face.

'Oh, before I forget,' said Raj. 'I got a new T for Musa. How is he?'

'He's...' Rebwar fought back some tears and choked on his words.

Geraldine took over. 'Someone's kidnapped him.'

'Fuck! No, who? OK, I mean, how much do they want?'

Geraldine grabbed Rebwar's hand. He was struggling with the situation. 'We're working on it.'

'He told me about his favourite T-shirt and how he wanted it.' He wiped a tear from his eyes, feeling his throat tighten and burn. He grabbed his beer.

'Hang on,' said Raj. 'What is his favourite T?'

'Oh, I dunno. There's so many.'

'No, no, I told him about the app. What three words. That's how we meet. Look, look.' Raj showed his phone to them. 'What's the T? Come on, remember.' Raj was, nearly jumping out of his seat.

Rebwar tried to think back. 'Something about Lazy, not lazy or...'

With his large round fingers, Raj tapped on his phone and found some pictures of T-shirts. 'What about this one?' He showed them one that had I'm Not Lazy. with a round computer symbol and text explaining it, saying just buffering.

'But that's five words and it's a T-shirt,' said Geraldine. 'I don't get it.' She shook her head a couple of times.

'Is that all he said?'

'Yes, yes, and then the man cut in.' Rebwar hoped Raj could work some kind of magic. 'How does this link to your app? Scan it?'

'No, no, it must be a code. I know. Wouldn't he have said "Hi Dad, doing fine, love you" or something?'

Rebwar thought back to the phone call and realised that he had a something. It was odd, why would he mention his favourite T-shirt? 'So where?'

Raj looked at the picture. 'There must be a clue.'

The bell for last orders rang. 'Look, I need to deliver the package. Can you two...?'

'Go. Don't worry,' said Geraldine. 'How are you supposed to get in touch with him?'

He just shrugged.

'Again weird, wouldn't they give some place to meet or something?' Geraldine went over and gave Rebwar a big hug. 'It'll be fine. We will find him.'

FIFTY-EIGHT

Geraldine had taken the two beers that Rebwar had left behind and was finishing them off as Raj was typing away on his keyboard. 'What if it's not what we're looking for?'

Raj ignored her and burped.

She answered with a longer one.

'There's one hundred and twenty-five permutations if we take the five words,' Raj said, running his fingers through his hair.

'And the symbol?'

He burped again.

'OK, you win.' She looked at the emptying pub and eyed up any pretty girl she could catch a glimpse of. It had been a long time since she had some fun.

Raj interlocked his fingers and cracked his knuckles. 'So, I've made a little script and run the names. Took out the locations outside the UK. Then narrowed the search area to London and its local counties around.'

She finished one of the pints. 'How many?'

He whistled and turned the computer around. 'Three that makes some sort of sense.'

'So I took this script... OK, I got these locations.'

Geraldine looked at the map. There was a golf club in Kent, a two-storey apartment block in Feltham and an airfield north of London. 'Fuck, still a plan. Too late for today. First thing tomorrow.' She looked at him and just saw a waiting smile. 'And you're coming with me.'

'No. Why?'

'You are. So, where shall we go now? Kebab?'

FIFTY-NINE

Rebwar stood in the hallway with a bunch of flowers and a bottle of red wine. Dinah had called him and told him he could deliver the package to hers. Jaleh was going to pick it up at the boutique first thing in the morning, as she was going there for a private view of Dinah's new collection. He still had mixed feelings about Dinah's role and a feeling of anger crawled through him. Dinah had excused herself for being unavailable, as she had been preparing the stock for the upcoming season. She wanted to make it up and make a surprise for him.

He wondered if Jaleh knew what was in that box or had there been a misunderstanding? It was pretty clear on the video, but maybe it was code for something. He still hadn't dared to open it. He convinced himself that he needed a couple of hours to think and make a plan for the next day. There was no point in running around like a rat in a cage.

He knocked on the thick wooden door and it opened to a warm smiling face. Dinah grabbed him and kissed him deeply till he had to break off to breathe. She wore a figure-hugging green dress that revealed her best attributes. It was short and thin to the touch. She grabbed the flowers and the bottle and walked over to the kitchen, put the bottle on the counter and inched up her dress to reveal a cheek, which she slapped. She giggled and blew a kiss at him.

She brought over two glasses of white wine. 'Now, let's not talk about work.' She tiptoed to whisper in his ear. 'Just us.'

There was so much that he wanted to say, but he needed this escape. And she wanted to brush the whole thing under the carpet. He drank the cool fresh wine, which, for the first time in a while, tasted of something. It was buttery, with hints of rose petals. It was probably what she had said about it, but he enjoyed it. 'I can smell some home cooking.'

She put her finger up and turned around and skipped to the oven. 'You'll see. Cheated a bit... A lot. But it's for you. Sit, sit.'

He went over and sat on the couch, sinking into it till his body was one with it. Aches and pains ebbed and flowed. Holding a tray, she made her way to the coffee table and knelt down in front of it. He scanned the little snacks: Kotlet, a small fried pattie with ground beef, mashed potato and onion; Sosis Bandari: traditional cocktail-sized sausages with a tomato paste and chilli pepper. He tried to pick a meat-filled dumpling called Joahpara but Dinah got there first and gently let him have a bite. Both sharing the taste. She kissed him and pushed him down on the couch, lifting his shirt. She kissed his belly and undid his trousers.

————

Rebwar woke up, and it took him a couple of minutes to get his bearings. Dinah was fast asleep next to him. He glanced at his watch and saw that he'd only been sleeping for a couple of hours. But he knew he would not get any more; his insomnia was going to make sure of that. He read a text from Geraldine. They had found three locations that they were going to search. He was going to let them get on with that, as he had to somehow either convince or abduct Jaleh. He needed her as his insurance to get his son. But he knew she would not come willingly. With her entourage, this was going to be a problem. He still had the hand grenade, but this time he was also dealing with ex-military. They were trained for such situations. He looked up at the ceiling, hoping that an idea would come to him.

SIXTY

Only a few Water Mill Way streetlights were on. Either this was the council's austerity measures or it was a forgotten area that didn't warrant their attention. It set the tone for their early rise. Geraldine mounted the kerb to park the car in front of the first address that Raj had found. She had hoped that the car's jolt would have woken him up. She looked at the block and counted six apartments. It was seven am and the street was still quiet. The days of milk deliveries were long gone. Back in her day, they were the scourge of stakeouts. Either the milkmen were too chatty for their own good or on the take or even both. She shook Raj's shoulder. 'Wakey, wakey.'

He stretched his large arms, which hit the car's roof. 'What's for breakfast?'

She had forgotten to pass by a local fast-food joint. 'Mate, you're going to have to work for it.' She pointed to the block of flats. 'You take the bottom two.'

'And...' He looked over. 'And knock on their doors and say, "Hello. Have you kidnapped my friend Musa?"'

'We went through...'

Raj shook his head like an annoying toy dog from some advertisement.

'I thought we had. OK.' She looked up into the proverbial heavens. 'I'm sure we did. You wear your rucksack and...' She reached into the back seat to get her handbag. 'Take this.' He took the lanyard and badge. 'And say you're doing a survey.'

He looked at it. 'That's not me. And what's ONS?'

'Office for National Statistics. And they never look at the picture. If they do, say you got mixed up with your colleague. Then ask if they have seen Musa. You'll get the hang of it. Easy.' She looked over at the building and opened the door. The air was fresh and there was a touch of frost on the parked cars.

Raj stepped out. 'Geez, it's freezing. Can't we wait—'

'Come on, you big wuss!' She walked off to the left side of the building where the entrance was. She expected to have to ring a few doorbells till someone would let her in. The lock on the door was broken. She held the door for Raj to catch up, held her index finger to her lips and pointed at the door he was supposed to knock on. Then she took the stairs to the second floor. There were two flats, and the furthest one seemed to have someone in it. She rang the bell. A woman shouted to her husband to get the door. It opened just a fraction for half a face to stare out. The latch was on. Still in his pyjamas and with bloodshot eyes, he asked who she was.

'Police.' She showed her badge.

The man ruffled his messy hair. A baby cried in the background. 'Can you come back later? A bit early?'

'We're looking for a boy.' And she brought out her phone and showed him a picture of Musa. 'Seen him or a man with a boy?'

'Who is it?' said the woman inside the flat.

He answered back to her. 'Oh, nothing, just... Nothing to worry about.' He turned back to Geraldine. 'No,' he said, tensely, and tried to close the door on her. But she had put her shoe in the gap.

'Who lives opposite?'

'No one. It's empty.' He pushed harder to close the door.

'Need your help here!' Geraldine pulled her shoe and the door closed. She went over to the other apartment. She lifted the mailbox flap and looked in. From the limited view, she made out bare walls and a small pile of unopened mail that spread under the door. She reached down and slipped out a few. They were addressed to a Mr and Mrs Patel. Judging from the number of letters and their position, no one had opened that door in the last few weeks. She took the stairs and went to the third floor to the flat above the couple that had its lights on. She pressed the bell, which buzzed. She waited but heard no sounds of stirring. She buzzed again and, at the fifth attempt, a middle-aged woman opened the door. A strong smell of cat piss passed Geraldine like a wave. Trying not to throw up, she showed her warrant card.

'You found Pascha?' she said with a broad smile showing red wine-stained lips.

'No, we're looking for a boy and a man.' She was glad to not have to go into the flat as it looked messy. 'Any suspicious activity? Neighbours?'

'Now that you mention it...' In a hushed voice and pointing to the flat opposite her, she said, 'He's a bit of a one. In and out at odd hours and all that. Sure, pay him a visit. But I didn't tell you that.' And, with that, she closed the door.

Geraldine looked over to the door opposite. Took a breath and went over. There was no bell, so she knocked, and that became harder as she waited.

An out-of-breath Raj joined her. 'Geez, you didn't tell me about the stairs. You done?'

She leaned on the door and put her ear to it. The she shouted. 'Police!' and banged again. She looked through the letter box and saw bits of furniture. She tried to open the door and saw Raj dangling a key in front of her, which she took.

'Courtesy of the old man. Said he had rented it out to some foreign bloke. Got a gun?' Raj looked at her, concerned, turning away as if he might make a run for it.

Geraldine inserted the key and turned it twice. The door opened and a man wearing only his boxer shorts stared back at them. He had a knife in his hand. She held up her warrant card at him. 'Put it down now.'

'What you want?' He pointed the blade at her. 'Show me papers.'

'Where's Musa?' said Raj,

The man turned to Raj with the knife.

'Listen to me,' said Geraldine. 'Put the knife down. Now.' He thrust forward and she had to step aside to avoid being stabbed. 'Sir, this is your last warning.' Raj had already gone around the corner to hide. The man slammed the door shut and tried to lock it, but with the key in the cylinder, he couldn't. 'Raj, give me your rucksack.' He passed it over by sliding it along the floor. She grabbed it and went to open the door. Using the rucksack as a shield, she stepped into the flat. She couldn't see the man. 'Sir?'

She heard some fumbling and steps coming from a room past the kitchen. The place was a mess, with clothes and fast-food boxes lying around. The man stepped out, hoodie up, partially covering his face. He swung at her, hitting the rucksack and slashing it. She retreated into the kitchen and he ran past and out into the hallway. Footsteps disappeared down the stairwell. She went into the bedroom, where she found clothes, cans and toilet rolls. It looked more of a squat than a lived-in home. For curtains there were a couple of sheets stuck on with duct tape. It reminded her of Zac's old place, her sister's excuse of a boyfriend.

'Who was that?' said Raj, peeking his head into the room.

Geraldine just shrugged and carried on looking for some clues. There wasn't much to go on.

SIXTY-ONE

On their way to the second location, Geraldine decided to go and check in to Baxendale Street and into that house where she saw Basar visit. She had regretted not going back to ask about him. Traffic had built up, and it had taken longer than they hoped, even with Raj constantly trying to find a shortcut. They had driven through a McDonald's and the leftover wrappers were all over the back seats.

'What's the plan this time? And we didn't talk about this one before you start.'

Geraldine felt like punching him. 'Stay in the car.'

'What if you need my rucksack again? And I've sent you my PayPal details.'

'It's a woman and we are going to... Stay in the car.'

'Is she cute?'

Geraldine turned into the street and drove past the address to park the car. 'Stay.' She went to the door. She was about to ring the bell but then went over to the front windows and peered in. The living room was empty but had a TV, sofa and some flowers. It looked lived in but not a tip. She rang the bell and waited. Raj was playing some tunes on the car's radio. She tried the handle on the door. It opened. She slowly peered in and said hello. There was no answer. Looking around, she made her way in. The place smelled of perfume, but there was a hint of something odd that she couldn't quite place. The house was small. There was a thin staircase ahead of her and a small corridor that led to the back. The wooden floor creaked as she made her way slowly in. As she pushed the door to the kitchen, it hit something and she couldn't open it fully. It was too heavy for her to heave any further.

She inched her head around the door. For a second, she stepped back, holding her mouth, and looked again to confirm what she had just seen. It was a corpse lying on the floor with its head missing. Blood had made a large puddle all over the black and white lino floor.

'Is that her?'

Geraldine jumped and nearly fell into the kitchen, holding onto a counter to steady herself. 'What the fuck!' She pushed Raj back. 'Get back in the car.'

'She's missing her head.'

'Raj, back. Not for you. And don't touch anything. Wipe whatever you handled.' She made Raj reverse out. 'Back, back.' Making sure he had done what he had been told, she made her way upstairs, slowly and carefully. There was a bathroom and two bedrooms. She looked around for some information about the victim. It looked like everything had been taken, as drawers and cupboards had been emptied onto the floor. All she could find was skimpy underwear and sex toys. In the bathroom there were different soaps, some makeup bags, condoms and a pile of fresh towels. The toilet seat was up and if she had a swab, she would no doubt have got some evidence of a man being the last visitor.

'I've found her,' said Raj, shouting up to her.

Geraldine looked downstairs. 'Who?'

'Fit Paula_12.' He showed her his laptop with some pictures.

She went downstairs. 'Did you know her?'

'No! Wish. Tamar's fitter; she's my future ex-wife.'

'All right, tell me in the car.' She reached for her phone and called Rebwar. 'Let's get to the golf club.' The phone went to voicemail and she hung up.

'Did you call the police?' asked Raj.

'No. It could tip someone off.'

SIXTY-TWO

The boutique was filled with clothes racks and Rebwar was about to light up when Dinah took his cigarette away. 'Outside my love. Got the box of sweets?'

Rebwar showed them to her. It was his third coffee, as he had slept little. He was also wondering how Geraldine was doing with their scouting. He'd tried to keep out of Dinah's way as she rushed around the shop rearranging clothes. The brown box was on the floor next to him, still unopened with its surprise.

Jaleh's black limo arrived outside the shop and Al stepped out to open the door for her. Rebwar's stomach tightened in anticipation. He had his options laid out but which one was he going to choose? He'd seen that there was a message from Hourieh. If he left that to fester too long, she would be calling around and then contacting the police. Dinah rushed over to the door to greet Jaleh. They kissed each other's cheeks and walked in.

Jaleh took off her sunglasses and she held them by one stem. 'Darling, this is sublime. What a line! Thank you for sharing. Going to make some men jealous.' And she looked over to Rebwar. 'Quite a catch.'

Dinah threw a kiss at him. 'I know, cute man.'

'Cute? I'd say a specimen of a man. Hunk.'

Rebwar looked away, slightly embarrassed at all this attention.

'Shall we start with the day or evening?' Jaleh scanned the collection and pointed at some flowing dresses. 'As always, let's have some fun.'

He hadn't anticipated this and thought she would want to check the package first. He went with the flow. The car had driven off. He sipped his coffee and found a seat.

'You seem quiet,' Jaleh said to him. 'Long night?' She laughed. Dinah handed her a couple of dresses to try. She went into the changing room to undress.

Rebwar had never thought of Jaleh sexually. She was a pretty woman, especially for her age. He guessed she was in her late fifties. With her toned body, she surely had a gym membership with a personal trainer. She also had been a single widow since her husband had passed away. She walked out wearing one of the famous silk dresses for which Dinah was known. Its satin red bounced off the mirrors. Jaleh's curves were accentuated by the cut and smoothness of the fabric.

With her dark eyes, she caught Rebwar staring and smiled. 'Down, boy! Oh yes, I can see myself getting some free drinks with this number.' She held her breasts. 'Think I need a trip to Turkey.' She looked over to Dinah and then Rebwar.

'What you think, my love?' said Dinah.

Rebwar struggled to find something appropriate to say.

Dinah turned to Jaleh and said, 'That dress shows them off. I don't like those perky fake numbers.'

Jaleh swung around and went back into the changing rooms. Rebwar was struggling with the show. He had to make a move. 'I've got the package.'

'Open it,' Dinah said, without hesitation or emotion.

He grabbed it and now wondered if it was some Persian art. He got a pair of scissors and cut the thick parcel tape. Jaleh walked out in another evening dress, again in silk, but this time black and white. The cut was more angular and elaborate. It had wide shoulders and a fitted waist to give her a commanding stance. Rebwar took out the bubble wrapped object. It was round. He put his hand in and it felt soft, which he didn't expect. He flinched a little and put the box down. Dinah brushed Jaleh's hair and tied it up.

They both looked into the mirror. 'That's for a ball,' said Dinah. 'Good movement and a waist to grab.'

Rebwar bent down and pulled the object out. Layers of bubble wrap made it impossible to see what it was. He pulled at the sticky tape. Jaleh went back behind the curtain to change again. He kept pulling bits of plastic tape and layers of wrapping. It was like a giant onion.

'Mind making a coffee?' said Dinah.

He put the package down and took the orders and went over to the machine. Two espressos and a black Americano with three sugars. It gave him a few minutes to worry about his son. He wanted to scream it to everyone, which was a possibility, he had thought long and hard about. But he couldn't risk his son's life by exploding like a series of loud fireworks. His hand trembled and he found a tray to deliver the hot drinks.

'Show me what's in that package,' said Jaleh, walking out in another outfit. This time it was a striped business suit.

Rebwar found a pair of scissors and cut into the plastic.

A red liquid oozed out, and he covered his mouth as the stench hit him. It was a woman's head.

'Jaleh!' shouted Dinah.

Jaleh covered her mouth and her eyes looked over in horror. 'The fuckers! How dare they?' Rebwar quickly covered it up again and put it back in the box.

Dinah turned over to Jaleh. 'It's not one of the girls?'

'No, but I'm going to call.'

Rebwar washed his hands in the sink and reached for his gun. He checked the chamber and counted the bullets in the magazine. It was full. He cocked the gun slowly and returned to the front of the shop.

'Can... What's the idea?' said Jaleh. 'Was this your doing?'

Trembling, he waved the gun for them to go to the back of the shop.

'My love! You're pointing a gun at us?'

'To the back. There's no time to explain. My son has been kidnapped.' Rebwar and Dinah both looked at each other, each waiting for the other one to say something. 'I've got to deliver Jaleh to a bastard who is holding my son,' he said at last.

'Rebwar,' said Jaleh, walking up to him, 'Let's think this through... I mean, I'm sure you have. But...' She looked at the gun which he lowered.

Dinah stepped closer to him. 'You should have told us.'

'What do they want?'

This hadn't been his plan. Why had he let them talk? In his head he would have duct-taped them quiet. 'Your head.'

Jaleh looked at the box that was behind him. 'Who are they?'

He shrugged and he sat on a bench next to him, exhausted. Dinah went over to comfort him.

SIXTY-THREE

Geraldine was glad to see the turnoff to the golf course, as she'd had enough of Raj's conversation. He had a way to wind her up and she didn't know how Rebwar managed. She'd even tried to tell him to shut up, but that only lasted a minute. She was sure he suffered from ADHD.

'You said you had a plan,' he said.

She gave out a sigh as she looked for a parking space, not that she knew much about golf courses, but she wouldn't have said that this was one of those clichéd courses where you saw lots of middle-aged men in plus fours. This one had a small, sloped-roof club house that seemed to have more in common with a holiday chalet than a manor house. Around the parking lot were three elongated sheds, one of which was a golf shop. People milled around the car park with their golf bags and electric caddies.

'Is this a sport?' said Raj, looking around. 'Look.' He pointed at a couple. Geraldine looked over, wondering what he was trying to get at.

'No, we're looking for Musa. Remember.' She parked

the car. 'Go and check the shop.' Geraldine thought that was the only place where Raj wouldn't be challenged.

'He won't be in there. We need to look in those sheds.'

She stepped out of the car. 'Go. Now.' Normally, she would have briefed a partner or explained her plan but unless it involved computers, she wasn't going to risk it with Raj.

'And where...?'

But she had walked away towards the main clubhouse. Not looking back so as not to encourage him to follow, she passed the main entrance and headed for a small shed she had seen on the way in. She went to the back and tried to open the door. There was a padlock but the wooden slats were loose and she kicked them down. There was a set of tools hanging off the walls, a workbench, small cupboards and cans of gardening products. She picked out a screwdriver and punched the plastic containers. She found a small can of petrol and got a rag. She soaked and lit it. She walked out as the fire took with a burst of heat and made her way back towards the clubhouse, walked into the main entrance and smashed the fire alarm. The man behind the reception asked her what she was doing. And she pointed over to the drifting smoke that was passing the windows.

People gathered around to find out what was going on. Word spread quickly and people vacated the building. She took the opportunity to get right into the clubhouse. She went back into the office area, looking for any hidden rooms. Whenever someone tried to make her turn around and make her way out, she flashed her warrant card. She got to the kitchens and found them empty. Her phone rang.

'Nice one. I'm in the car park and spotted a man and boy.' Raj caught his breath and went on. 'He's wearing his hoodie so can't see his face. The man's got some sunnies and a thick coat. I spotted them coming out of one of the sheds.'

'Coming!' Geraldine ran out onto the grass and passed people congregating in groups. She spotted Raj in front of the shop and she made her way to him. He pointed at the suspects, who were making their way to a parked car. Smoke partially obscured them and as she crouched down to try to see, a car's engine started. Through the smoke came a white car. She held up her badge and the palm of her hand. The man swerved onto the grass but drove on. She shouted for them to stop, but he just carried on. They took a left back onto the tarmac and down a row of parked cars. Her eye caught Raj running on the other side of the parking lot. There was a screech of tyres and the sound of a horn. She ran towards it to see Raj in front of the car with a golf club.

The driver had his window down and was shouting at him. As she got closer, he slammed the car into reverse. Geraldine stood her ground. The back of the car hit her and she was taken up onto the boot. The car stopped sharply. and she slid off the back of the car and onto the ground. He drove forward again. Raj, shouting and raging, smashed the golf club into the bonnet and then into the windscreen. Feeling a little shocked, Geraldine picked herself up.

The man stepped out of the car. 'You prick,' He took his coat off, which made him look thinner and smaller. 'What do you think you're doing, you fat wanker?'

Raj looked at him, his face lost in a rage. Geraldine grabbed the man's arm and swung him around. She jabbed his jaw and then his nose. This stunned him and blood trickled down his face. Geraldine took out a pair of hand-cuffs to put them on his left wrist. She secured the other end around the car's door frame. With his free hand, the man swung out.

'Stop, Dad, stop!' came a girl's voice from the passenger seat.

Geraldine looked into the car to see a teenage girl. 'Raj, Raj,' She signalled to him to cut it out. He threw the club away and screamed. People had come over to look at what had happened.

'Bitch, get this off me!' yelled the man, who was trying to pull himself free.

Raj swung and hit the man in his ribs. 'What did you just call her?'

Geraldine went over to grab the club off him. 'Let someone else deal with him.' There was a little too much attention now and they needed to leave. She pulled Raj over to the car.

'Let me go, he's—'

Geraldine slapped him. 'Listen, we need to find Musa. And not get arrested. OK?'

He nodded.

'Geez, you're a walking, talking headache.'

'But I just—'

She got in the car and started it.

SIXTY-FOUR

Rebwar stopped by a barrier at the North Weald Airfield and lowered the window to talk to the guard. He told him he was delivering a package. He checked the rear-view mirror to glance at Jaleh sitting in the back. Geraldine had finally managed to reach him to tell him about her progress. On hearing about the last possible location, the alarm bells had rung. Jaleh mentioned that they owned a couple of warehouses and the site of the illegal fight was just a stone's throw from there. What worried him was that this implicated Jaleh and her gang. He struggled to read her. He was so emotionally involved that he couldn't trust his judgement anymore. There was a risk that he might not see the wood for the trees. If someone told him that Jaleh had killed Izah, he would believe them. The guard raised the barrier and they drove off to the left around the perimeter road of the airfield. The sun was setting and lit the dark clouds with a palette of red and yellow, but his eyes were on the businesses and signs that they passed.

The car's headlights picked up a sea of reflective yellow and green: rows of ambulances that had been parked and looked to be in different states of disrepair. 'Are they yours?' he said.

She shook her head.

He stopped the car and stepped out. 'You stay here.'

A small plane passed by overhead and landed on the runway, its engine drowning out any possibility of him shouting for his son. He checked his gun and cocked it. Looking for signs of footsteps and activity, he kept his back to the vehicles. He opened the back door of the first ambulance he came to to find it gutted of its contents. He switched the torch on his phone and he methodically checked each ambulance. By the time he got to the last one, the sun had set.

They drove off, following the concrete track. Warning signs for taxiing aircraft and rights of way were at every junction and corner. They passed a line of old double-decker busses by a metal fence. Their headlights shone through the windows. They all looked abandoned. They carried on towards some large hangars with planes in front of them. On their right were two rows of small aircraft. A car appeared ahead and drove towards them. Its headlights temporarily blinding them. He slowed the car down, trying to get a view of the driver. The windscreen reflected the few lights that lit the airfield. As it passed, he got a glimpse of a woman.

'Stop!' said Jaleh. 'The planes...'

He looked over to the parked aircraft. Beneath them, a pair of legs moved around. He carried on until he could see a man.

'Lanny! I knew it!' said Jaleh.

He stopped the car behind one of the small planes. They both got out and he reached out his gun. 'Stay behind me.' But Jaleh just walked ahead, shouting Lanny's name.

Lanny turned round and saw them. He squinted and shaded his eyes. 'Nice surprise. What brings you here...' He noticed Rebwar's gun. 'You got my package.'

'Yes,' said Jaleh. 'Was that meant to even things out?'

'Jaleh, like your detective said, you've got a mole.'

Rebwar took a few steps closer. Beside the plane was a couple of black holdalls. 'It wasn't her.'

'If we are to make this work, I want a clean house. Now—'

'What's the plane for?' interrupted Jaleh. 'Got a smoke?' Lanny laughed. Rebwar hesitated. 'You take me for an idiot. What's your game?' She headed for the bags.

Lanny put his arm out to stop her. 'No, I've got a delivery.'

'My son's been kidnapped,' said Rebwar, still pointing the gun at Lanny.

'I know...' Lanny looked at them both, waiting for a reaction.

'Where is he?' Rebwar cocked the pistol. 'Take me to him. Now!'

Lanny raised his arms, 'Let's be rational. Now—'

Concrete blew out next to Lanny and a shot rang out. 'I don't know!' Rebwar's eyes caught something coming to his left. He looked over to see Basar standing next to another plane with two holdalls. As Rebwar turned with his gun, Basar dropped the bags and ran off. Lanny bolted in the other direction. Rebwar shot at Lanny, hitting the plane. Jaleh went back to the car. Rebwar turned around and aimed at a running Basar. An incoming car headlight dazzled him. He went after Basar, who was heading towards an enormous hangar next to some piled up containers. He hadn't had time to process what was going on, but he was going after him to find out. Behind him, Jaleh started the car, its headlights throwing shadows of him, Basar and Lanny running.

Basar opened a side door and disappeared inside. When Rebwar got there, it was locked. In his frustration, he shot the door. It was futile, and he knew it. You had more chance of injuring yourself from a ricochet than opening it. He ran around, looking for another entrance. At the front of the hangar, the huge sliding door was slightly ajar. Hearing footsteps echoing inside, he carefully approached the wheelie bin-sized gap. The smell of aviation fuel and oil came through as he darted his head in and straight out again. Thundering thuds hit the metal doors and sparks flew out from the edges of the door. He was going to have to find another entrance; this one was too exposed. He blindly pointed his gun inside and shot off five rounds then rolled across the opening and ran to the other end of the large sliding door. At the corner, he carried on making his way down the side of the building till he found a window. Using the butt of his gun, he tapped the glass, until it cracked open. Using his leather jacket to cover the shards, he climbed into an office. He inched the door open and listened for movement. Apart from some dim emergency exit lights, the place was dark. Crouching, he made his way into the hallway. Feeling a sticky substance, he checked his hand. It was blood. Drips and smears led down to a closed door.

SIXTY-FIVE

Geraldine and Raj

Geraldine stalled the car as she stopped in front of the North Weald Airfield gates.

'Look...' Raj pointed at his now wet hoodie.

With a big sigh and then clenching her jaw, she said, 'It'll dry.' She wound down the window.

'It's new and stained.'

'Yes, hello,' said Geraldine to the man in the gatehouse. She looked ahead at a small air traffic tower. 'Need to talk to the boss.' And she showed the man her warrant card.

He stared at them both and stepped out of his cabin. He grabbed her card and studied it. 'What's this about?'

'Urgent police business.'

'And he is?'

She looked over at Raj, who was now speechless. More of a lost puppy than a colleague. 'Witness. Now, who's your boss?' She tapped the door panel.

'Yes... DC Smith...' He gave her card back. 'So... See the tower ahead. Mr Barnes... he's the boss.' The gate lifted up.

Geraldine started the car and went over to look for somewhere to park.

'Witness?' said Raj.

———

After arriving up a couple of flights of stairs, they arrived up in the air traffic tower which had a commanding view of the area. Apart from the instrument panels and a couple of reading lights, it was dark. The landing strip was lit with a series of white, red, amber, and green lights. The man was looking out.

'Mr Barnes?' she said to a red-faced middle-aged man with two sets of glasses on his head. The second pair was lodged in his thick grey hair. His short tie barely made it over his round belly.

'Yes.'

'Are you in charge?'

'You are?'

'DC Smith, and...' She looked over at Raj and turned back to him. 'We've got a live kidnapping situation and we suspect the victim is being held on this airfield.' She handed him her warrant card.

Barnes put down his mug of tea. 'A what?' He picked up her card.

'Raj, what's the coordinates?'

With his now white-stained hoodie, Raj approached with his laptop and placed it on a table, opened it and pointed to the screen.

Barnes, put on his reading glasses, checked her card and looked at the screen. 'That's in the taxiing lane. Sure that's right?'

Geraldine looked over at the airfield. 'Who owns those buildings over there?'

'That's...' He put on his second set of glasses. 'International Shipping Ltd.'

Geraldine's frustration was rising. She was desperate for some kind of a breakthrough. 'Seen any suspicious activity? Or where would you keep someone captive? Can't be many places. Seems busy, no?'

'Look, DC Smith, this is a small airport. I just handle the ground traffic. What goes on in those businesses... not really on my radar.'

A man appeared on the stairs. He looked out of breath and was holding on to the bannister.

'Lanny,' said Barnes. 'You might be able to help these people.' Geraldine looked over at him. He was well dressed in a sports blue jacket, jeans and black gloves. 'They are from the police and are looking for...' He looked over at Geraldine.

'We've got a live kidnap. We are pretty sure the victim is being held here.'

Lanny slowly walked over, looking at Barnes.

'Lanny, any ideas?' said Barnes.

'Sorry, no I mean, who?' He gave a concerned look at them both.

Geraldine stepped closer to Lanny, noticing the beads of sweat trickling down his forehead.

'In a rush?' 'No, officer. Who are you looking for?'

'A boy has been kidnapped and is being held somewhere on this airfield.'

Lanny took out a white handkerchief. 'That's dreadful.' He patted his wet brow. 'Wouldn't know where to start.'

'Yes, that seems what everyone is telling me. Are there any empty business premises?'

Barnes said, 'You'd have to check with the office but it's closed.'

Geraldine wanted to slap them and make them search the place but she had no authority to do it. It was like taking to a brick wall. She turned around and walked off. Raj had to gather his things quickly and run after her.

SIXTY-SIX

Rebwar had followed the trail of blood to a bathroom and between the sound of prop planes revving their engines, he heard fumbling noises punctuated by grunts.

'Hakan... ' said Rebwar, crouched down on the floor with his back to the wall. The response was three gunshots, which blew holes in the surrounding plasterboard.

'*Madar Ghabah*[1] ,' Hakan cursed as his gun's trigger clicked a couple of times.

Rebwar peeked into one of the blown-out holes and saw Basar slumped on the floor. Basar slid the pump action stock and aimed at Rebwar, who rolled out of the way. Another click but no shot.

'You're out!' shouted Rebwar. 'Where's my son?'

'Die, you dog!' The metallic sound of interlocking parts resonated inside the small room. With laboured breathing, Basar snarled. 'Damn you!'

Rebwar peeked again and saw that Basar had put the barrel of the gun in his mouth. Holding out his gun at him, he ran in. 'My son?' Basar pulled the trigger. Rebwar looked away. There was another metallic click. Basar wept in frustration as he tried and tried again. Then Basar laughed manically with an air of menace and joy until his pain made him stop. In Persian, he said. 'I know you. Farrouk?'

Rebwar went over to snatch Basar's gun away. He checked it. He'd run out of cartridges. 'What about Farouk? The dog is dead.'

Basar tried to pull himself up until his wound stopped him. 'You got lucky.' He looked at his side, which was bleeding out.

'Tell me where my son is and I'll save you.'

'You have no idea, Izah...' His breathing became erratic and his eyes rolled. 'I... we did it. Idiot like you. No idea, detective... he told me stories.' He smiled. 'Farrouk... you two he told me about the commander. Oh yes, he solved that one.'

Rebwar went up to him and grabbed his jacket to stare into his eyes. 'Where's Musa?' He shook him, trying to get an answer out of him.

'It was him in that cell with you... Farrouk told me.' His eyes rolled over and his head fell back.

Rebwar slapped him. 'What about Farrouk? Go on then. As you want to tell me. Tell me.' He grabbed Basar's jaw.

'He was my jail. Shit card player like you... We had you. Like a rat in a cage. I had you.'

Rebwar pressed on his wound, which made his eyes pop out and he gasped. 'One last chance... Musa?'

'He's here...' Basar laughed and coughed. 'I know where the commander is. How does that make you feel?'

Rebwar struggled to stay focused. Old stories that he had long buried were being dug up. 'One more time. Show me, point...' He tried to pull Basar up but he was a dead weight. His body was as limp as a sack of sand. His head dropped and Rebwar lifted it and shook him. 'Hey, stay with me! Basar, did you hear me?'

'Is he dead?'

Rebwar turned around to see Jaleh by the door. He tried again to lift Basar but it was futile. He hit him in frustration.

'Stop, stop. He's gone,' said Jaleh walking over to him.

Rebwar held his forehead. 'Who is he?' He searched Basar's pockets to find a playing card.

'Some drugged-up fool that kept my addict daughter happy.' Basar's body slumped down on the floor. 'Or that's what I thought.'

'Where's Lanny?'

'I lost him.'

'He played us, with him and Craig. How?'

Jaleh kicked Basar's dead body. 'I was consumed with revenge.'

'You stopped me.' He pointed at her. 'And now my son is missing and that piece of shit knew.' He showed her the card – a joker. It glowed in the dark like the ones Musa had. 'And he killed Izah. Your son-in-law to be. That's how rotten...' Jaleh walked out of the door. 'Hey? Call your dogs! We need to search.'

SIXTY-SEVEN

Geraldine drove around the northern part of the perimeter where lights lit the taxiways and the main runway. She told Raj to look out for planes.

'Look out!'

She slammed on the brakes and their seatbelts held them back as the car came to a standstill.

'No, no, it's...'

'What?'

'A light... how am I supposed to look out for planes when I've no idea what they look like?'

'They've got wings and fly—'

'In the night!'

Geraldine slammed the car into first gear and headed across the runway to the other side, where a series of small sheds and hangars were. 'Bloody needle in a haystack!'

The two then looked left and right as they passed parked planes and tractors. She stopped by a small green hangar with a rusting container next to it. Both knocked on the metal panels and shouted Musa's name. After going around the building and finding nothing, they made their way back to the car. Raj noticed something and ran into the grass just off where the car was parked. Geraldine thought he was trying to pick up some litter that was being blown in the wind. He came back holding what looked like a piece of paper.

'You lost something? KFC receipt?' He came over and showed her a playing card, at which she shrugged.

Raj smiled and waving it at her. 'Musa's!'

'It's a three of diamonds. There are millions of them.'

He moved the card out of the car's headlight. 'Look!' The card glowed in the dark. 'I gave him these cards.'

Geraldine looked over in the direction of the wind. There were a couple of large hangars, old and new planes, and more containers. She got in the car and started it before Raj had even shut the door. They drove across the grass and towards the other side of the airfield. The car bounced along the uneven turf and she lost control. It skidded to the left, she corrected but it went violently to the right and came to a stop. She slammed the accelerator and the driving wheels just spun. She tried to reverse, but mud flew across the windscreen.

Raj opened the door and stepped out. 'Who taught you?' She just showed him the middle finger and walked off. Raj spotted another card. 'King of hearts.'

She just hoped that they didn't find a full set before finding Musa. Engines roared in the distance as aircraft landed and flew off. As they made it to the tarmac, she spotted a card and picked it up. Ace of clubs. She looked ahead. There were three aircraft, none looking airworthy. One had its engine missing, another its wings, and the last one was on its belly. Behind were some bushes. They carried on, following the trail. A row of stacked containers appeared. They both looked at each other and picked up the pace.

'Two!' Raj held the cards up.

There were about thirty or more of these metal containers piled up five high. Around them were some Portakabins. Despite the wind and roaring engines, they shouted Musa's name. Looking on the muddy ground, they scanned for cards. One darted past her and she tried to work out where it had come from. The wind swirled around her, picking up leaves and plastic bags. She couldn't make sense of the direction. She spun around, looking up. Nothing, just square shapes. It made her dizzy and she closed her eyes.

'G! G! Over here!'

She opened her eyes, trying to locate Raj. He was waving behind one of the rows. He pointed to a pile of cards. Above them was a stack of containers four, five high and all facing in different directions.

'Look!' Raj pointed to a card falling, spinning card.

She still didn't know which one to go for or how they would get up there.

'The green one!' shouted Raj, jumping. 'Musa?'

It was three stacks up, and she started looking for a ladder.

SIXTY-EIGHT

Rebwar passed through the small opening of the hangar's doors and then helped Jaleh to step out after him. His breath was expelled by a massive hug. He extended his hand onto the metal panel to steady himself. It was Musa squeezing him. He returned the gesture, feeling his beating heart drumming into him. Rebwar treasured the moment and felt Musa's warmth. He kissed his hair.

'Son, thought I'd never...' Musa looked at him, his face covered with tears and bloodshot eyes. 'You all right? Did they hurt you?' He just shook his head and hugged him again, resting his head on his shoulder. Seeing Geraldine and Raj, he said, 'Where was he?' Raj pointed to the containers behind them. 'Sorry, son. So sorry you had to go through that.' He held Musa's shoulders and looked him up and down. 'Sure they didn't harm you?'

'Did Chelsea win?' asked Musa.

'Come on, enough of this family gathering,' said Jaleh. 'We need to find that traitor, Lanny.'

'Did you just say Lanny?' said Geraldine.

'And you two are?'

'They work for me,' Rebwar said. He turned to Geraldine. 'Lanny's he's in with Hakan and Craig or was.'

'He's over there!' Geraldine pointed towards the air control tower, which was across on the other side of the airfield. 'Matey with Mr Barnes. You could have called me—'

'The rotten bastard!' Jaleh reached for her phone.

'Son, you OK?' said Rebwar.

'Dad, can we go home?'

'Sure, Geraldine, can you take him?'

She looked over at her car. 'Sure. Aren't you—'

'No. Not letting him get away.'

Jaleh finished her call. 'Lanny's got a new plane.'

'Mus, let them find some justice,' said Raj. 'I'll get an Uber. and we'll pass by a KFC.'

Musa's face lit up and he nodded vigorously.

Rebwar was about to question the rationale of the plan but decided to trust Raj and find Lanny. 'The bags?'

'What bags?' said Geraldine.

Rebwar looked over to the parked planes. 'They were loading them onto the plane.'

'He didn't have them when I saw him.'

'They were mine!' Jaleh took out her car key and walked off.

Geraldine mouthed *'What the fuck'* at Rebwar.

'Later,' he said. 'You search that building.' He pointed to a small flat-topped building by the parked planes. He followed Jaleh to her limo. 'I'll drive.'

She ignored him and got behind the wheel. Rebwar secured his seatbelt and they drove off at speed across the runway. He held on to the grab handle above him as the vehicle swerved to avoid a landing plane. Just leaving the vicinity of the tower was a two prop plane.

'That's him!' And she sped up towards it. Its engines revved up and headed for the runway. 'Shoot him.'

Rebwar lowered the window and shot his gun. But Lanny was getting away and his plane crossed the runway. Bits of paper flew by them and one stuck to the windscreen. It was a dollar bill which Rebwar reached for. More and more of them passed them by.

'The bitch!' In the distance was Geraldine, throwing money into the air. 'Shoot her!' Jaleh headed for her and so did the plane. He grabbed the steering wheel off Jaleh. 'Get off, you idiot!' she yelled. The car swerved towards the plane, which was now parallel to them. Jaled wrestled the wheel but Rebwar managed to pull it further. The front of the van clipped the wing of the plane, which made it yaw up. Its opposite wing caught the grass, and it flipped around, the propellers hitting the ground. Sparks and debris flew in all directions. The van went off the runway and onto the grass. Jaleh slammed on the breaks which made it sink into the wet ground. It slid to a stop. Rebwar opened the door and went over to the crashed plane. Lanny was trying to get out. Broken parts littered the area. Liquid was seeping out of the engines.

'End of the road.' Rebwar held his gun at Lanny.

'Sure you got any bullets left?'

'Care to find out... Why?'

Notes flew by them.

'Kill the fucker!' said Jaleh, walking over to them. 'Give me the gun now.'

'No. This stops here.'

'You stupid? You belong to me. You're not going to get away with this. I've got your balls.'

Rebwar felt an urge to put a bullet in both her and Lanny.

Lanny hobbled out of the plane. 'I'll take my chances.'

The two looked at each other and rushed him. Rebwar shot Lanny in the chest and he fell back onto the tarmac. The pistol's slider had not returned and was in its rearward loading position. He'd shot his last bullet. Jaleh's nails scratched his face. He flipped the gun around, held it by the barrel and hit her skull with the grip. She fell to her knees. Rebwar was ready for her to try again.

'You'll regret that. Now help me.'

Geraldine arrived and pushed Jaleh to the ground.

'Get off me.'

Jaleh tried to resist, but Geraldine had her knee in her back, pinning her down. Rebwar passed her some zip ties. He felt his face. Blood was trickling down it. Everything was catching up on him. He took a breath and looked at the scene: Lanny dead by his smashed plane, the stuck van, dollar bills swirling around them. In the distance were sirens and blue lights. It was over, but not over.

SIXTY-NINE

The sun was setting over the river Thames. Red, blue and white hues were being picked up by the gently flowing water. Rebwar and Geraldine were sitting on one of the benches outside the Rutland Arms. They faced the last of the warming rays and took a moment of silence to appreciate the sight. A crowd had gathered around and people were leaning on the wall that ran along the river or standing with their drinks on the pavement. They chatted or took selfies as the streetlights turned on. Further down was the famous Hammersmith Bridge, a Victorian suspension bridge. It had a gothic feel to it and the lighting accentuated its features. Geraldine had chosen the spot that for many was one of the famous tourist hangouts. Canal boats were moored along the tidal banks with people living in them. Festive decorations sparkled around the exterior of the pub and the windows had been sprayed with white powder to make it look like snow.

Rebwar drew on his cigarette. 'Any news from our friends?'

'A bit. They can't deal with your visa as they have a backlog.'

They had released Rebwar and Geraldine from the local police station without too much of a fuss. But Rebwar was waiting for them to take him in for an interview. He looked around for some suspicious faces. People were in a festive mood and having their Christmas parties. Some wore coloured paper tissue crowns and party blowers. Some were still in their company lanyards and others were slumped on tables. 'At least they are thinking of me.'

'What happened to that gun Jaleh had on you?'

'The one she used to kill the Chief Policeman, James?' He stubbed out his cigarette in the ashtray. 'She's got it somewhere with my prints on it. Think she'll go to jail?'

'If they find her useful, then no. But I hope, for your sake, she does. Woman scorned and all that.' She sipped her beer. 'Unlucky on the ammo front. How did your other half take it?'

Rebwar ran his fingers through his hair. It had been him or their situation and her ruthlessness had surprised him. 'Been avoiding Dinah. Not sure she's going to forgive me...'

A man in a dirty Santa's hat came by asking for money, his unwashed scent making them hold their breath. Rebwar took out three cigarettes and gave one to the man. 'Merry Christmas,' he said and went to the next people.

'Why that head?' said Geraldine. 'Did he have some-thing against prostitutes?' She dragged on the smoke.

'Lanny wanted to send a message to Jaleh that he knew that Hakan was shagging around. Also, by killing her, he was making sure she wasn't going to gossip about who Hakan really was.'

'And I thought he was just a druggie loser... close... an Iranian convict you say?'

Rebwar nodded.

'And he knew your former colleague, Farrouk?'

'Cellmates he said.'

'Why kidnap Musa?'

'Wanted me to kill Jaleh and free up the throne.'

Geraldine stretched out her legs across the bench. 'What a rotten family! But I guess it comes with the territory. I mean, I can't talk... look at my sister. Oh! It was a boy. Arthur, Now I've got a nephew.'

Rebwar picked up his beer. 'Congratulations.' He clinked her glass and she just rocked her head left to right. 'And to Izah Sasani, poor guy who was duped by Basar, pretending to be some businessman. Dunno if he was trying to be kind to his sister or to protect her from him. But he walked straight into that trap, with Craig and Basar murdering him.'

'And Jaleh didn't thank you for that. Did she?'

'No. Done your Christmas shopping?'

'What do you get a newborn?'

Rebwar had to think back to when Musa had been a baby. It seemed another lifetime ago; they didn't have much then. 'Pacifier.'

DID YOU ENJOY THE BOOK?

Thank you for reading my book and hope you enjoyed as much I did writing it. If you could find a moment to leave a review for which I would be eternally grateful for. This helps other readers to find this book and share the buzz. It only has to be a few words, a rating or even a helpful vote on a reviewer's comments. It all helps us indie authors to get the word out.

ALSO BY OLS SCHABER

The Contact

Sign up at www.olsschaber.com and get your free novella.

A prequel to the Rebwar series where we meet his first contact Clive. A dramatic inciting incident sets off a chain of events where Rebwar is left to pick up the pieces.

Rebwar - The Missing Parts

(Book 1)

Ex-Iranian police detective Rebwar hides from his past behind the wheel of his London Uber. But when an enigmatic organisation threatens to expose his identity, he has no choice but to lend them his skills. And when his missing persons assignment leads only to a severed foot, he'll have to connect it to a body to prevent being deported.

When he finds his quarry's wife in bed with another man, Rebwar is forced to revive his old interrogation methods to extract a confession. But when the case is closed despite body parts still appearing, he's convinced there is more to the murder than his superiors want known. Determined to learn the truth, his private investigation uncovers a conspiracy that could see him torn to pieces

The Gipsy

(Book 2)

Rebwar struggles to recover from his last brutal case. But with his illegal migrant status used by his shadow organisation bosses to hold him under their thumb, he's stuck working at an East End car wash... until the owner is gunned down before his eyes. And when his handler wants him to find out why, he's forced back into the underbelly of the city's deadliest streets.

Going undercover as a delivery man, Rebwar follows the clues to a disturbing human-trafficking operation. But when he runs into an old adversary willing to get their hands dirty, the desperate military man worries he's walking right into an unmarked grave.

Can Rebwar destroy a smuggling ring before he's the next to eat a bullet?

Rebwar - Plan B

(Book 3)

Iranian ex-detective Rebwar still struggles to gain his footing in London. Barely making ends meet driving an Uber, he can't keep his marriage from fraying. And when the shadowy agency blackmailing him orders an investigation into one of their own, he's caught between domestic stress and clandestine murder.

In over his head when a key political figure is killed, Rebwar walks a knife's edge of danger pursuing the truth. But when his main informant disappears, he exposes a plot for him to take a fatal fall.

Can Rebwar finally unmask his sinister employers before he loses his family... and his life?

Rebwar - Dr Gul

(Book 4)

London. Rebwar feels like he's hit rock bottom. After his wife took their son and left, the former Iranian soldier finds himself stuck in a dead-end job as a security guard and still under the thumb of a clandestine organisation. And when the next mission he's assigned is to uncover who killed a man and dumped him in the sewer, it quickly gets personal when the victim is revealed to be an old friend.

Surprised to learn his acquaintance was recently fired from his position at a pharmaceutical company, Rebwar falls down a rabbit hole into a high-stakes drug ring. And after discovering his estranged spouse was having an affair with the deceased, the desperate immigrant is in a race against time to find his broken family before they're crossed off the hit list.

Can he rescue his loved ones, or are they soon to be wasted?

Ols Schaber, The Missing Parts: Rebwar. Kindle Edition.

ACKNOWLEDGMENTS

I must thank the people around me that have made this series possible. I feel so lucky to have them there and they encourage me to keep going. It's quite an undertaking writing a good yarn and even more to self publish. I couldn't have done it without them. My amazing wife Tracey, to my editor Ed Handyside, my brother Fred, and so many other great friends. You know who you are.

NOTES

Chapter 3

1. A Persian saying 'What flower bouquet did you give to the water?' which means 'What did you do wrong?'

Chapter 4

1. Iranian secret service

Chapter 25

1. Major General
2. Soldier

Chapter 26

1. Soldier
2. Major General

Chapter 31

1. Son of a Bitch

Chapter 45

1. The festival is celebrated in Iran and other historically Persian-influenced regions, including Azerbaijan, Afghanistan and Tajikistan. The longest and darkest night of the year is a time when friends and family gather together to eat and drink.

NOTES

Chapter 48

1. Soldier
2. Major General

Chapter 51

1. Khoresh e fesenjan: Stew flavored with pomegranate syrup and ground walnuts.
2. Serious Organised Crime Agency

Chapter 66

1. Son of a Bitch

CPSIA information can be obtained
at www.ICGtesting.com
Printed in the USA
LVHW010328200723
752857LV00003B/98

9 781838 227845